THE PHONE RANG AGAIN

Barbara Price picked up the receiver. "Price."

"Ross Melton has just been killed," the President of the United States said without preamble.

"Yes, sir. We're already working on it."

"Have you found out anything?"

"Nothing specific that we can go on."

"Hell, the whole DEA network has been ripped from one end of the globe to the other," the Man said. "There have been twenty-seven attacks on our people in the past two hours."

"A slight correction, sir. Forty-one attacks," Price replied, "and we already have the DEA's files. At this point I'd say we know considerably more than they do."

"What are the possibilities that all the drug syndicates are working together on this?"

"Astronomical."

"Ross Melton was a friend of mine," the President continued. "I want you to put your teams on this as soon as you can, Ms. Price. And I'd like you to ask our special friend if he'd look into this with us."

"He called earlier, sir. He's going to be in Hong Kong within half an hour. He has his own agenda."

Both of them knew what that meant. The body count was about to increase in that region of the world, and the scales would

DON PENDLETON's
MACK BOLAN.
STONY MAN
V

A GOLD EAGLE BOOK FROM
WORLDWIDE.

TORONTO • NEW YORK • LONDON
AMSTERDAM • PARIS • SYDNEY • HAMBURG
STOCKHOLM • ATHENS • TOKYO • MILAN
MADRID • WARSAW • BUDAPEST • AUCKLAND

First edition October 1992

ISBN 0-373-61889-1

Special thanks and acknowledgment to
Mel Odom for his contribution to this work.

STONY MAN V

STONY MAN

V

CHAPTER ONE

Hong Kong Harbor

DEA section chief Bobby Caine stood in the shadows near the dock and glanced at his watch. It was 8:18 p.m. Elverman was almost twenty minutes late.

Acid bubbled in the section chief's stomach, and he scowled at the night. He was twenty-nine years old and too damn young to be worrying about ulcers. He took a bottle of antacid from the pocket of his trench coat and swallowed two big gulps. It didn't help immediately. It never did anymore.

The walkie-talkie in his other pocket vibrated for attention. He took it out, slipped the earphone into his ear and thumbed the transmit button. "Go."

"City Mouse, this is Country Mouse. Over." Mitchell Elverman's voice sounded as laid-back as ever.

Caine figured if Elverman survived another three years in the trenches of Hong Kong and mainland China, a lot of the cockiness the younger man exhibited would be worn away. That had been his own experience. He'd come to Kowloon with a hard-on for danger, bad guys and exotic women. By the time he reached the beat in Victoria, he'd known all three and had lost his appetite for most of them.

He keyed the walkie-talkie. "Go, Country Mouse. Over."

"The convoy's five minutes from your twenty. Over."

"We're on top of it. But you're twenty-five minutes late. Over." He raised an arm over his head and made a circle with his fist closed.

"Nothing to worry about, old hoss," Elverman replied with a West Texas twang that was done badly. "Tsu-wang had some trouble picking up the delivery. With the way you boys have been busting the pipeline from the mainland recently, old Shih Ti figured the raw product might be worth a little more. Hell, ever since he started getting CNN at his hut through the satellite dish, he's been developing the killer instincts of a mako shark when it comes to business. Over."

Men moved in the shadows at Caine's silent command. He saw only some of them, and those solely because he knew their positions and what to watch for from each one.

"Understood, Country Mouse." The section chief unbuttoned his trench coat and freed the safety strap over his .451 Detonics Magnum Scoremaster. "You got the back door, so you make sure my hindsight is twenty-twenty. Over."

"Roger that, City Mouse. Country Mouse out."

The earphone buzzed in Caine's ear. Leaving it in place, he pocketed the walkie-talkie again. He stepped up to an easy jog and threaded through the parked forklifts and crates awaiting the morning shipping crews.

The target area was a two-story warehouse owned by the House of Chang trading company. The company had a two-hundred-year history of import and export work, with no hint of the opium trade ever being involved. As far as anyone knew, the company and its owners had always flourished from legitimate business.

But that had been before Elverman's report two weeks earlier.

Caine paused by a stack of crated television sets and scanned the outside of the warehouse. Under the tin skin was a teakwood skeleton that dated almost from the days of the inception of the business, additions made as the holdings of the House of Chang grew. He reviewed the blueprint of the structure in his mind. A small office was in the northwest corner, and the rest was open space where goods could be stacked. A skylight gleamed on the near side of the pointed roof, looking like an angled, rectangular pool of water. Above it black clouds skated across the face of an anemic moon.

Satisfied, he checked the nearby buildings on either side of the warehouse. Even though he couldn't see them, he knew Wills and Murray would be up there in position, their sniper rifles ready to provide covering fire.

The Scoremaster was in his hand before he knew it, then he realized he'd heard a sound behind him. He whirled and sought cover at the same time, holding his fire when he recognized Makibi Li.

"Christ," Caine whispered to his Hong Kong PD contact as he dropped the pistol out of target acquisition. "You know how close you came to getting popped? What the hell do you think you're doing sneaking up on me like that?"

"I didn't sneak up on you. I was here before you were. You just didn't see me." The man stepped away from the stack of textiles and joined Caine by the televisions. A wicked Skorpion machine pistol was slung across his shoulders. He scanned the terrain with a small set of infrared binoculars. "What about Tsuwang?"

"Coming." Caine quickly relayed the news he'd gotten from Elverman.

Li nodded, never taking his attention from the warehouse. The sign over the double doors of the warehouse wobbled and squeaked, exposing Chinese characters and their English translations from the shadows.

"You've never mentioned who your contact is," Li said after he finally lowered the binoculars.

"No." Elverman was Caine's secret. The Agency had dropped the man onto the scene in deep cover more than eight months earlier, and from the very beginning Elverman had shown a flair for undercover work in the outland bush area where the poppies were grown and harvested by feudal Chinese bandits like Shih Ti. He'd penetrated Tsu-wang's organization in short order and started turning useful intel almost immediately.

"Do you trust him?" Li asked.

"His information's been on the money so far."

Li gave him a short nod. "And his successes have come more closely together of late."

"So?"

"I am a cautious man," Li replied. "I do not trust luck. It is how I have remained alive in this business for so long." He focused on Caine with the deadest pair of eyes the section chief could ever remember seeing.

"Your choice," the DEA agent said. "In or out. But you better damn well hurry. My men and I are going to hit that shipment the instant it enters that warehouse. I don't want to be tripping over your guys when that goes down."

"You won't be." Li removed a hand unit from his pocket and spoke in rapid-fire Chinese.

Even with four years of exposure to the Cantonese dialect, Caine couldn't keep up with the two-way conversation. He was nervous, wondering if their communications would be overheard by Tsu-wang's people. But Li had probably been worried about the DEA communications, too. The walkie-talkie buzzed in his pocket. He reached in for the transmit button and moved the channel down to the frequency his team was using for the operation. "Go."

"Contact, Ax Handle One. Over."

"Roger that, Ax Handle Six. How many? Over."

"Four trucks. Make that four trucks, Ax Handle One. Over."

"Body count? Over."

"No can do. I count two in the cabs, but the rear decks are covered with tarp. Over."

"Acknowledged. Let them come. Over."

Li was giving orders of his own.

Caine hit the transmit button. "Okay, team, this is for pay dirt. These people don't know we're coming, and I want this to go down by the numbers so nobody on our side gets hurt. We're not looking for prisoners here, just taking product off the street. If they go ballistic, take them down hard. Ax Handle One out." His hand trailed across the extra magazines for the Scoremaster snugged on his belt as the four suspect trucks whined into view.

The vehicles entered the docking area in single file at less than twenty miles an hour, took a right and headed west across Caine's field of fire. He kept the .451 Detonics Magnum propped on the television boxes. Perspiration trickled down his cheeks, and his stomach tried to tie itself into knots.

A man got out of the lead truck, ran to the double doors of the House of Chang warehouse and unlocked them. Before he had completely pushed them open the first truck was rolling inside. The three others followed closely behind.

Caine looked at Li. "Ready?"

The man nodded and swept the Skorpion from its rig.

They hit their transmit buttons at the same time, already in motion. "Move in!" Caine ordered. He tore the earphone loose and shoved it into his pocket.

Zigzagging through the stacked goods, the DEA man raced across the open street, Li running abreast of him. Engines strained, coming closer now as ground units swept into the area with their lights out. Three marine cruisers under Li's command sped into the harbor to shut off any attempts at escape by water. In the distance the throb of helicopter rotors could be heard.

Caine flattened against the galvanized tin of the wall. He knew he was outlined by the lighter metal, but was secure that his sniping team had given them the field. Holding the Scoremaster in two hands, he nodded at the agent standing beside the door who swung the door open. They'd broken the locks on an earlier recon.

The section chief trotted through the door with the Scoremaster pointing the way. He sprinted down the row of crates to his right and paused to peer around the corner.

The four trucks were parked two by two. The lights created a dim glow that revealed the men as two-dimensional shadows. More men clambered out of the back of the vehicles and swept the tarp aside to bare the metal rib cage beneath. All of them carried automatic weapons.

Glancing back over his shoulder, Caine saw Li shake his head slightly, as if doubting the reality of the scene before them. It had been hard convincing the Hong Kong policeman to come along, since he'd been sure the House of Chang was being falsely accused.

The DEA man chose his spot, took a fresh grip on the Scoremaster and aimed it at the ceiling.

"Positioned," the agent behind him called out softly.

"Ready," Li confirmed.

Caine squeezed off a round at the ceiling. The crack of the bullet sounded twice, once as it was touched off, then again as it smashed through the galvanized tin roof.

Immediately the spotlights the recon team had installed less than an hour earlier flared into life. White light poured onto the trucks from six different locations.

"Freeze!" Caine ordered in the loudest voice he could manage. "This is Agent Caine, DEA!"

Li called out a similar order in Chinese.

The narcotics traffickers scurried out of the lights, muzzle-flashes flaming as the measured roars of autofire filled the warehouse.

A burst chewed into Caine's cover and showered splinters over him. He put two rounds through the guy hammering his position and watched the body go flying back. Two men tried to flee, but Li stepped from cover long enough to burn them with a blistering figure eight.

DEA snipers lining the upper reaches of the warehouse made short work of the Chinese traffickers. Caine was aware of the ruby dots of laser sights sweeping among the men. Bodies sprawled to the ground whenever the dots moved on. By the time he finished his second clip, still unsure if he'd even hit anyone else, the battle was over.

Nine surviving men threw out their weapons and stepped into the open with their hands on their heads. Caine seated his fresh magazine and walked out to confront them. "On your faces!" he ordered.

They got down.

DEA agents and Hong Kong policemen flooded the scene, handcuffing the nine men. Thumbing the earphone into place, Caine asked, "Anybody on our side hurt?"

"We got two down," Carson radioed back, "but neither one is in any kind of real trouble."

Caine looked into the nearest truck bed at the stacks of metal cases. "Anyone get away?"

"Nobody penetrated the outer perimeter," Carson answered. "There are two bodies outside."

The section chief glanced at Li.

"No serious injuries," the Hong Kong man reported.

They climbed into the back of the truck together. Li took out a pair of bolt cutters and snipped through the lock. When Caine opened the lid, they both saw the pillow packs of raw opium settled neatly inside.

The DEA agent did a rapid calculation of the number of containers on each truck. "Another good bust," he told Li.

"So it would appear."

"Bobby!"

The outright fear in Carson's voice drew Caine's attention immediately. He looked at the agent and saw him standing on the ground at the rear of the truck with a white block of C-4 in his hand.

"The trucks are wired!" Carson said.

"Everybody out!" Caine yelled, aware that Li was giving orders beside him. They started to dive from the truck. The concussive blast caught the section chief in midair. He never heard the series of explosions that killed him.

Washington, D.C.

THE BLUE RACQUETBALL screamed off the wall hard and low. Ross Melton, reigning antidrug czar by presidential appointment, raced after it. He was in his early fifties, a silver-haired man a shade over six feet tall and less than five pounds overweight. He prided himself on keeping in shape, used it as part of his public image in his stand against drugs. He also used the ordinary-guy appearance to keep himself in the good graces of the press, which was why he was dressed in conservative sweatpants and a red designer T-shirt.

He returned the ball with a vicious forehand designed to pull his opponent to the left of the court, then dropped back to the forgiving center himself. House member Jeff Jameson, a representative of California and on the board of the chief appropriations committee Melton had to deal with for funding the drug war, was twenty-something years younger, but had a weak backhand.

Jameson also had a flair for sports clothing and wore a neon-green tennis outfit that drew the attention of people walking past the Plexiglass windows that lined one wall of the room. He fielded the ball and placed it high on the wall.

The ball bounced once, just past midcourt. Melton closed in and set himself. As he'd figured, Jameson failed to come back to center court, leaving himself wide open for a return down the right sidewall. "The score's nine to two, right?" he asked, then smashed the ball with enough force to challenge Jameson's backhand again.

"Yeah." Jameson was breathing raggedly.

Melton kept the smile off his face. The cocky young representative had already learned that racquetball wasn't entirely about being younger and faster. There was a good deal of strategy involved, as well.

Another backhand saved the congressman. The return was lower this time, with more spin on it.

"Your favor?" Melton kept the return to Jameson's backhand, drawing him farther out of position to the forehand wall.

"Yeah."

They exchanged volleys again.

"How about," Melton offered, "if I win this game, you push the appropriations committee for my budget, no questions asked?"

"Fine," Jameson said with his cocky grin. "Game in six."

Melton took the rebound, caught it low before it had the chance to make the first bounce and smashed it hard enough to pull it straight back and low three-quarters of the court back.

Jameson had no chance at a save and went skidding and tumbling to the floor when he dived for the ball.

"Game," Melton said, "in twelve." And he set to work, chopping methodically at the congressman's offense and defense. Jameson still wasn't easy prey, and having something on the line brought out the best in him.

Thirty-two minutes later Melton took the game fifteen to nine. Jameson took it better than he'd expected and even offered to spring for breakfast.

When they left the court, Norris was waiting on him with the briefcase phone. "Excuse me," Melton said.

Jameson nodded and headed back to the health club's receptionist. From this morning's verbal fencing between the two Melton had already figured the congressman was going to be oh for two before he left.

Norris was six-four and drew attention in his full suit. The haircut was military, and the black wrap-around sunglasses were pure Hollywood. Still, Melton knew he'd have had to look hard and long before he found a more competent aide and bodyguard.

He took the briefcase to the nearest table, sat down and opened it. The news had to be bad, or Norris would never have taken the chance that some media person would see him taking the call. He picked up the receiver and activated the scramble. "Melton."

"Time to come home, Chief," Pat Haynes said tensely. "The shit's hit the fan. At last count we've got nineteen teams that have been hit on domestic and foreign soil."

A cold fist seemed to close around Melton's heart, taking away the brief moment of victory he'd had with Jameson. "How bad is it?"

"Stats are still coming in. At present we have forty-seven dead, another fifty-eight injured and twenty-three missing. And those are just the ones we know about."

"I'm on my way." Melton hung up, closed the briefcase and marched toward the double doors with Norris close behind, pausing only long enough to let Jameson know he wouldn't be accompanying him. Outside, his mind wouldn't leave the situation alone. He wondered who was dead, who still lived. He knew most of those men. God, he was friends with a lot of them.

His four-door sedan waited in the parking lot. It looked like an undercover vehicle, like one of those he used to ride in before taking the appointment. They'd coined the term "drug war" during his predecessor's term. And in spots around the globe deadly battle zones had been drawn.

Now it looked as if somebody was trying to make it official.

He opened the door, tossed the briefcase into the back seat and keyed the ignition. Norris got in beside him. He put the car into gear, shrilled out of the parking space and steered for the exit.

Melton's peripheral vision picked up movement as he coasted to a stop to pull onto the street, and he turned to face it as the short hairs rose on his nape.

"Son of a bitch!" Norris yelled while reaching for the gun in his shoulder holster.

A man stood across the street beside a van, a tube across his shoulder as he sighted it directly at Melton's vehicle. A four-year hitch in the Marines and time spent in the reserves had made Melton aware of what a LAW was.

A puff of whitish-gray smoke flared from the back end of the tube. Melton didn't see the warhead as it rocketed across the street between the staggering traffic. He knew only that it struck the front of his car with impossible force and spread a sheet of flame across the shattered windshield. Then his world went black.

CHAPTER TWO

Stony Man Farm, Virginia

Tense silence filled the computer room, punctuated by Aaron ''Bear'' Kurtzman's deep voice calling out instructions. His people responded with a minimum of conversation.

Barbara Price watched with a mixture of pride and trepidation. As mission controller of America's premier antiterrorist groups, she knew Stony Man Farm went into direct action only when the stakes were at their highest and the chances for coming through a situation unscathed were at their slimmest. It looked as if one of those times had arrived again.

Less than six minutes earlier the news about Ross Melton had hit the radio stations. The television crews had it now, responding more quickly than the Washington, D.C., fire department.

Kurtzman had parked his wheelchair at his station, which was in the center of an immense horseshoe-shaped desk covered with electronic hardware. Built more along the lines of a village blacksmith than the cybernetics specialist he was, Kurtzman's attention seemed to be everywhere at once as his fingers tapped the keyboard in front of him.

Over Kurtzman's broad shoulder Price watched in fascination as window after window of information scrolled open on the oversize VGA monitor in front of the big man. At the other end of the long room three wall screens displayed different information. The center wall was filled with a split screen, depicting two different views of Ross Melton's burning car. Paramedics were held back by the orange flames and roiling black smoke. Police units struggled to keep back the crowd while a foot patrol moved among them, seeking witnesses.

The screen split into thirds, with the new video camera view being provided from a helicopter. A massive yellow fire truck trundled down the blocked street between police cars and yellow-striped sawhorses, then deployed yellow-slickered firemen trailing thick white hoses. When the water hit the flames, it beat the fire down, turned the smoke white and changed to steam.

The wall on the left side was using taped versions of the current transmissions to piece together different views of the crime scene. Price knew from Kurtzman's orders that Carmen Delahunt was even now prepping a visual roll call for every face that had been captured by the video cameras. Not everybody would be identified, but it was conceivable that they could spot the person or persons responsible for the attack. At the very least it would give them a pool to search through as information continued to narrow their focus. Delahunt was old-line FBI, culled from the expert ranks at Quantico. Price knew the perky redhead wouldn't miss a trick in putting the file together for optimum speed and coverage.

To the right, Huntington Wethers, the black ex-professor of cybernetics at Berkeley, chewed on the stem of his dead pipe and sorted through the list of strikes against the DEA. Kurtzman had "acquired" them through a means of his own less than an hour ago. Price knew that being an effective mission controller sometimes meant knowing when not to ask how or where the troops got their information or materials.

From what she had gleaned from the DEA files, Price had been astounded at the damage the agency had suffered in the past five hours.

The phone rang.

Glancing at the lighted extension number in front of her, Price knew it wasn't the call she was waiting for. "Price," she said into the mouthpiece.

"I'm returning your call," John "Cowboy" Kissinger said. Even though he knew part of what was going on in the outside world at present, the Stony Man weapons specialist sounded laconic.

"Like to get away from the Farm for a while?" Price asked.

"What farmboy doesn't?"

"I need you to take a team and pick up Hal. He's vacationing with his wife at Calvert Cliffs, Maryland. I haven't been able to contact him, so I'm assuming they aren't at the cabin. He won't know you're coming."

"I'll find him."

"Damn quick," Price urged. "I don't like the way this is shaping up. With Melton out of the way a lot of people might be looking at Hal as the number two man temporarily. Could be the teams lashing out at the drug squads are looking at him, too."

"I'll let you know something as soon as I know something." Kissinger broke the connection.

Cradling the phone, Price checked the right wall screen. The list was growing, layered in more details as Wethers pursued intel along the different channels covertly open to the Stony Man hardsite. A line of satellites in space gave them access to the world in an electronic heartbeat.

She read down the list of strikes. A fighter jet, possibly an F/A-18 Hornet, had been taken down off Florida. There were no known survivors. A mined drug shipment had taken out a police team near Moscow. Snipers had cut down a Berlin police unit as they closed in on a drug factory. A confiscated shipment of heroin blew up in the faces of a narcotics squad in Marseilles and had taken out the traffickers, too.

The list went on, and the cold, calculating feel of it left frost along Price's spine.

It was either a monstrous and carefully orchestrated strike launched across the globe or it was an astounding series of coincidences. Some new events were still coming in. It was hard to guess how many others were still out there.

The phone rang again. This time it was the call she'd been expecting. She picked up the receiver. "Price."

"Ross Melton has just been killed," the President of the United States said without preamble.

Price looked at her watch. Actually Melton had been killed twelve minutes ago. "Yes, sir. We're already working on it."

"Have you found out anything?"

"Nothing specific that we can go to work on."

"Hell, the whole DEA network has been ripped from one end of the globe to the other," the Man said. "There have been twenty-seven attacks on our people in the past two hours. I'll have the DEA release the particulars to your groups within the hour."

"There have been forty-one attacks," Price replied, "and we already have the DEA's files. At this point I'd say we know considerably more than they do."

The President seemed surprised.

"But that's not the whole picture," Price went on. "There have also been attacks launched against the international agencies targeting the drug trade. Interpol has even taken hits in its information-gathering circles. Domestic agencies within Britain, Switzerland, France, Germany, Italy, Japan and Australia have also been hit in ways similar to the ones the DEA has experienced."

"You make it sound like a conspiracy."

Price grimaced. "I couldn't think of a better word to call it, Mr. President."

"What are the possibilities that all the drug syndicates are working together on this?"

"Astronomical."

"Exactly. Those people are motivated by greed. They'd never agree to do anything together. That circumnavigates the profit potential."

"True. But when you rule out the possible, only the impossible remains. There's no way all of this could have happened without some kind of guiding hand."

"Investigate it discreetly, Ms. Price. The Europeans operate under the notion that America is responsible for the drugs now turning up in their backyards."

Price knew that. Switzerland and Russia were two of the foremost dissenters about the drug shipments that had been penetrating their borders. Those countries felt that if the United States could deal more effectively with the home problems, they wouldn't have been affected. Price figured it was an ostrich syndrome those nations had chosen to employ to keep from dealing with their own problems. Confronting the drug issue on home territory was no easy matter, and admitting it existed was the hardest step.

"Ross Melton was a friend of mine," the President said. "He was a good man, a family man. I've met his wife and daughters. They're going to be devastated by his death. I don't want his killers to escape retribution, nor do I want the other people who've fallen to go unavenged." He paused. "I want you to put your teams on this as soon as you can, Ms. Price. And I'd like you to ask our special friend if he'd look into this with us."

Kurtzman looked up, letting Price know he'd been monitoring the exchange.

"Yes, sir."

"I want to exact our pound of flesh from these bastards," the President went on, "and the sooner the better."

Price finished the conversation, hung up and turned to Kurtzman. "Get me Able Team and Phoenix Force. We can fax them the files we've already generated and let them work on those. I want them up and moving in ten minutes."

Kurtzman nodded and turned to his computer. His fingers worked the keys as he spoke. "What about Striker?"

Striker was the code name for Mack Bolan, the Executioner and the "special friend" the President had referred to.

"He called earlier," Price said as she picked up her clipboard of hastily jotted notes to add others that were rapidly coming to mind. "He's going to be in Hong Kong within half an hour. He has his own agenda."

Both of them knew that meant the body count was about to increase in that area of the world, but this time the scales would be shifting back the other way.

Bogotá, Colombia

THE NOONDAY SUN burned bright and hard across the jungle, sparkling off the winding river that bisected the foliage. Crouched in the fork of a tree, David McCarter peered through the telescopic sights of the Heckler & Koch PSG-1 sniper rifle. The cross hairs fell across the first of his targets.

Through the scope magnification Tomaso Alonso's features seemed even broader than the faxed sheets from Stony Man Farm had shown them to be. Alonso was Gaspar Cota's second-in-command. Cota had been one of the first in the struggle to fill the void left by the death of Luis Costanza the previous year.

McCarter stifled a flame of anger that tried to disrupt his cool when he saw the ragged peasants huddled around the raw coca packages Alonso and his men had forced them to carry through the jungle to the river. The battle against Costanza and the Medellín cartel had been a holding action, and the Stony Man teams had known that going in. The cartel was a monster with many heads. Cut one off and another grew in its place. Costanza had been a threat because he'd been on the verge of turning it into a single organism with one mind.

Dressed in stained shirts and torn cotton pants, the peasants shifted uneasily in the shade provided by the trees on the riverbank. Seven wooden carts sat with their wheels sunk into the muddy water. The long poles sticking out in front of them were worn smooth by the countless hands that had pulled the carts through the vines, creepers and long grasses for many years. Human labor was still the cheapest form of energy in the country.

McCarter shifted, trying to relieve the bite of the rough bark chewing into his side. It was futile movement, and he sighed with frustration, then accepted it. Before signing on with Phoenix Force he'd been a member of the British SAS, so he was no stranger to discomfort. He blocked the low hum of pain from his mind and waited.

"Phoenix Two, this is Phoenix One. Over."

McCarter hit the transmit button on his ear-throat headset. "Go, Phoenix One. Over."

Yakov Katzenelenbogen's voice was a calm whisper. The Israeli was an ex-Mossad agent and was schooled in tense situations that tended to go awry.

"Phoenix Five has confirmed the approach," Katz said. "We are go after your first shot. Over."

"Roger, Phoenix One. Phoenix Two out." McCarter wiped his palm on the leg of his jungle camouflage fatigues. It didn't help much. With the humidity being what it was his clothing was already drenched. He settled into line behind the gun butt as the blatting engines of the approaching plane became audible.

He marked off his field of fire one last time. At last count there had been twenty-seven armed men with

Alonso. The peasants numbered about forty, but they expected no resistance from them.

The cross hairs bisected Alonso's face. Between the Phoenix warrior and his target were nearly four hundred yards of jungle. The distance was outside the comfortable edge of a sure head shot for the average sharpshooter with the particular weapon that McCarter held. But the position was necessary for the pincer movement Katz planned to employ. Tactically spread out in a half-moon around the river rendezvous, Phoenix Force planned to make a clean sweep of Cota's group before moving on to its next objective.

McCarter's peripheral vision picked up the plane coming in from the east. The sound of the warbling engines echoed out over the river. An experienced pilot himself, he identified the plane as a Piper. The pontoons hung ponderously under the wide body, making it look like a fat silver-gray sea gull against the blue sky.

The Piper shed altitude gracefully, came almost to a stop over the turgid water, then settled onto its surface. White waves cut through the dirty brown water and trailed behind the pontoons in twin vees. The pilot cut the engines, brought the craft around sideways almost fifty feet past his designated landing area, then kicked the door open and slowly floated back down the river toward Alonso and his people. Just before he drew abreast of the waiting transport group, the pilot heaved out an anchor. It caught in the silt-covered river bottom at once, bringing the plane to a bobbing halt within feet of the loading area. Moving to the back of his craft, the pilot kicked open the cargo door, which fell into the water with a splash.

Alonso's shouted commands started the peasants moving. They grabbed packages of coca, placed them on their heads and walked into the water toward the anchored plane. The level never rose above their chests.

Staggered along the river's edge, Alonso's troops didn't seem inclined to get wet. They stood smoking and talking in small groups, nonchalantly holding their weapons. They hadn't had to fear the government troops or roving bandits for months.

McCarter drew in a breath, locked onto Alonso's mustache and focused on making the shot. The distance and windage had already been calibrated. His finger took up the trigger slack. He let out half his breath, held it, then squeezed the trigger. The big sniper rifle slammed into his shoulder.

He didn't bother to track his success. From the moment he'd fired until the instant the Colombian drug force heard the first shot he still had time to kill again with anonymity.

The cross hairs found the pilot and came to a rest over the guy's chest as he stood on the starboard pontoon. McCarter squeezed the trigger again, and the man went spinning from the plane.

By the time he fired the third round from the 20-round box, the Colombians had begun to scatter. The bullet caught the latest target high in the shoulder and shoved him facedown into the shallow water. Another bullet caught a man in the calf as he ran, whirling him around. McCarter punched the fifth round into the man's upper body. He moved on, hunting targets, but found most of the survivors dug into the thick foliage.

An explosion erupted from the side of the Piper. A belch of flame and thunder struck the starboard pontoon, shearing it from the craft. Destabilized, the plane tipped over and dipped a wing into the water. As the Piper turned over on its side, the wing stabbed into the river bottom and lodged. Before it had the chance to come to a full rest another explosion ripped into the plane and broke it in two.

McCarter knew the handiwork belonged to Gary Manning. The big Canadian was Phoenix Force's demolitions expert. Manning possessed an affinity for anything explosive.

The headset crackled in McCarter's ear. "Phoenix Two," Katz called. "Over."

"Go, Phoenix One. Over." The Briton took aim and put three carefully placed rounds into coca packages left by the fleeing peasants as a way of warning. The wrappings tore, scattering gray-white globs of paste over the black earth.

"Get clear. Out."

"Roger, mate. Out." McCarter slung the sniper rifle, then lowered himself through the tree branches with acrobatic ease until he was on the ground.

The sound of small-arms fire and the steady thump of Manning's M-79 grenade launcher rolled toward him. He stashed the big rifle in a preselected clump of brush, grabbed a fistful of his combat harness and shrugged into it on the run. He carried his Browning Hi-Power in a shoulder rig. Bandoliers of 12-gauge double-aught rounds for the Mossberg 590 Military 9-shot he carried crisscrossed his Kevlar vest. Other pouches carried grenades, extra pistol magazines and more ordnance that he might need. A Gerber combat knife rode in a boot sheath. An impact-resistant helmet was secured to ride high on his back.

He moved at a military jog, alert to the sights and sounds around him. Taking the amber-tinted aviator glasses from his pocket, he slid them on, then tapped the transmit button on his headset. "Phoenix Five, this is Phoenix Two. Over."

"Go, Phoenix Two. You have Five. Over." Calvin James sounded unhurried despite the twin cracks of the Beretta M-21 he carried that echoed over the comlink during his transmission. The black warrior had been seasoned on the streets of Chicago, then received a deadly education as a U.S. Navy SEAL before being further schooled by the professionals in Phoenix Force and at Stony Man Farm.

"Alonso? Over."

"Down and out," James replied. "It was a pretty shot. Over."

"We aim to please. Over and out." With Alonso out of the picture the Colombian troops would be slow to regroup and would be more apt to retreat. It didn't make the assignment easy, but it did keep them in one place and confused longer.

A yellow flash caught the Briton's attention. He glanced up and saw a golden monkey scamper fearfully toward the higher tree branches that formed an emerald canopy over the area. A multicolored parrot burst from hiding and went squawking across the open space. The Mossberg pumpgun came up automatically as he broke left and took cover behind a tree.

Two armed men burst from the bush less than twenty feet from McCarter's position. The Phoenix warrior whirled around the tree, fired from the hip and cut down the lead runner. He racked the slide and pulled the trigger again as bullets from the second man's weapon chipped splinters from the tree. The 12-gauge load caught the man squarely in the face and sprawled him brokenly on the ground. McCarter thumbed replacement cartridges into the shotgun's breach and went on.

Katz called for positions. The team radioed back in order, using the coded sector map they'd generated before setting up perimeters on the operation. McCarter automatically fixed them in his mind.

A peasant stumbled out of the foliage in front of him, suddenly saw him and realized there was no place to run. The old man dropped to his knees and held up his empty hands beseechingly.

"Go," McCarter commanded in Spanish. He waved the shotgun. "I'm not here to hurt you."

Not wasting any time, the old man pushed himself to his feet and continued on his way.

As the jungle thinned, McCarter found he could make out details around the river. The remaining half of the Piper was on fire in the water. Thick black smoke sailed in a widening column, pushed by the southeasterly breeze. The tail section had either sunk or floated from view. Bodies stretched out across the coca packages and the dark earth, bloodstains turning the ground black in places.

Most of Alonso's troops had taken refuge among the trees fronting the river. Scanning the tree branches above eye level as he neared, McCarter spotted the warning flags Manning had posted earlier. He slowed, picking his spot to keep out of the circumference.

A burst of 9 mm fire raked up dirt clods at his feet and sheared through small branches in front of him. Throwing himself forward, the Briton tucked and rolled, cursing silently when he landed wrong and crushed the breath from his lungs. Before McCarter could get to his feet one of the Colombians stepped around the tree he'd chosen as a defensive position.

The man appeared to be as surprised as McCarter and tried to fall back to use the AK-47 he carried.

The British commando surged up from the ground, unable to bring the Mossberg pumpgun around. Instead, he crashed the barrel of his weapon into the man's lower face. Teeth broke. He hit his opponent again, gained some room and yanked the shotgun free. He stroked the trigger even as the Colombian raised his assault rifle. The 12-gauge charge at close range shredded the man's shirt and knocked the corpse back into the brush.

"All set? Over." It was Manning's voice.

"Dug in, mate," McCarter answered as he hunkered down in expectation. He pulled the helmet on his head, then took a double-fisted grip on the shotgun. "Over."

The other three members of Phoenix Force chimed in right behind him.

"Fire in the hole," Manning announced.

At first it seemed to McCarter that everything had taken place in silence. Huge clumps of earth along the riverbank flew into the air, then rained to the earth in smaller chunks. Some of the underground charges had been placed in the water as well, which created even more spectacular visual effects. They'd been planted and timed to create a massive shrug of power that spilled the emplaced Colombians into the open. Then the sound rushed back in to fill the vacuum, the harsh crackle of thunder slamming out flat and loud across the river.

"Go!" Katz ordered.

McCarter was in motion at once, racing for the downed Colombians. Perspiration covered his face, and he could feel the crust being created by the flying clouds of dust. Debris continued to rain down on him, pinging against his helmet.

Two crossed trees lay in front of him with broken branches woven together. A head popped up, eyes wild with fear, followed instantly by a rifle barrel.

Before McCarter could take evasive action a round black hole appeared between the Colombian's eyes, then the head snapped back from view.

"Ah, Rafael," McCarter whispered to himself as he raced toward the trees, "remind me to buy you a pint after this bloody bit of business is finished."

Rafael Encizo was the remaining member of the team. Cuban-born, the man had been witness to a number of turbulent times in his home country while struggling against the Communists and Castro. His cunning and training had come from the heart and the battlefield rather than a professional military background. Katz had assigned him to run backup on the play from high in a tree behind the open sights of a Beretta M-21 sniper rifle. Evidently he'd wasted no time climbing into position.

McCarter stretched out his left hand and vaulted the fallen tree, going to ground at once. He rolled, carried by his momentum, and kept the shotgun close to his chest. Movement blurred in front of him. Identifying one of his opponents, he dropped the barrel of the Mossberg and squeezed the trigger.

The initial charge staggered the cartel man. Pumping the slide, McCarter's second round put the guy down. The Briton levered himself to his feet, then saw Katz come scrambling through a torn haze of branches to his right.

"You all right?" Katz called.

"Right as rain, mate."

The Israeli nodded, then swept a line of death from his Uzi. The 9 mm Parabellums jerked a man from hiding and spilled him over another corpse.

The ground was shredded from the explosives. The amount of carnage seemed unbelievable to McCarter even though he'd seen Manning's handiwork up close and personal many times before. The Canadian was absolutely lethal in his chosen field.

Return fire was scarce now. McCarter went forward confidently, flanked by Katz. He'd tried counting bodies but had to give it up. The explosions had made that impossible to do with any kind of accuracy.

He could see the brown water through the trees now. The surviving bit of the Piper had floated down river, still ablaze. Autofire drove him to cover behind one of the overturned carts. Bullets thunked into the solid wood.

Katz lay flat behind a corpse, pinned down by the steady stream of bullets. "Rafael," he called over the headset.

"Here."

"Do you have the position of the men firing on David and myself?"

"Yes, but I'm unable to pick them off from here."

McCarter scanned the riverbank and caught the floating white smoke of gunfire trailing from a shrub-covered hill at the water's edge. "Looks like the last pocket of resistance, mates." He set the Mossberg down beside him, slipped the Browning Hi-Power from shoulder leather and steadied himself. His skill with the pistol had earned him a place in the Olympics. He placed his shots carefully, breaking the pattern of autofire enough to allow Katz to get out of the line of fire. But he was unable to put any of the men down.

"We're running out of time here," Katz said.

McCarter silently agreed. Cota wouldn't take the assault lying down. And the narcobaron had access to a small cadre of attack helicopters that could be rapidly deployed.

"Calvin?" Katz suggested.

"On my way."

Knowing what to expect, McCarter shifted, thumbed a fresh magazine from his combat harness and slowly fired through the remainder of the clip. It was close enough to keep the cartel people worried, but not enough to scare them out of position. All they had to do at this point was to wait, and they knew it.

Katz sat and watched with hawklike intensity. "Gary?"

"Yes."

"A diversion, if you please. On my mark."

"Just say when."

"Rafael?"

"Go."

"Whomever Calvin isn't able to take out is your responsibility."

McCarter watched in helpless anticipation. Calvin James was an incredible swimmer. The SEAL training had made him that, but it hadn't bulletproofed him. James would be a sitting duck if anything went wrong.

Then he saw a hand break the river surface less than twenty feet from the bank. He started to tell Katz, then heard his leader's voice calmly speaking into his ear.

"You have your mark, Gary."

Instinctively McCarter tracked the egg-shaped object out of his peripheral vision. It fell yards short of the hill despite the Canadian's best efforts. McCarter didn't think he could have made a throw even that far.

The grenade popped loudly, then hissed a bilious red smoke into the air. A cloud quickly gathered and drifted back over the Colombians. They fired blindly into the smoke, obviously expecting a charge.

Like some kind of creature from a horror movie, Calvin James surfaced in the river, the Uzi subgun in his hand spewing death. Trapped by the cross fire, the surviving Colombians scrambled for the top of the hill. The Phoenix Force members opened fire, grimly aware that Calvin James's life hung on their skills.

In seconds it was over.

McCarter slipped a fresh magazine into the Browning while James waded to shore. Manning helped them confirm the kills while Encizo kept watch. They turned over everything from the dead men's pockets that seemed of interest to Katz, then switched their attention to the coca packages scattered across the battle zone.

Two of the wooden carts still held most of their load, so Manning shouldered them into the river. McCarter and James threw the other packages in after the carts. Nearly eight minutes passed before they were certain they'd destroyed them all.

"Saddle up," Katz ordered as they regrouped. "There's still a lot to be done today. Rafael, you have point."

McCarter volunteered to bring up the rear. He paused in the middle of the gentle incline that led toward the river. As he looked over the dead men and counted the blood price Phoenix had exacted from Cota's army, he knew it was only the beginning. For the team to be unleashed like this, too many good people fighting the drug wars had already died. There was no way to get them back. They'd been told to exact a pound of flesh from the jackals thought to be responsible for those deaths. And David McCarter was willing to make sure every ounce weighed in.

CHAPTER THREE

Victoria, Hong Kong

An unmarked police car screamed around the corner, flattening a row of metal trash cans by the side of the road. After a showy fishtail, the driver recovered, downshifted and continued his pursuit of the black van only yards ahead of it.

"Windshield's busted," Jimmie Lee Santee said into the microphone cupped under his chin. Standing against the crowd of Hong Kong natives behind him and behind the police lines, the man looked like a misplaced cowboy. He wore a white cowboy shirt, a gray Stetson, jeans and boots. A red handkerchief and cowhide gloves stuck out of a back pocket.

Near the back of the crowd Mack Bolan watched Santee. He'd had the man's name in his records for some time as a possible resource. There were other names, but Santee happened to be the most accessible at the moment.

The big cowboy was crowding sixty. The night might have been kind to him and smoothed out some of the wrinkles and age lines, but the Executioner's intel in his war book had the man pegged. Santee was ex-cowboy, ex-television star and ex-Texas. Now he managed props for low-budget and Vietnam-era movies shot in Hong Kong, Thailand, the Philippines and Taiwan. Santee was also known to dabble in black market goods.

"I said the damn windshield's busted," Santee repeated loudly.

The unmarked police car and black van roared past and screeched to a stop at the other end of their planned flight path.

Santee knuckled up a fist and strode toward the director's chair. "A blind man could see that windshield. There ain't no way you can cover that up in the edits. I told you them damn fool trash cans wouldn't work. You have to either reshoot this scene or scratch your interior shots from the driver's seat."

Bolan drifted along in the man's wake on the other side of the waiting crowd. His combat senses were alert and picked up the undercover police working the movie. He carefully avoided them. The DEA murders were only hours old, and there had been some concern that whoever had killed the agents might try for the movie people as a bonus. It hadn't taken the warrior long to discover that the rumor was being circulated by the movie people themselves to increase interest in the drug war film they were producing.

The Executioner halted under a darkened neon sign and waited in the shadows. He couldn't hear the conversation between Santee and the young director, but he could tell it obviously wasn't going well for the older man.

Two men stepped around the director and started forcing Santee back. The gesture Santee used for the director was universally recognized. The crowd crowed its delight and cheered enthusiastically, then seemed genuinely dismayed when Santee turned and left.

When the prop man cleared the crowd, Bolan fell into step beside him.

"Do something for you?" Santee asked brusquely.

"I'm in the market for a gun."

Santee didn't break his stride. "I don't know you, mister, and I don't do business with folks I don't know."

"That's what I was told," Bolan said, "but the guy who told me that said I should mention November 29, 1950, Chosin reservoir."

"A bloody bit of fighting that was," Santee replied. "This feller tell you to mention anything else?"

"Red Emma."

"Fair enough, old hoss. You got any dinero?"

"Yeah," Bolan replied.

"My goods come expensive."

"I'll pay what's fair, and I'll know fair when I hear it."

Santee laughed, then led the way to a travel trailer hooked up to a big Chevy pickup. He fumbled with the lock for a moment, then went inside.

Bolan followed.

The trailer was small and compact. It was neater and homier than the weathered exterior led an on-looker to believe. A tiny kitchen filled the front third, and a sofa and chair took up some of the living space that wasn't occupied by padlocked closets.

"What are you looking for, son?" Santee asked as he opened one of the closets.

"A long gun," Bolan replied.

"You hunting?"

"Soon." Dressed as he was in a black turtleneck and black jeans under a dark trench coat, Bolan knew there wasn't much about him to let the man guess his business.

Santee pulled a rifle from the closet, unzipped the protective cover and handed over the weapon for inspection. Bolan stroked the barrel with a fingertip and inspected the film of oil on his skin.

"That there," Santee said, "is a Parker-Hale Model M-87 target rifle. She's calibered in .308 Winchester. Got a mounted bipod and 'roll-off' scope mounts. Damn fine gun."

"It is," Bolan admitted when he handed the rifle back. "Trouble is, I'm looking for something domestic."

"Don't want to stand out in the herd?"

Bolan nodded. "Something like that."

Santee put away the Parker-Hale and moved down to another closet door. On the wall above this one was a picture of him in full western regalia on the set of *The Six-gun Marshal*. "Most of these movie stars nowadays like them stylized pieces. Me, I was cut out for lever-action and Kentucky windage. Had to learn this new shit just to stay in the business."

"They have their place."

"I suppose." Santee took out another rifle and stripped it. "This here's as local as you get. The SVD Dragunov is a Russian sniper rifle first introduced in 1963. Chambers a 7.62 mm round in a 10-round clip. That's four feet of killing machine you're holding there, friend."

"I'll take it."

Bolan chose a Makarov 9 mm for his side arm. Santee had a paddle holster that fit and threw it in free. The Type 56 Chinese-made AK-47 wasn't a surprise. The warrior had seen the movie heavies weaving them around earlier. The price for all three weapons was a little high, but Bolan paid it, anyway.

"Them serial numbers is faked," Santee said as he put the money away in a fireproof box tucked behind a piece of false siding near the ceiling. "You get caught with them guns, the local law's gonna light a fire under your ass wanting to know where you come by them. If you send them my way, I'll just be sending them on again. And chances are, I won't be in town more than another hour. Got me a little vacation lined up. Me and the director have got a creative difference going on. I figure I'll either go fishing for a few days, or I'm liable to kick his ass up between his ears."

Bolan slung the rifles over his shoulders, concealing them with the trench coat. His rental car wasn't far, and the opening numbers for this operation were falling fast.

"Offer you a cup of coffee, son?" Santee asked. "Help take the bite out of that wind."

"Sure."

Santee took a pack of foam cups from a drawer. When Bolan accepted the coffee, he noticed the glass jar of what looked like plastic coins. He reached inside, took one out and found they were plastic replicas of Texas Rangers' badges.

"Mementos mostly," Santee said as he hunkered down behind the bar. "Used to give them away to the kids who came to watch me on the set during my TV show. Damn movie career cost me two marriages and some of my best years. Still can't just chuck them things away like I ought to."

"You mind if I take a few?"

"No, son. Go ahead and help yourself. Kids don't ask for them no more nohow."

Bolan dropped a handful inside his trench coat pocket. "It might be an idea to put them away for a while after tonight."

Santee sipped his coffee. "I like the cut of your style, son. You're here about them DEA boys, ain't you?"

The question was as blunt and as forthright as a prairie wind. Bolan didn't try to dodge it. "Yeah."

"I knowed it as soon as I seen you. Your eyes got the look of somebody about to do something that needs doing." Santee grinned. "Shame I ain't twenty years younger."

"I ride alone," Bolan said.

"Understand just how you feel."

"I have a couple of other questions."

"Ask them."

"Who's the guy on the set who supplies the nose candy to today's stars?"

"That'd be Ryan Jeremie." Santee spelled it.

"He's connected with the local distribution people?"

"Yes, sir. As connected as they come. Hustles a little Triad action in the States for Keran Tat when he needs to. Pictures himself as a real wheeler-dealer."

"And where will I find him?"

Santee checked his watch. "Hell, it's past midnight. The set's due to wrap soon as they finish this scene. Old Ryan'll have himself a party going at the Blue Lotus. Sounds like a yuppie's kind of place, don't it?" He added an address. "Security's pretty tight there, son. Keep your head down and your powder dry."

"You, too," Bolan said. He left the trailer, made sure he wasn't followed, then headed for his car. After stashing the rifles in the trunk, he slid behind the wheel, keyed the ignition and headed for the Queensway nightlife.

"WHERE CAN I find Ryan Jeremie?"

"There."

Bolan tipped the waitress, then moved across the crowded dance floor to the bar. He put his back to the wall as he took a seat. He had a clear view of Ryan

Jeremie and the crowd of people the man held in thrall.

The bartender drifted over, a petite woman with a British accent and flaming red hair. The warrior ordered a bottled beer and drank it slowly as he watched the movement around Jeremie.

The man obviously enjoyed being the center of attention. He was slim and slightly horse-faced, with sandy blond hair fashionably styled and flashing green eyes. Confidence oozed from every pore, and jewelry gleamed on his fingers and wrists. Despite being unbuttoned, his suit coat hung just right.

Occasionally a camera flash would go off and most of the fifteen people gathered around the long table would automatically go on point. It didn't take much to figure out that most of the crowd was used to being on the business end of a camera lens.

Thirty minutes passed. During that time, more people arrived, a few departed, and Bolan got a table. He ordered a ham and cheese on rye from the waitress and had ten minutes to digest it before a Chinese man in a dark blue suit came to collect Jeremie.

Making his excuses, obviously intending to return in only a few minutes, Jeremie left the table and followed the other man to a bank of elevators. Bolan figured his check, added a tip, then moved to intercept Jeremie and his companion.

The Blue Lotus was on the third floor, above two stories of shops and family businesses offering personal services. The eight floors above contained apartments for foreigners on extended business stays.

"What floor?" a tired maid asked as Jeremie and the man stepped into the cage.

Bolan stopped the closing of the double doors with one hand.

"The eighth," Jeremie told the woman.

"Sorry," Bolan said. "I'm going down. Didn't notice the arrow." He released the door after checking the button display in the chrome interior's reflection. Buttons for two other floors before the eighth were lighted. As soon as he moved back, another elevator dinged open.

He entered, then punched eight. Since Jeremie's car had to make stops, the Executioner arrived first. He stepped off at the eighth floor and loosened his jacket. The Makarov filled his hand. He kept it hidden in the folds of his trench coat and knocked at the door nearest him. When no one responded, he let himself in with a credit card, then pulled the door almost shut behind him.

The room was dark and filled with the smells of soaps and disinfectants.

He listened intently, recognizing Jeremie's voice when the man got off. The dealer's conversation with his companion was muted and low and didn't carry strongly enough to reach the warrior.

A key rattled in a lock, then hinges creaked softly. The Executioner checked the hallway, found it empty and saw the Chinese man disappearing into a room on the left four doors down. He bolted, lifted the Makarov and snapped off the safety.

"What's going on?" Jeremie demanded.

As he rounded the doorway, Bolan had a brief impression of the Chinese man reaching for a hidden weapon while trying to shut the door. There was another Chinese inside the room, sitting on the bed next to a briefcase.

"Oh, shit!" Jeremie yelled as he dived for the floor.

Still in motion, Bolan fired twice through the door, the rounds taking the hardman high in the chest and punching him backward. The Executioner's foot collided with the closing door and kicked it open again.

The man inside the room had his pistol in both hands and took deliberate aim. Bolan fired instinctively, running through three of the remaining seven rounds in the clip. One bullet took the gunner in the left shoulder and jerked his arm so that the pistol fired into the wall. The other two caught him in the throat and forehead, knocking him through the sliding glass doors behind him.

Car horns drifted up from street level almost immediately. Knowing there was no way the shooting had gone unnoticed, Bolan reached down for Jeremie and roughly brought the man to his feet. He flattened his prisoner against the wall and gave him a quick frisk that turned up nothing.

"Move!" he ordered.

"Man, there's a quarter-million dollars lying on that bed."

"You care enough about it to stay here and die with it?" the Executioner asked in a graveyard whisper.

"Not me." But Jeremie's eyes didn't leave the briefcase.

"Walk," Bolan commanded, "and keep walking. Try to escape, and I'll drop you and walk over your body." He reached into his pocket, placed one of the plastic Texas Ranger badges on the dead man's chest, then followed Jeremie into the hallway.

A few curious heads had popped from the doorways of nearby rooms, vanishing as Bolan and Jeremie made their way down the hall. An elevator dinged to a halt as they reached it. Four people were inside, dressed as if they'd just come from the dance floor downstairs.

Bolan grabbed Jeremie by the collar and slammed him into position to hold the doors open. "Out."

The new arrivals didn't hesitate after seeing the gun in the Executioner's fist. Even though it hadn't pointed in their direction, they assumed the threat was there.

Once inside the cage, Bolan pressed all the buttons. The doors closed and the elevator started its descent. He pocketed the Makarov, making sure Jeremie saw him do it. "Try anything and I'll put you down."

"And if I do what you say?"

"You get to live. Is that simple enough?"

The man nodded.

"Put your hands down."

Jeremie did.

The cage stopped on the seventh floor, and Bolan pushed his prisoner out ahead of him.

"What the hell's going on up there?" an older man asked. A handful of people had gathered in the hall and stood in small groups.

"Don't know," Bolan replied as he hustled his prisoner toward the fire escape. "But hotel security seems to have everything under control now." He had Jeremie get the door, and they started down the stairs. "What do you know about the DEA hits down in the harbor?"

Jeremie clung to the railing fearfully, stumbled and barely managed to catch himself. Using his greater weight and leverage, Bolan kept the man moving. The ruse with the elevator wouldn't last for long.

"Nothing."

Bolan spun the man around the landing, then headed down another flight of stairs, gathering speed. "Somebody knows."

"Not me."

"Keran Tat?"

"It's not his way."

"Then he can find out who."

"Tat doesn't run the action in the harbor," Jeremie said. "Nobody does. Costs too much to hold control over it. The Triads cut one another to pieces over it for years. Now they leave one another alone."

"Tat can find out."

"He won't."

"You tell him it's going to cost him more and more the longer we have to wait." Bolan deliberately used the pronoun. With what he planned to set in motion it could easily seem like the organized efforts of a small group. The possibility would give the Triad boss more to think about and more to fear. "He operates the Baiyun Textile warehouse in Guangzhou. We'll contact him there. If he's not there when we call, he can mark off another piece of his organization."

Jeremie stumbled as they reached the next landing. Bolan slammed the man against the wall to help him keep his balance. A low groan escaped Jeremie's lips, but he kept his feet moving.

"You also tell him that when we call all we want is the answer we're looking for. Anything else and we'll assume he's just trying to stall for time. We're going to keep on hitting him till he delivers."

"What if he doesn't know?"

"Then he's going to have to find out."

"He won't let you get away with this."

"He doesn't have a choice at this point."

"Do you know who you're fucking with here?" Jeremie's eyes were wide.

Bolan halted the man at the second-floor landing. Harsh, angry voices were drifting down from the upper stories. He put himself nose to nose with his captive. "Yeah, I know. But he doesn't know me." He took one of the plastic badges out of his pocket and pressed it into Jeremie's hand. "Give that to him. Tell him he'll be seeing more of them real soon."

Jeremie's hand made a fist over the badge.

"And you tell Keran Tat that if he doesn't have the answer soon enough, we'll take him out, too, and move on down the line till we find somebody who does know the answers. Understand?"

"Yeah. I sure do."

Bolan pushed Jeremie backward, controlling his fall as he tripped over the stone steps, and eased the guy into a sitting position. "If you don't deliver the message, I'll come back for you."

Wrapping his arms around his knees, Jeremie shivered and nodded.

Bolan turned and sprinted down the final flights of stairs. The sounds of pursuit were growing closer. In minutes he made it to street level without being seen, then let the night take him away.

THE INTEL BOLAN HAD in his war book on Keran Tat's organization was sketchy at best. The Chinese opium lord had risen to power slowly, inheriting the position from stronger men who had gone before him. But once he'd reached his present status, Keran Tat had worked hard to maintain his hold on the business. People who had gone up against him had died in quick succession.

The Executioner left his rental car five blocks from the waterfront hotel, hid the Dragunov sniper rifle under his trench coat and walked. He paid for a room on the third floor in small bills to give the sleepy hotel clerk even less reason to remember him, and went up.

Once in his room, he raised the window, stepped out and took the skeletal metal fire escape to the rooftop.

Usually when he moved on an operation, Bolan did a series of soft probes and recon work. A section of his war book was filled with neatly written rows of rumor and half-truths about Keran Tat's business holdings. His preliminary testing of Tat's organization would have separated the facts from fiction. He wasn't entirely flying blind, but the guesswork made things uncomfortable.

On the rooftop he kept low and crept to the edge of the building. The moon was full and was reflected from the dozens of miniature ponds formed by collected rainwater on the tar-and-pebble surface. Everything else was masked by shadows, which absorbed the Executioner as he took up his position.

He wasn't sure what stance the DEA and the United States would take on the murder of the agents in Hong Kong. Nor was he sure exactly how widespread the violence was. Confused reports from Colombia, Paris and Switzerland—among others—continued to pour in through the news sources. He'd listened to them during the flight over, mentally cataloged them and filed them away.

From his brief talk with Barbara Price he'd gathered the Stony Man mission controller was only waiting for the call that would allow her to unleash Able Team and Phoenix Force. The President wasn't the kind of man who would let something like this pass unchallenged.

For himself, there was no confusion. The Executioner had come to Hong Kong to do what he could do to make certain the people who had fallen would be avenged.

The warrior took a pair of night glasses from a pocket of the trench coat and scanned the harbor. Sampans and flatboats littered the water. He moved through them swiftly once he found his bearings. A previous recon had allowed him to locate the vessel he searched for, and assured him that his prey was still aboard.

The *Yellow Lion* was a fifty-two-foot American motor-sailer berthed in private docking. She looked sleek and expensive, her name written in English and Chinese across her bow. A group of men stood guard amidships, dressed in dark clothing.

Bolan adjusted the magnification of the field glasses. None was the man he wanted. He waited patiently, moving on to scan the lighted windows of the boat.

In less than ten minutes Fai Shan stepped onto the deck, flanked by a bodyguard. He recognized the man from the pictures he'd studied. Shan was Tat's number one man in the Hong Kong-Kowloon area. Now in his forties, Shan had been picked from the gutter at an early age and groomed to be Tat's personal aide. The word Bolan got was that Shan was so close to the old man that it seemed as if they were blood kin.

When in Hong Kong, Shan traveled aboard the *Yellow Lion*. The boat was off-limits to the local police, and it was generally accepted as truth that Shan never transported contraband aboard the vessel. Women were another matter. From the reports Bolan had, Shan possessed a brand of lust that exacted an expensive price. At least nine women in the past two years had taken a cruise on the motor-sailer and were never seen again. Two of them were Western, an American and a Briton.

Bolan put the field glasses away and reached for the Dragunov. On board the vessel one of the bodyguards walked to the starboard side to reel in the line attached to the dinghy. Shan stood on the deck and put a cigarette in his thin-lipped mouth.

Bolan hunkered behind the butt of the sniper rifle and gazed through the PSO-1 telescopic sight, which featured a graduated range-finding scale. Although not fashioned for night work, there was enough moonlight to see fairly well. The warrior put the range at two hundred seventy yards, then locked in his shot.

The dinghy bumped into the bigger boat and the man began to tie it alongside. Stroking a lighter in his cupped palms, Fai Shan bent to light his cigarette. As the illumination touched his target's face, the Executioner took up slack on the trigger and fired. Both eyes open, tracking in case the men moved more quickly than he'd anticipated, Bolan zoomed in on his second target. The big rifle bucked against his shoulder again, kicking the projectile out at 2,733 feet per second.

Locking in on his third target as the man lunged for the safety of the cabin entrance, the Executioner squeezed the trigger. The bullet caught the man in a hip and spun him away.

Sporadic muzzle-flashes gave away the fourth man's position. When the gunner tried to race to the cabin, Bolan picked him off with two quick shots that caught him in the chest. The body tumbled into the dark water.

Spotting the remaining man diving into the harbor, the Executioner waited. A silvery spiral of air bubbles surfaced before the man. When his face came into view almost twenty feet from the vessel, Bolan put a round between the man's eyes. The body sank out of sight.

Bolan unhurriedly put the scope back on Fai Shan's ruined face. He bracketed the man's head with the four shots remaining in the clip. The bullets dug splinters from the polished deck.

Satisfied, he recharged the weapon with one of the extra magazines, dropped one of the plastic badges onto the rooftop and started for the fire escape. The police teams would be able to triangulate the source of the shots from the bullets he'd placed into the *Yellow Lion*'s deck, and they'd find the badge. He was certain once they knew of it that Keran Tat would soon learn of Shan's death and the badge, as well.

The blitz was under way.

"KERAN TAT?" Mack Bolan stood in the shadows of the public phone. Hong Kong was still vibrant around him, painted with neon colors. A few blocks away sirens could be heard screaming their way down to the harbor.

"Wait," a voice instructed.

Bolan glanced at his watch, logging the time. The fact that Keran Tat might try to trace the call didn't bother him. He'd be gone before anyone could arrive. But he didn't want the drug lord to guess that he was being menaced by only one man.

"Hello," an aged voice said.

"Keran Tat?"

"Speaking."

"I called to let you know Fai Shan and four of his men are dead." The second hand on the warrior's watch started to sweep the second minute.

There was a pause. "So I have been told. What do you want?"

"The people behind the DEA hit."

"I do not know these people."

"Then find out." Bolan broke the connection and walked back to his car.

CHAPTER FOUR

Los Angeles, California

"I see two guys on the outside," Carl Lyons said into his ear-throat headset. He rested easily against the safety belt encircling the power line pole, his spiked boots thrust deep into the wood. "Outside perimeter at ten and three, with your position being twelve."

"I read you," Rosario Blancanales's calm voice responded in his ear. "Gadgets?"

"Two guys at the front door," Hermann Schwarz replied. "Standing guard between the garage and the south wing."

Lyons lifted the minibinoculars that hung around his neck and scanned the outside of the house again. A pool, placidly blue, occupied the center courtyard in the middle of four buildings roofed in red tile. The garage sat off by itself while the other three buildings formed an L behind it. With the way the land fell in Pacific Palisades, construction of the home had been expensive. To level that much ground was costly.

But the money hadn't meant much to the people living inside the dwelling.

Lyons picked up the two men standing in front of the gate of the wrought-iron fence that secured the ground. Both were dressed in street clothes and wore dreadlocks. Neither appeared to be armed, but the Able Team leader knew they were packing.

The house belonged to Merripen, a Rastafarian drug dealer scarcely removed from the Jamaican jungles. The file Kurtzman and Price had forwarded read like a horror novel. As a general rule, the Jamaican posses were run by a guy strong in the magic of the island's particular brand of voodoo. The members weren't only loyal, but they feared for their lives, as well.

Merripen was ruthless. An unofficial estimate, cross-referenced through the LAPD, the Los Angeles Sheriff's Department and the FBI, held the man's kills at thirty-two. And he was only twenty-eight years old.

Lyons had a healthy respect for the Rastafarian and his organization going in. He knew from experience how deadly they could be.

"Got them," Lyons said softly.

"Makes the head count somewhere around eighteen," Blancanales stated.

Lyons didn't detect any worry in his comrade's voice. Rosario Blancanales and Hermann Schwarz were jungle fighters, hailing back to Vietnam and Mack Bolan's Pen-Team Able. They'd seen death close up, grinned in its face and spit in its eye.

Blancanales—called Politician by his friends because of his talent for using words with as much skill and precision as a sniper used bullets—sat in the back of the white Ford van, which had local power company markings on its sides. He was running logistics and backup while Lyons and Schwarz pulled recon.

"Eighteen," Schwarz repeated. "Don't worry, Pol. I'll see if I can talk Ironman into saving you one or two." He laughed lightly.

Nicknamed Gadgets, Hermann Schwarz was a deadly, crafty individual. There wasn't anything electronic that he couldn't use to create some kind of communications device or a booby trap.

Lyons unslung the binoculars and stashed them inside his jacket. "Okay, the prelim count stands at eighteen. If we wait around, they could up that, or we could end up chasing Merripen through the streets. And that definitely isn't on my list of things to do."

The leader of Able Team was an ex-LAPD detective, drawn from the ranks when Stony Man Farm had been formed to battle the increasing threat of terrorists. Like the other two men, he had shared a previous history with Mack Bolan. Only his role had been as an adversary. During the early days of the Executioner's war against the Mafia, Lyons had been one of the cops assigned to the Hardcase corps, given the responsibility of bringing the soldier in dead or alive. Then and now he'd earned his nickname of Ironman by being one of the wildest players on the field.

"Let's do it," Blancanales said.

"Pussyfooting has never been our style," Schwarz added. "And I'm getting damn tired of pretending to read these gas meters."

Lyons looked south and saw Schwarz's jumpsuited figure less than a block from his position. "We're on it. Give me some time to get into place."

"You got it."

Navigating carefully, Lyons shinnied his way down the pole. He kicked off the spiked boots and dropped the belt on top of them. Then he pulled a pair of tennis shoes from the heavy toolbox he'd carried from the van and put them on. Beneath the loose-fitting jacket he wore a Kevlar vest and a combat harness. His Colt Government Model .45 rode in shoulder leather. He took the holstered Colt Python .357 from the toolbox, then belted it around his lean hips. Incendiaries were attached to the webbing and were in his pockets, as were Speedloaders and extra magazines for the pistols.

The last thing he removed from the toolbox before abandoning it was a .45ACP Ingram MAC-10. Then he strode toward Merripen's house.

The houses were close together, separated by cultivated bushes and trees designed to enhance a feeling of privacy that didn't exist above the second floor of most residences. He crossed one of the winding two-lane streets cutting through the neighborhood, then fell back into the bushes to mask his approach. Once inside the perimeter of the verdant growth, he shed the power company jacket and the ball cap.

Less than five minutes later he was at the back of the house overlooking the patio and the kidney-shaped pool. The hallway connecting the master bedroom to the living room ran as a separate corridor. Through the hallway windows he could see the two men beyond the wrought-iron gates. The other rooms were closed off from view.

He tapped the transmit button on his headset. "Ready."

"Show time," Schwarz radioed back. "Keep a close eye out there, Ironman. I learned this one from *Fall Guy* reruns."

"Terrific," Lyons muttered.

An engine raced and rubber shrilled. The two Rastafarians posted at the gate looked up in idle curiosity.

Lyons balanced the MAC-10 in both hands as he caught sight of Schwarz's pickup racing down the street. Then he lost the truck when the road dipped in front of the house.

Abruptly the vehicle was back again, this time on the other side of the two sets of windows. The pickup slewed off the street, fishtailing sideways for a moment as the transmission shifted downward and the tires sought traction. Sunlight glanced off the chrome bumper behind the reinforced steel bars welded across the front of the truck.

One of the Rastafarians had time to level a pistol and get off a few shots before the pickup was on top of them. Lyons sprinted for the house.

The two gate guards ran for their lives, then the pickup shot through the wrought-iron gates. Twisted metal bounced high over the truck's hood, spiderwebbed the windshield, then spun away. Unable to find traction on the concrete surface surrounding the pool, the truck took a nosedive in the deep end. A second later Gadgets broke the surface with a CAR-15 clenched in one fist. A triburst hammered a Rastafarian drawing down on him, tearing him loose from the stone column that had helped frame the gate.

Lyons fired the MAC-10 from the hip. Glass shattered from the floor-to-ceiling window in front of him and he charged through. "Pol?"

"Go."

"Gadgets is inside."

"I heard. Don't worry. I'll be there."

Lyons slid through the glass fragments and didn't bother trying to stop until he slammed into the opposite wall inside the hallway with his shoulder. He lost his breath for a moment, and swirling black dots crowded into his vision.

Dropping to one knee, he raised the machine pistol as a figure staggered in from the living room area at the other end of the hallway. The man was a Rastafarian, and he held an AK-47 in his arms. "Hey, mon!"

Lyons squeezed the trigger. The burst caught the man in the chest and punched him back inside the room.

"Shoot," Lyons advised. "Don't talk." He scrambled back to the master bedroom and yanked a grenade from his combat harness. When he looked, two men with automatic weapons were headed into the bathroom. Lyons knew from the blueprints that another door in that room led to the courtyard and pool.

The rear man saw him and fired a burst that ripped into the hallway door casements. Lyons ducked out of the way, pulled the grenade's pin, counted down and heaved the spherical explosive into the room.

One man managed a warning yell, then the grenade went off and swallowed the sound. Debris flew out into the hallway, settling over Lyons. He coughed and waved a hand in front of his face.

More autofire sounded in the courtyard. Lyons tapped the transmit button. "Pol?"

"Three seconds, Ironman."

"Just remember who the good guys are." Lyons ripped a smoke grenade from his vest, pulled the pin and flung the bomb toward the living room.

The grenade skittered across the hardwood floor and exploded just across the threshold. An inky black cloud spewed out and filled the room. Voices screamed challenges, and sporadic autofire chewed at the hallway walls.

Standing beside the three windows overlooking the courtyard, Lyons peered through. The pickup had tilted forward and sunk straight down so that the rear third of it jutted skyward. Two more Rastafarians were stretched across the sunbaked tiles. Schwarz was pinned down behind a stone bench he'd obviously overturned for protection.

A glance at the peaked roof of the garage showed Lyons that Blancanales had gained his position. The barrel of the M-21 Beretta sniping rifle spoke with authority. Then a vicious line of autofire drilled through the roof tiles.

"Anytime you want in on this, Ironman," Schwarz transmitted, "you just step right on in."

"Just catching my breath," Lyons replied, recharging the MAC-10. He took a pair of grenades from his harness, then slammed the machine pistol into the bullet-fractured window. Shards of glass fell from the frame and shattered against the tiles.

At least a half-dozen stray rounds thumped into the walls near Lyons's position. He pulled the grenade pins, then lobbed the orbs over the swimming pool into the hedges lining the wall of the family room. A gunner attempted to bolt through one of the windows. Blancanales's rifle boomed in the courtyard and cut the man down.

Taking a double-fisted grip on the MAC-10, Lyons raked the side of the house, emptying the clip in a sustained burst that ended only a heartbeat ahead of the explosions. The concussive force generated by the grenades folded the side of the wall in and brought the roof tilting down at an angle.

On the move and out of magazines for the machine pistol, Lyons dropped the MAC-10 and drew the Colt Government Model. He raced toward the smoke-filled living room, going over the blueprints in his mind to get his bearings.

Once inside, he was blinded by the acrid smoke. The dining room was at twelve o'clock. The kitchen was at three. He couldn't hear anything from either direction.

Finding the wall to his right, he put the pistol in his other hand, then trailed his fingers along the textured surface to find the door leading to the hallway and the utility room. Someone touched him in the smoky darkness. When he didn't get an immediate electronic feedback from his headset, he knew it wasn't Schwarz or Blancanales.

He swung the pistol at what he considered to be head level but missed. He closed his other hand in the guy's shirt. A gun went off between them, and Lyons felt the solid impact of a bullet kick into his stomach. The Kevlar kept it from penetrating, but the expended force took his breath away and made his head whirl.

The gun went off again, but the bullet disappeared without touching either of them. Stepping in closer to his opponent, the big ex-cop lifted a leg and kneed the guy in the crotch. The man could bob and weave and swing his head around, but his midsection wasn't going anywhere. The guy screamed in pain.

Lyons kneed the gunner three more times in quick succession, then fell forward with him, feeling the hot muzzle of the man's pistol on his cheek. He swung the Colt Government Model, connected blind and heard the other pistol go thumping away.

Coughing, choked by the smoke, Lyons swayed to his feet and gave the guy a quick frisk that turned up another pistol and a long, thin-bladed knife. After disarming him, he picked the man up from behind and put him in a chokehold, screwing the barrel of the .45 into his ear. He felt the man's arms go up in surrender.

"Ironman," Blancanales called.

"Go," Lyons answered as he stumbled into the hallway. It was clearer there, and he could see two-dimensional shapes. Farther on, the collapsed roof blocked the hallway.

"Hey, you be putting the gun down now," a voice ordered.

Lyons swung toward the utility room, barely making out a hardman through his tearing eyes.

"Ironman," Blancanales repeated.

"Busy," Lyons growled.

The Rastafarian seemed hesitant to shoot. Lyons wasn't. He aimed at the gold medallion on the man's chest and dropped the hammer. The golden disk disappeared and the man bounced off the wall behind him, then slumped to the floor.

"What did you want?" Lyons asked as he looked for a way out. In the end he followed the twisting trail of smoke winding through the shattered windows that lined the hallway.

"The locals are on their way," Blancanales said. "Are we clear here?"

"Yeah. Get the van and let's move out."

"What about Merripen?"

In the courtyard, his vision only fuzzy now instead of blinded, Lyons looked at the man he had. Merri-

pen had scarred cheeks and smoldering hazel eyes. He
looked at Lyons through red-rimmed, hooded lids.

"You be a dead man walking," Merripen promised.

"Not today, asshole." Lyons keyed the transmitter.
"We got lucky with Merripen."

"That's the Carl we know and love," Schwarz said.
"When detailed planning and strategy go out the
window, there's always luck."

Still recovering from the smoke and the painful
bruise under the Kevlar vest, Lyons didn't reply. Instead, he leathered the Colt, used the handcuffs at the
back of his belt to secure his prisoner, then shoved
Merripen at the ruined gate as Schwarz took up point.

Bogotá, Colombia

"HER NAME," Yakov Katzenelenbogen said as he
passed out the colored computer printout, "is Maria
Alfaro."

Gary Manning studied it and committed the face to
memory, then pushed it at Calvin James.

Katz stood with his back to the wall of the small
room Colombian F-2 intelligence let them use as a
base of operations while in the country. The walls were
barren of information and surrounded a desk, a rectangular table and seven wooden chairs. A coffeemaker was set up near the door, a leaning tower of
cups standing beside it.

The Phoenix Force leader shook an unfiltered Camel cigarette from the pack, caught it between his lips and lighted it. He looked over his team and knew every man there was bone-tired. Despite the success of the earlier mission the trip back had been excruciating.

Cota's forces, according to their F-2 liaison, were in disarray.

"She's a good-looking woman," James commented as he handed the contact sheet to David McCarter.

"She's DEA," Katz said. "Undercover."

"I assume she must be operating within Cota's organization," McCarter observed, then handed the sheet to Rafael Encizo.

"Yes. The agency had managed to slip two people into Cota's operation almost a year ago."

"A year is a long time to be in deep," Encizo commented.

"Hell, mate," McCarter said, "three months can be a bloody lifetime when you're in with the wrong crowd."

"What about her partner?" James asked.

"He was found out and killed by Cota's forces two months ago," Katz replied. "The agency was reluctant to admit this, but Kurtzman accessed some files they had hidden. Once Price confronted them with our knowledge of the situation they had to own up to the truth."

"But Alfaro is still operational?" James asked.

"The DEA believes so. They recovered the body of the other agent, but they've had no contact with Alfaro since her partner was murdered."

"Her partner didn't give her up?" Encizo asked.

Katz regarded the stocky Cuban. After being involved in the bloody politics in Cuba's efforts to overthrow Fidel Castro, Encizo was used to the abrupt changes of wind from companions who were supposed to be friends.

"The other agent wasn't tortured. He was killed by a single bullet from behind."

"How does Alfaro fit into Cota's little group?" McCarter asked. He reached back into the ice chest they'd been given as a welcoming present from the F-2 people working the trenches and took out a can of Coca-Cola Classic. He cracked the ring and the hiss echoed in the room.

"She's his lover," Katz replied.

"Tidy little arrangement," Manning commented. "Could be she's working this to get the best of both worlds. With Cota she gets to live the life of Riley, and maintaining her connection with the DEA, she's more or less granted immunity if the guy gets busted."

"Unless she ends up dead," James said. He took the picture from Encizo and looked at it again.

"Our primary mission," Katz said, "is to take Cota down, gather information if we can about the recent drug enforcement agencies hits and get out of here in one piece. If we're able, we're going to bring Alfaro out with us."

"If not?" McCarter asked.

"Then she finds her own way home. We do the favor as long as it doesn't slow us down."

James passed the contact sheet back to Katz.

"Any questions?" Katz asked.

"When do we go?" Encizo asked.

"Now."

The men of Phoenix Force stood, gathered their duffels and started for the door.

Katz lagged behind them for a moment, long enough to place the picture of Maria Alfaro on top of the other fax sheets they'd received from Stony Man Farm. Then he gathered the documents and dropped them into the wastepaper basket beside the desk. Using his lighter, he fired up a paper napkin left over from the quick lunch they'd had brought in, then dropped the flaming paper into the bin. The picture of the female DEA agent blackened around the edges and curled in on itself as it burned.

She was very pretty, Katz admitted. Alfaro was in her mid-thirties, with a chiseled face cut in smooth lines and a nose that stopped just short of being too long. Her cropped ebony hair offset her olive complexion very well. The only jewelry she wore were diamond-chip earrings.

A gentle woman, an onlooker would have thought. But Katz knew differently from reading her files. Maria Alfaro had learned how to go for the jugular. If she had turned, she would make a formidable foe.

The fire erased her image but not the possible threat. When it was out, Katz poured a bottle of seltzer water over the glowing embers, then stirred them around with a telescoping pointer he'd found in the desk. Satisfied, he grabbed his duffel and followed his men.

CHAPTER FIVE

Stony Man Farm, Virginia

Barbara Price stared at the piles of hard copy spread over her desk. Even as advanced as the Stony Man computer equipment was, coupled with the deep-space satellite links they had access to and with Kurtzman's deft hand guiding the intelligence acquisitions, she felt as if they were missing something in their search.

A pounding headache had taken root between her temples. She opened her desk drawer long enough to take out a bottle of pain relievers and shake two out onto her palm. She recapped the bottle and swallowed them dry.

Kurtzman had his team working like a well-oiled machine, gleaning information from news services and tapping domestic and foreign intelligence circles. Numerous leads had been cultivated. At present none was leading anywhere definite.

The reports had tripled. The death toll had almost doubled. Both were still rising.

She turned to look at the television monitor at the back of her office, which was tuned to CNN. She'd switched the voice off, but the picture broadcast footage from different hot spots. Keeping up with the location tags as the reporter gave a summary of events was almost a full-time job.

The murders ran the gamut of violent death: shootings, bombings, one-on-one assassinations and group carnage. Their invisible enemy was skilled in every one.

Then she realized she'd been thinking of their opponents as someone other than the visible heads of the drug empires around the world. Subconsciously, she knew, she'd already rejected that theory. But if it was someone else, she was puzzled as to whom it might be.

Brognola had been right. They needed to broaden their scope because they were getting lost in the microcosm they'd chosen to blame. They needed to know the "why" in order to figure out the "who." Once they knew that, they could work on eradicating the threat.

She reached for the remote control and clicked the television off, then left the office and walked into Kurtzman's theater of operations.

The big man was at his post, hands playing across the keyboard like a virtuoso giving the concert performance of his life. Screen after screen of information flashed onto the monitor in front of him, then divided into individual windows and kept moving.

Price came to a halt behind Kurtzman and waited patiently.

"Hey, Barb," the Bear called, "frustrated yet?"

"Past my eyeballs a long time ago."

"Good. I was beginning to think I was the only one." Kurtzman pushed himself from his work station, rolled down the ramp, then reversed direction and rolled to the coffeemaker. He filled his chipped ceramic cup with Born to Hack written on the side. "Coffee?"

"No," Price answered immediately, then hoped it hadn't sounded that sudden. Kurtzman's coffee was known and deplored by any who'd had the misfortune to drink it.

Kurtzman didn't appear to be offended. He pulled a container of orange juice from an ice-filled plastic tray and tossed it to her.

"Have you heard from Leo?" Price asked. Leo Turrin had been a Bolan ally since his Mafia days.

"Yeah. Five minutes ago. He got a lead through one of his Mafia connections." Kurtzman rolled back up the ramp and hit the keyboard. The screen opened up and showed profile and full frontal shots of a grizzled old man with a fringe of hair around a bald head. The gunmetal-gray eyes looked as if they'd been set back in dark hollows. He was neatly dressed in a bronze three-piece suit.

"Liborio Parrella," Price said.

"Right." Kurtzman nodded. "Used to go by Packy Parrella back in the good old days."

"I thought he was retired or dead." Price sipped her juice.

"A real dinosaur," Kurtzman agreed. "Parrella was one of the guys who couldn't make the change to legitimacy the way so many of the Italian Mafia did after the heat came down in the seventies."

"He ran drugs in Florida."

"You know your history." Kurtzman tapped the keyboard again. The monitor screen flicked to page after page of what was evidently a long document. Reproduced black-and-white pictures from newspapers broke up the lines of copy. Parrella had been decades younger. "When his peers tried to sink into legal holdings, Packy struggled to keep an iron fist on Miami. He'd gotten his start in the pre-Castro days in Cuba in the late fifties and early sixties. A shooter. Very dangerous guy. But Packy wasn't prepared for competitors like the Colombians and Rastafarians."

"You mean people he couldn't scare away through intimidation."

"Right. Packy's boys would kill one guy, the Colombians would kill three or four of his right back. He's been walking with a cane since 1983 when an assassination attempt was almost successful. Unable to get any support from his cronies, he closed up shop, bought an isolated mansion in the Tarpon Springs area and left Miami behind."

"So what's Leo onto?"

Kurtzman shrugged. "He said maybe nothing, but he didn't want to sit around the Farm waiting to see what everybody else found out."

"Send Charlie Mott and a support team down there. Special Justice ID in case any inquiries come up.

Is there any way we can get a message to Leo to let him know they're coming?''

"He's flying chartered air. I can have someone try."

Price nodded. "Do it. I trust Leo's instincts. If he smells something fishy, it's probably there."

Kurtzman made a note.

"Has Able Team checked in?"

"They're at the L.A. Sheriff's Office interrogating their prisoner. We'll know something when they know something."

"What about Phoenix Force?"

"They're in the field staking out Cota."

"And Striker?"

"No word. But I've been keeping an eye peeled for news reports coming out of Hong Kong. It's been a busy night for the local police. Seems gangster types are running a high mortality rate right now."

Price looked at the wall screen at the opposite end of the room. Akira Tokaido, lean and compact, his punk-cut ebony hair jutting forth defiantly, worked at his console, eyes focused on the monitor as he arranged intel being siphoned in from the various world police agencies. "From what I've seen the attacks against the drug enforcement agents have slacked off."

"I've noticed that, too."

"Yet police aggression has picked up, and they're having a high success rate. And instead of retaliating immediately it seems the drug organizations are more confused than anything."

"Doesn't make sense, does it?"

"No." And that was the thing that bothered Price most of all. She knew the answers were out there. It was just a matter of finding out where to look, and having the time to do it. She had the uncomfortable feeling that the whole scenario was locked securely on someone's timetable. Figuring out why would give them the goal that someone had in mind, and perhaps a means of shutting the operation down.

L.A. County Sheriff's Department, California

"THERE'S PAPER on this son of a bitch from out of Kingston, Jamaica," Sheriff Orrin Conagher said, "besides our own outstanding warrants."

Carl Lyons nodded. He'd taken an instant liking to the big lawman. Conagher was tough-minded and wouldn't cut any corners for anyone not respecting his turf, but he was also a guy Lyons felt he could deal with.

They talked in the sheriff's office, with the blinds closed on the two windows overlooking the bullpen. Conagher rested easily in the old-fashioned swivel chair behind the organized chaos topping the large desk. He was a lean man, well into his graying years. Close-clipped hair made the bushy mustache under his hooked nose stand out even more. Broad shoulders stretched his white western shirt, and Lyons couldn't help thinking a five-pointed star should have been pinned on the guy's left breast to complete the image.

"I'm not here to pony up a jurisdiction dispute," Lyons said, leaning against the closed doorway.

"Now that really relieves me, Agent Lydecker," Conagher said without a trace of sarcasm. "Really, it does."

"I just want a chance to go one-on-one with the guy before we sink him into the system and lose him."

"Seems like you had that chance before we caught up to you." Conagher put one footed boot on the desk, then crossed it with the other. He reached out and brushed imaginary dirt from the polished tops.

"No chance at all," Lyons replied truthfully. After leaving the Pacific Palisades estate, a sheriff's department helicopter had picked them up at once. Within minutes they'd been surrounded by three cruisers with flashing lights. Merripen had crowed exultantly when the deputies removed him from Able Team's custody.

"My investigators are still searching through the wreckage you people left of that home. They had to ship in additional body bags. Now I don't know where you usually work, Agent Lydecker, but that kind of shit doesn't cut it in my town. When the Justice Department contacted my office, I'd assumed we'd be pursuing some kind of joint venture here. Instead I find you and your boys out playing suburban vigilante."

"Would you have been willing to back our play?"

"Hell, no. You boys ever stop to realize how many people could have been hurt during that little fracas?"

"Nobody got hurt."

"You were lucky."

"Maybe," Lyons said. "Or maybe we're just that good."

"Hell." Conagher ran a hand through his hair. "I bet you think you're tougher than hemorrhoids, too."

Lyons grinned. "On most days."

"And you bear a striking resemblance, son. No glory in that."

"I've been told that, too."

"Looks like I'm not covering any unexplored territory here."

"No."

"How much trouble can you cause if I refuse to let you see Merripen?"

"Enough that you can pass it on to your grandchildren," Lyons replied. "I've got paperwork lined up and waiting for my call."

Conagher's eyes narrowed. "Then why haven't you called?"

"You're not a man I want to push, Sheriff. I respect you, respect the job you're doing here. But I have my own agenda."

The sheriff dropped his feet to the floor and leaned forward to touch his intercom. "Barnes."

"Yes, sir?"

"Where's Merripen?"

"Showers. They're delousing him now, Sheriff."

"I'm on my way. You tell them to keep him there."

"Yes, sir."

Conagher stood and hitched his gun belt around his hips. A Smith & Wesson .44 Magnum rode in seasoned and worn Sam Browne leather. "You're going to get your interview with this guy, but I'm going to be on hand for it."

"I don't have a problem with that. If I get anything out of Merripen, chances are it'll be something that takes me out of the county."

"You're working those drug enforcement deaths, aren't you, son?"

"Yeah."

Conagher opened the door. "I suspected it from the moment you and your team blew in through my front door."

"We're still working on our subtlety."

A grin twisted the sheriff's lips. "Well, you damn sure aren't letting the effort get the better of you."

Lyons smiled back and preceded the man out the door. They walked side by side between the rows of desks toward the hallway and the waiting elevators. The county jail was a huge, multistory affair made of steel, brick and glass. Even the dim lighting in the hallways was oppressive.

"How much do your people know that they aren't telling?" Conagher pressed a button for one of the lower levels. The elevator doors closed and dropped away.

"Nothing yet."

"That for show, or is that for real?"

"The last I heard," Lyons replied, "that's for real."

Conagher nodded and scratched his chin in open speculation. "Scary thought."

"Yeah."

"I'm just an old country boy, and I guess I'm prone to such thinking," the sheriff said. "But the notion that some of these newspaper people got—that this is just a bunch of random strikes—is purely unadulterated bullshit. For what it's worth and as corny as it sounds, I think there's some kind of conspiracy going on."

"The drug empires scattered around the world aren't generally known for their congeniality. Especially to one another. These guys take each other out."

"Get enough stakes on the table, son, everybody will be inclined to take up a hand sooner or later. And you're talking about a hell of a lot of dinero out there."

"There's a lot of product out there, too," Lyons said. "Contrary to what the users believe, there's not a drug shortage in the streets. That's just a myth the pushers use to drive up the prices."

"Could be." The elevator coasted to a stop. Conagher held the doors shut with the button. "But you keep something in mind. I lost five good men this morning who were working surveillance on Merripen and a couple of other people. You find out something workable in this neck of the woods, you give me a call."

"I'll do that."

Conagher released the button, and they went out into the hall toward the showers and general processing. Lyons's stomach rumbled, reminding him that he hadn't eaten in hours. He grimaced when he remembered that Blancanales and Schwarz were waiting for him in the cafeteria. Even a cup of hot coffee sounded good now.

They went through the doors at the end of the hall and into the lab. A man in a white coat was sprawled beside a desk, a bloody hole punched through his chest.

"Son of a bitch," Lyons breathed. He raked the Colt Government Model from shoulder leather and scanned the perimeters. Nothing moved.

The .44 in his fist, Conagher sprinted to the desk, checked the man, then reached for the phone. He punched a two-digit number.

Hissing noises came from the large, open shower area to Lyons's right. He moved into place along the wall.

"Seal the building," Conagher said into the receiver. "I want every manjack identified and in place in five minutes. No one goes in or out." He hung up and crossed the room to back Lyons.

Mouth dry with anticipation, the Able Team warrior peered around the corner of the shower. The muzzle of the .45 followed his eyes automatically, tracked across the room.

Merripen was to his left. Stripped naked, suspended from an electrical cord tied around the spewing shower head, the Rastafarian slumped midway to his knees. Someone had cut his throat with a broad-bladed knife, exposing the white bones in his neck.

Lyons crossed the shower room floor to the opposite end of the room, which overlooked another section of the lab. No one was there.

He turned back to Conagher and shook his head. He walked into the spray bouncing off the corpse, then reached out and turned the knob to shut off the flow.

Merripen's sightless eyes were filled with false tears from the shower head. Whatever information the man had possessed, if any, had died with him.

CHAPTER SIX

Victoria, Hong Kong

From under the cover of darkness, Mack Bolan reached for the first perimeter guard. The soldier clapped a big hand over the guy's lower face, then pulled him from sight.

The guard tried to fight, panicked at having his breath cut off so suddenly. He clawed at the hand that held him, ignoring the Uzi hidden by his leather jacket.

Before the man could remember his weapon or manage to break free long enough to call for help, Bolan slammed the blade of the Cold Steel Tanto between the man's third and fourth ribs. The guard spasmed, struggled momentarily, then collapsed.

Bolan knelt beside the corpse and searched it. He ignored the Uzi and the .357 Magnum the guy was carrying. He didn't have room for the extra weight.

When he found the light-amplifying goggles in the guy's gear, he mentally readjusted his assault on the factory. He stripped the 9 mm ammo from the body, recovered his knife, cleaned it and put it away, then picked up the body.

The Executioner was dressed for the night. He wore a skintight blacksuit, with the Makarov riding his hip. The AK-47 was slung over his back, barrel pointed down so that it could be brought quickly into play.

Supporting the corpse, he walked to the rear entrance of the factory, put the dead face next to the sliding spy hole, then knocked loudly.

Bolan had observed the process earlier from across the street. Rain poured down on him, beaded up against the oily sheen staining the metal door. He drew the Makarov and held it at the dead man's back.

"What?" a gruff voice demanded in English.

"Coffee," Bolan said in a low voice. He'd heard the guard speak English. "It's cold out here."

The spy hole slid to one side.

Bolan held the dead man close enough to the view that the man on the other side of the door couldn't see anything else. There was no guarantee it would work, but the security on the operation was lax.

"Come in and get it," the man said. The spy hole slid closed. "But you're going to have to drag your ass right back outside no matter how cold and wet it is."

"Sure."

The metal door swung back.

Bolan shoved the corpse into the doorway to block any attempt the other man might make to close the entrance.

"Oh, shit!" The guy peered past the dead man and saw Bolan for the first time.

The Executioner slammed the guard with the corpse. Driving his legs hard, he pushed the man across the small room into the wall. The guard flailed for the pistol snugged in shoulder leather. Holding the guard against the wall with his own weight and the weight of the dead man, Bolan screwed the muzzle of the Makarov into the corpse's lower back and pulled the trigger twice.

The body helped suppress the detonations. What sounded like two loud hand claps echoed in the small room. The bullets erupted through the dead man's abdomen at an angle, thudded into the other guard's chest and killed him.

Bolan let the bodies slide to the concrete floor. He cleared the action of the pistol, making sure no flesh or material had gotten caught inside that would make the weapon jam later. He took the time to put two fresh cartridges into the magazine and lock the door, then went on.

While on recon, unable actually to penetrate the building or get hard intel, he'd sketched the possible interior a number of ways until he was satisfied he'd covered most of them. The factory produced ceramic knickknacks, things that flooded souvenir shops around the world. But its main export was China White. Despite the influx of cocaine in the United States, heroin was still the international drug of choice.

He'd automatically logged his entry time on his watch. Less than two minutes later he had the overview of the building's interior in his mind and had located the fuse boxes.

Once he'd gone beyond the short hallway leading from the rear access room, the building opened up into a large area that contained dozens of wooden racks of ceramic statues, cups and other items in various stages of finishing. Two guards, more interested in chatting with each other than in maintaining effective security, circulated between the racks.

Another hallway jogged more deeply into the guts of the building. Bolan let the Makarov guide him.

The cutting room for the heroin was to the right. Almost twenty feet by thirty, the room was used for storage, but kept few supplies on hand. The warrior figured the supervisors ordered new supplies daily and used most of them by the end of the business day.

He peered through the rectangular window set into the door. On the other side a dozen men and women worked diligently diluting the opiate powder at three tables. They were a mixed bag of Orientals, Caucasians and blacks—nine women and three men. Most of them showed considerable skill. All of them were stripped and worked naked to prevent theft. Four Asian men with machine pistols stood guard.

Making sure he couldn't be seen, Bolan finished his inspection of the room. Two windows at the back had steel bars over them. The door from the hallway was the only entrance that allowed free movement.

The warrior fell back, his mind already clicking with the new variables, turning a fresh stream of numbers on the blitz.

Following the hallway in the opposite direction, he found the fuse boxes set against the wall in a room where boxed goods were stacked and ready to be shipped. Bills of lading were already in place.

Besides the fuse boxes, an old-fashioned gasoline generator occupied a corner, set apart by a wire mesh cage. He smashed the lock on the cage with the butt of the AK-47. The inner mechanism shattered, and the lock snapped open. A five-gallon jerrican rested against the wall. When he shook it, he found the container was half-full.

He uncapped it, took a ceramic mug from one of the boxes and filled it with gasoline. He unsheathed his combat knife and cut slits in the protective pipes enclosing the electrical wiring that led to the fuse boxes. Using care, he poured the contents of the mug into the slits, then poured another mugful on the exterior of the pipes and the wall. He found a hand towel on one of the crates. He rolled it into a ball, then soaked one side of it with gasoline.

Fisting the jerrican, he retreated to the doorway. He lighted the towel, waited until he was certain of the flames, then flung it at the fuse boxes.

The gasoline whooshed as it caught. Flames raced up the wall and consumed the wiring.

On the move, Bolan raced back down the hallway to the cutting room. A fire alarm pierced the low hum of the factory. People yelled at one another, filled with confusion and sudden fear.

Less than ten feet from the cutting room door the Executioner tucked the jerrican against the wall, then donned the light-amplifying goggles.

The light died and sparks spewed from the fuse boxes, creating a flurry of images against the metal door. Bolan drew the Makarov. Controlled shots beat the bursts the AK-47 would put out. Unseen for now, his enemies could use the muzzle-flashes to track him down.

The goggles turned the world into monochrome landscape, totally colorless, filled only with a series of gray tones that threatened, in places, to overlap.

A man ran out of the cutting room with his machine pistol raised against his shoulder, obviously heading for the bigger room where the emergency lights were working. He paused in the doorway and yelled orders in Cantonese, pointing to the fire raging in the storage room. He never saw the Executioner when he passed him.

Bolan lifted the Makarov and fired two shots that kicked the man sideways. The gunner stumbled against the doorframe, then slowly sank to the floor. Someone returned fire, but the bullets never entered the hallway.

Three armed men remained in the cutting room. Bolan raced to the door, the 9 mm pistol up and questing.

One of the gunners rounded the corner, holding his machine pistol in front of him. He obviously didn't see Bolan, didn't know he was there until the soldier put his hands on him. The machine pistol sprayed a burst into the ceiling, bringing down acoustic tiles in a shower of tiny snowflakes.

Bolan grabbed the guy's shirt with his free hand, pulled him forward over his thigh and tripped him. Propelled by his own weight and momentum, the man slammed into the wall. Before he could move the Executioner pressed the barrel of the Makarov into his throat and fired two rounds. He dropped the kicking body and moved into the cutting room.

The remaining two men were in corners on the opposite side of the room. They yelled out questions that only added to the confusion of the situation.

Bolan moved toward them. One man must have caught sight of the warrior backlit by the fire in the storage room. The guy brought up the Uzi and fired a long burst.

The Executioner got off a single shot, putting the round squarely between the man's eyes. The corpse toppled back into a heap as the machine pistol clicked dry.

The last man swung his weapon around in a blistering arc that swept three-quarters of the room. Chunks of cinderblock were gouged from the walls and fell across the floor.

Anticipating the response, Bolan dropped to a prone position just ahead of the spray of bullets, rolled onto his side and drew target acquisition on the man. He squeezed the trigger twice. The rounds hit the man's heart less than an inch apart.

He shoved a fresh magazine into the pistol as he got to his feet. "Get out!" he commanded. He reached down and tipped over a table to let the people huddled underneath it know he was aware of them. "Get out now!" He fired two rounds into the ceiling to hurry them.

They rushed from the room, clawing at one another in their frenzy to escape.

Working quickly, Bolan kicked over the other two tables. Heroin spilled to the floor, creating a white powder mosaic of waiting death.

Bolan knew the drug could overcome him if he breathed the powder. He held his breath until he cleared the room.

Whirling in the hallway, he grabbed the jerrican, opened the cap, then threw the container into the cutting room. It skidded across the floor on its side, coming to a stop against one of the overturned tables. The contents sloshed out and filled the air with the pungent aroma of gasoline.

Bolan fired a short burst into the can. Sparks ignited the vapor trapped inside the container, and it went off like a small incendiary. Gasoline sprayed over the walls and quickly caught fire, creating flaming waterfalls.

The warrior went out the back way as police sirens cut through the night. He paused only long enough to scatter some of the Texas Ranger stars across the two corpses he'd left in the back room. No one tried to stop him.

KERAN TAT ANSWERED the phone himself on the second ring. From where he stood in the phone booth Bolan could see the glow from the fire that was starting to consume the factory. He'd counted two fire trucks before he'd quit the scene, and more had arrived since then. Between the electrical fire and the gasoline fire he was certain nothing of the building or its contents would be saved. He drank from his first cup of coffee. A second sat steaming up the window near his elbow. The night's pace was wearing him down, but he knew it was having its effect on Tat, as well.

"You just lost the heroin factory," the warrior said without preamble.

"So I've been told."

"Sounds like you've got a pretty good ear out on the street."

"I have people who look after my assets."

"That's good business."

"Yes."

"I'm in the market for good business."

Tat didn't say anything.

"How much did you just lose?" Bolan asked.

"I've not yet been told."

"From where I was standing it looked like a lot."

"I'm sure it was."

"It's going to be a lot more."

"You're an idiot," Tat snapped. "Every time you strike at me you run the risk of dying. You're pursuing a fool's errand. Instead of one enemy you now have two. How much longer do you think your luck will hold out?"

Bolan set aside his empty and reached for the second cup of coffee. "As long as I want it to. I've been in risk management a long time."

"I wonder how you'll talk when you're brought before me. Will you beg for your life? Or will you plead for a merciful death?"

"There's something you should consider," Bolan said in a graveyard whisper. "How long do you think it will be before I get bored with punching holes in your organization and come after you?"

Tat was silent.

"Get me a name," Bolan said. Then he broke the connection and left.

CHAPTER SEVEN

Bogotá, Colombia

"Yeah, that's good," Gaspar Cota groaned. He lay back on the king-size water bed and trailed his hands across the woman's naked flesh as she moved above him, smothering him with her heat.

She straddled him, working hard for her money, her palms flat against his chest as she rose and fell with increasing force and momentum. Lifting his head, Cota glanced at the mirrored tiles covering the wall on the opposite side of the spacious bedroom. He studied the smooth lines of the young woman's body as she worked, ignoring the gray-haired man's seamed and wrinkled face peering out just below her shoulder. It was this damn business, with all the pressures and complications of the past few months, that was turning him into an old man. He was forty-three, and his father had kept a head of black hair until his early sixties.

"Come on," he urged, "bring it on home now. I don't have time for you to be taking a breather up there and you damn sure aren't being paid for it."

The woman's mouth flattened into a thin, hard line for a moment. Then the sugar-coated smile dropped back into place, and she renewed her vigorous movements.

Cota closed his eyes and inhaled the odor of their mixed colognes and wet sex. The climax pulled at him, teetered for a moment, almost lost to the constant state of worry that plagued him these days. Then the orgasm struck like summer lightning. The breath emptied from his lungs as he lunged against the woman. He shuddered, wrapped his arms around her and felt incredibly small.

"Oh, yes," the woman murmured, sighing. "Make me a woman all over again." She held him, kissed his face and lay down with him against the silk sheets of the water bed.

He clasped her to him, trying to ignore the pounding of his heart as it tried to punch through his chest. It was the drugs, he knew. He could no longer use the cocaine as carelessly as he'd done in his youth. And now he could no longer live without it.

The woman moved slowly away from him, crawling to the side of the bed for the serving cart parked there. He watched her from behind heavy lids, remembering a time when his lust would already be building again as he gazed at her lean haunches.

She poured him a glass of champagne from the ice-filled bucket, then turned her attention to the small mound of white powder resting on the oval mirror next to it. She used the single-edged razor blade with precision, laying out the lines of coke in minutes.

Cota gathered the pillows behind his head and watched. He sipped the champagne, no longer gulping it back as he had when he first came into his wealth. The days of sleeping in a hut in the jungle and being satisfied with plump peasant girls was over.

Or were they? He had all but forgotten those long-ago days. But now, with what had been transpiring around the globe in the past twelve hours, those memories were coming back even sharper. Last night he'd even dreamed he was walking through a cemetery in a thunderstorm, his feet dragging through the mud until he stumbled at last upon the tombstone that had drawn him. His fingers traced the carved name, and he knew before the jagged streak of lightning showed him that it was his own.

He grabbed a corner of the blue silk sheet and mopped the sweat from his face. The woman noticed him. "Is anything wrong?"

"No." Cota finished the glass of champagne and tossed it onto the carpeted floor. The draperies, the mahogany bedroom suite, the chrome-and-glass desk tucked neatly into the corner by a glass-enclosed bookshelf showcasing a number of rare books that he'd never looked at, all spoke of the wealth he'd accumulated. No one would ever take that from him. He wouldn't allow it.

"You look as though you've seen a ghost."

"There are no ghosts here," Cota said louder than he'd intended. But there were. The ghosts of those he'd stepped on, the ghosts of the men who'd gone before him in building drug empires of their own, all stained his existence. It wasn't something that clung to any one room, or even this mansion. It was something that permeated the product that he sold every day. Many people, including his own countrymen, called cocaine the white death. He was beginning to think the nickname might possibly hold a kernel of truth. But he wouldn't give in to it easily.

He moved to the edge of the bed, swaddled in the expensive sheets, not wanting the woman to see him in his reduced state of arousal. She handed him one of the hundred-dollar bills tucked in the wineglass near the cocaine-covered oval mirror. He rolled it expertly, tucked one end into a nostril, then inhaled. The drug flushed into his system at once, filling his synapses with a deluge of pleasure. It erased the jittery paranoia that had been plaguing him most of the day. He took in another line, then switched nostrils. Only when he was finished did he hand the rolled bill to the woman.

She licked her lips in anticipation, held her hair back, then bent over the mirror. The line of white powder quickly sped up into her nose.

Studying the lines of the woman's back, the gentle sway of her heavy breasts, Cota felt the desire flow slowly back into his body. The fear left him. He was a strong man, strong enough to hold on to everything he now had, and strong enough to take still more from anyone he wished to.

The woman's eyes looked glassy when she turned to him. She smiled. "How much man are you, Gaspar?"

"Too much man for any one woman."

"Prove it," she said. A finger slid into her mouth. She purposefully flicked it with her tongue until it glistened, then she dipped it into the cocaine. Moving slowly, she daubed it onto her nipples. Then she reached for him, bringing him down to suckle her.

He took her breast into his mouth and felt the cocaine stutter through him, numbing his gums and tongue. He closed his teeth, nipping her hard enough to raise a muffled groan. But she refused to let him go. Already he was erect again. He pushed her back as he turned his attentions to her other breast.

She fitted herself to him and started gentle rocking motions that helped him thrust home. Then the phone rang.

A chill crept down Cota's back despite the cocaine and the tender flesh of the woman. When he glanced at the phone, he saw that it was his private line.

The woman continued to move beneath him, her breath hot in his ear. Cota untangled himself from her and pushed her roughly away. He picked up the phone cautiously, as if it might bite him. "Yes."

"Chief, there's a man on the first extension who wishes to speak with you."

"Hector, I've already told you I'm speaking to no one today."

"He told me you would speak to him."

"His name?"

"He didn't say."

"And you'd let this nameless man speak to me after I've told you I want to be left alone?"

"This man says he has something you want to know. Something he refuses to tell anyone else."

"About what?"

"Alonso."

Cota felt the desire leak out of him like the air from a punctured balloon. He threw his legs over the side of the bed and tried to unclench his fist from the phone.

"This man says he knows who killed Alonso and destroyed the cocaine shipment today."

"It was American federal agents," Cota replied. "This I already know. Everyone who lives on the streets knows that."

"He says he knows more. He says you're in danger, as well."

"Have you traced the call? It could be one of the federal agents."

"Yes, I did. It's coming from the Cayman Islands."

Cota considered the information. He had friends in the Caymans, people whose own financial interests would be hurt if his were hurt. And he couldn't ignore the direct threats against his life. International police agencies were extracting their pound of flesh from drug empires around the world. He'd assumed Alonso's death to be a response from the American DEA based in Colombia relating to the deaths of three of their agents during the night, but in light of today's developments that might not be true.

Cota hadn't ordered the deaths of the agents. It hadn't been necessary. His information was such that he knew who they were and had neutralized their threat to him months ago. But whoever had killed them had done so in territory recognized as Cota's.

The DEA had apparently waited only hours before claiming vengeance against Alonso.

"I'll speak with this man." Cota cut the line, then stabbed the extension button with his finger. "Hello."

"Wait," a man's voice said.

Cota looked at the blond whore.

Her eyes gazed with vague disinterest at his crotch as her fingers played with the gold chain around her neck. Her jugular beat frantically, showing the results of the drug slamming through her system.

Cota wrapped the sheet around his loins and listened as the phone was passed to someone new.

"Ah, my friend Cota."

The drug lord recognized the voice at once, but couldn't put a name to it. Memories stirred in the darkness of his mind, made more inaccessible by the cocaine. "What do you want?" He listened hard, not wanting to admit his ignorance of the other man's identity. The accent was Southwest American but held traces of British influence.

"From you," the man said, "I want nothing. I'm taking everything that you have that interests me."

"You've taken nothing from me, motherfucker."

"Haven't I? What about your freedom? Do you feel safe leaving your house these days, amigo?"

"If you think you're so much," Cota said, "then come to me and we'll see who has the biggest balls. I'll show you sights seen by few other men—the other end of your own cock."

The man laughed with honest amusement.

Unable to restrain his anger, Cota pushed up from the bed and paced the floor. The sheet dropped away from him, but he ignored it as well as the woman's incurious gaze. "There's a price on your head, bastard. You won't escape my wrath."

"Threats. You were always good at threats, Gaspar. But Luis Costanza was the better businessman. He built an empire that threatened nations last year, and today he's in the grave. He gathered people, shaped them into an organization that was formidable. You break them down, prey on them like a shark, with no sense of the greater picture. He was by far a better man than you are, and in the end he couldn't stand against the agency players, either."

"You speak in riddles."

"On the contrary. I called only to say goodbye. You and your kind, you're like dinosaurs, and you're on the way to becoming extinct. If the narcowarriors don't crush you, I will."

"You think you know me? You think you can call me in my own house and threaten my life?"

"I've just done it."

"Fuck you, man. The DEA, the DAS, F-2, the Justice minister, none of those can touch me. You think you can call me from the Cayman Islands and get me to shit myself with your threats? I'll have the eyes from your head."

"Sleep tight, Gaspar." The man chuckled.

"We'll see who has the last laugh, amigo. When I'm pissing on your grave, I'll remind you. I know all about Maria Alfaro and her ties to the DEA. Maybe I'll send you her lying tongue for a souvenir." Cota slammed the receiver into the cradle, then punched the button for the home switchboard.

"Yes, chief."

"No more phone calls," Cota ordered. "And round up Mando and Oalo. We're going hunting." He put the phone on the nightstand and glared at the prostitute. "Get up. Your work here is done today." He reached into his wallet and threw a fistful of money at her. The woman grabbed for the bills as they settled over her naked body.

Opening his walk-in closet, Cota chose a fresh gray sharkskin suit from the racks and dressed. Maria Alfaro still burned brightly in his inner-directed anger. Never before had a woman made so much of a fool of him. And he had loved her. He could never forgive himself for that. He'd chased after her as if he were a lovesick boy, never thinking that she might betray him.

He shut off the whirling thoughts. Behind him the woman was sucking up another line of coke, never once considering her nakedness. Cota had always believed all women to be whores. His own mother had been one, and she'd become pregnant with him by their village priest. But it had taken Maria to show him the final truth of his beliefs.

Taking the shoulder holster from the shelf, he buckled it on, then slid a Smith & Wesson Model 4506 .45ACP into the soft leather. He pulled on the jacket and checked himself in the mirror. After he dusted the white powder film from his thick mustache, he thought he looked impeccable.

"OKAY, WE'RE in motion now." From the foliage covering the hill to the west Calvin James surveyed Cota's villa through a pair of high-power field glasses. The setting sun drew ragged streaks of color across the white buildings, turning the crimson roof tiles to bloodred pools. Dressed in a jungle camouflage jacket and dark brown slacks he knew he'd be hard to spot by the sentries guarding the mansion and outbuildings, especially with the sun to his back.

A long white limousine rolled to a stop in front of the main building. A moment later four armed guards escorted Cota to the car.

James increased the magnification and inspected the vehicle as it sped toward the main gate. The way it sat on its tires let the ex-SEAL know it was heavily armored. He didn't doubt for a moment that the windows were bulletproofed.

"Where are they headed, Calvin?" Katz prompted.

James tracked the car to the highway. Three dark sedans trailed in its wake, drawing clouds of red dust after them. He hit the transmitter as the limousine turned. "South. Into the city. I see a white limo and three blocker cars."

"I've got them, mate," David McCarter said smoothly.

James flicked the field glasses to sweep through the eastern side of the rugged terrain that framed the twisting highway to Bogotá three miles distant. But even though he looked carefully he couldn't see the Briton.

On the highway a motorcycle pulled onto the concrete ribbon and eased into the pace set by the limo and the three sedans.

James capped the field glasses and quietly faded back up the hill to the Kawasaki motocross dirt bike that was his transportation for the operation.

"Puts a crimp in our plans to light up Cota's home life this evening, doesn't it?" Gary Manning asked.

"Or it might have given us an even better opportunity to take the man down," Rafael Encizo replied.

"Well, Katz," Manning asked, "do we sit tight, or do we pursue?"

The Phoenix Force commander didn't hesitate. "We follow. But at a distance. If Cota's trying to leave the country, I don't want to miss him."

"Being in motion like this ourselves," James said, "puts us in a vulnerable position, as well."

"It's a risk we'll have to take," Katz replied. "We're operating with a number of unknown factors at present. With Cota out of the picture there will be a vacuum in the power hierarchy here. Observing how it's filled could teach us something about what's going on here and in other countries."

"I've got more versatile transportation than the rest of you," James said. "I'll be second man up after McCarter. We'll switch off when I get there until we can set up a surveillance pattern with you guys."

"Agreed," Katz said.

James took his jacket off, reversed it to the dark leather side and put it back on. He carried a Beretta 92-F in a paddle holster at his back. Taking the Uzi machine pistol from the saddlebag strapped across the motorcycle, he slung it around his neck, concealing it with a tug of the jacket zipper. Then he pulled on a pair of protective gloves and strapped on his helmet, careful to leave the ear-throat headset in place. The Kawasaki's 125 cc engine caught on the first kick.

It jounced and bucked as it followed the rough terrain leading to the highway. James turned south and cranked the accelerator.

"Was there any sign of the Alfaro woman?" Katz asked.

"Negative," James answered. He felt comfortable on the motorcycle, stetched out lean and taut as the road whizzed by under his booted feet. "If we intend to get her, we might have to raid Cota's fortress, after all."

"We stick with our primary mission," Katz said. "There's more at stake here than one life." His words hung in the air.

James tried to keep the images that trickled into his head at bay. He remembered the woman's picture, tried hard not to think how she'd look with her face twisted in pain while Cota and his men torutured her if her cover had been blown. But it was just as bad thinking about what he'd be forced to do if they found her and she was dirty.

He tucked the bleak thoughts away and concentrated on catching up to McCarter and changing places with him before one of Cota's men realized they were being tailed.

Stony Man Farm, Virginia

"WHO'S THIS?" Barbara Price asked.

Kurtzman tapped the computer keyboard and brought the digitized picture to the forefront of his monitor. "George Russell."

The man had soft features, and his face was made rounder by the rimless glasses he wore. Weak, watery blue eyes stared forward without expression. A just-shaved sheen covered his jowls.

"And who is George Russell?" Price asked.

Kurtzman looked up at the mission controller, amazed at how run-down she was beginning to look. Dark bruises seemed about to surface under her bloodshot eyes, and her complexion was definitely paler than it had been that morning. He started to say something to her about getting some rest, but quickly checked himself. Price was a trooper and would stick it out until the bitter end. It was one of the things that made her valuable. And his remark, as she would definitely point out, was sexist thinking. Mentally he shrugged and gave up. "George Russell was the lawyer retained by Merripen and the Rastafarians when they set up shop in the United States." He tapped the keyboard again.

The picture of Russell evaporated and was replaced immediately by a street scene where the law offices of Russell and Associates figured prominently. They were on the lower level of the building, flanked by a barber shop and a Vietnamese restaurant.

"Doesn't seem like Russell's basking in the glow of economic prosperity," Price observed.

"That's just the cover," Kurtzman said. "On the surface Russell appears to be your average ambulance chaser. Twenty years ago he was a young assistant district attorney who got caught making deals. Charges were brought forth, but nothing stuck. Some of the deals were pretty political and would bring heat down on a lot of people who should have known what was going on. Russell went into business for himself and made a meager living doing public defender work. He lost more cases than he won, but he made a lot of connections."

The image on the monitor rainbowed and became another view. This one showed Russell in a courtroom, obviously objecting to something in front of the judge.

"Recognize the man beside Russell?" Kurtzman asked.

"No."

"Maybe this will help." Kurtzman entered new commands.

The courtroom scene vanished and was replaced at once by a splitscreen showing an older man with dark curly hair and a deep tan in frontal and profile shots. The shirt collar was obviously from some penal institution.

"Still don't know him," Price admitted.

"Leo would," Kurtzman said. "So would Striker and Hal." He studied the cruel face. "His name was Gus Giancola."

"Any relation to Pepsi Giancola?"

Kurtzman's mind locked onto the name from the past, still felt the hurt that came attached to it. Evidently Price had covered all the past Stony Man involvement since coming on board the team. Pepsi Giancola had figured into the death of April Rose. "They were cousins."

"You said 'were.' "

"Gus Giancola is dead. Has been for more than a decade."

"So he had nothing to do with that other business?"

"No." Kurtzman moved the computer file onward.

Another picture took form, this one showing Gus Giancola with Liborio Parrella in a small Italian restaurant, seated across the table from each other.

"Gus Giancola was one of Parrella's thugs?" Price asked.

"Yeah. Surprised me, too, when I was flipping through the file Hunt Wethers assembled on Russell."

"What put you onto Russell?"

"Not Giancola or Parrella. Russell's been minding some of the drug action in L.A. for years," Kurtzman said. "Nothing that would completely dirty his hands, though."

"He siphons off the money," Price said.

"Right." Kurtzman hit the keys.

A succession of business profit and loss statements filled the wall screens at the other end of the room.

"He's been a busy guy," Kurtzman said. "And he's good at what he does. Most of these businesses are legitimate. To a degree. But none of them actually make the money he reports to the IRS every year."

"So Russell's laundering drug profits through these businesses?"

"Yeah. RICO has files on most of them, but they haven't proved anything that will stand up in court yet. I know. I glanced at their files earlier. They've done some in-depth studies. However, I have an added edge because my systems aren't under the same scrutiny their systems are. I traced the money back to the Cayman Islands and to Switzerland."

"And?"

Kurtzman smiled. "Our boy Russell has been cutting himself a bigger piece of the pie lately."

More electronic data tracked across the monitor.

"He's double-crossing the people he's been representing?" Price asked.

"And bleeding them dry." The monitor froze on several pages of documentation from a car import agency based in Glendale, California. "This is one of the businesses set up as a front for the Rastafarians," Kurtzman said. "Notice the profit potential for the past three years."

The profit showed a healthy six figures, depicting a slight gain for each successive year.

"Now, eight months into this year, here are the comparative figures." Kurtzman filled the screen with two financial statements laid side by side. Windows opened up on each document. "Last year's profit margin showed a little over eighty thousand. According to the figures generated from this year's estimate, the car import business was already one hundred ten thousand in the red."

"Evidently Merripen didn't check up on Russell often enough," Price commented.

"This is one business," Kurtzman pointed out. "I haven't been able to find out all that Russell is handling, but I've found about twenty other businesses that he's laundering drug profits through. The rough figure that I'm able to come up with is at least five million dollars that he's managed to spirit away."

"And that's only counting the money that shows up on the company books."

"Right." Kurtzman shifted in the wheelchair, trying to relieve the ache sinking into its accustomed position between his shoulder blades. "This is one for the bean counters at RICO. It'll be a long time before the dust settles on exactly what Russell has done and to whom he's done it."

"When did most of the action start taking place?"

"Six, seven months ago. Of course, you can bet he was planning on it a long time before that."

"So what precipitated Russell's change of heart?"

"I haven't the vaguest clue." Kurtzman gestured at the computer. "I can define actions that have taken place, catalog thousands of them, mix them any way you want in seconds, but motivation is something the programming doesn't know a damn thing about."

"I was thinking more along the lines of what Russell is doing with all this extra money," Price said.

"From what I've seen he still lives at the same address and his bank accounts are hitting about the same marks as last year. Three months ago he bought a new car, but reviewing his past years, that's the same time he buys a new one every year."

"He could be tucking it away in hidden accounts."

"He'd better be," Kurtzman stated. "Once the people he's doing business with find out what he's done to them, he's going to need all the running room he can get."

Price nodded. "Something like this seems out of character for the guy you describe."

"Yeah."

"So if he changed, I think it's safe to assume that the reason for him to change came from without, not from within."

"Meaning someone's got him by the short hairs."

"I'd think so. We need to find out who." She paused. "Hal said it would come down to this."

"He's logged a lot of years working through stuff like this," Kurtzman said. "Long before they had anything like the computers we have access to. I guess we take them for granted, but Hal, he still remembers what a hunch feels like."

"What about Russell's connection to Parrella?"

"I haven't found anything incriminating yet, but the phone company records show they maintain a relationship."

"Keep looking." Price smiled. "I've got a gut feeling about that myself."

Kurtzman grinned back.

"In the meantime notify Charlie Mott and his crew that Leo could be heading for rougher waters than we'd assumed."

"Okay."

"Another thing."

Kurtzman looked up expectantly.

"Did Merripen get his one phone call?"

Kurtzman saved the current file and reopened the one he had on the Rastafarians. He scanned the data quickly. "Yeah."

"And who did he call?"

"George Russell. His lawyer."

"Then he turned up dead just a short time later. That's too damn convenient for me to believe. Put Able Team on Russell without letting the sheriff's department know. Maybe they can sweat some information out of him. The man sounds as if he might be ripe for it."

"I'm on it," Kurtzman said. He heard Price's footsteps retreat behind him as he sank back into the cybernetic heart of the Farm. The electronic pulse swallowed him, and he became larger than just a man trapped in a wheelchair.

CHAPTER EIGHT

Bogotá, Colombia

David McCarter stopped at a darkened street corner. Night had dropped over the city like an ebony curtain. Traffic was sparse. Most of the citizens had bedded down early, afraid of being caught in the nocturnal activities of the cocaine cockroaches that scurried out at night to prey.

He took a folded map and penflash from inside his bomber jacket, switched the light on and played it over the map. Tapping the headset transmitter through the open faceplate of his motorcycle helmet, he asked, "Calvin? Where are you, mate?"

James gave him the street and the heading. McCarter scanned the maze of streets, trying to fathom where Cota and his entourage might be headed. They definitely weren't making for the airport, which made for some relief and some increased anxiety at the same time. With the airport out of the picture the team wouldn't have to be concerned about taking the drug lord down in the next few minutes. But it conjured up some wonderment about where Cota was going and what he was going to do once he got there. The guy was definitely acting like a man on a mission.

Katz's voice was quiet and controlled when it came over the radio. "Calvin, David?"

"Yo."

"Yeah, mate."

"I think it's time the two of you peeled back and let Rafael and I take over the tailing. With the onset of night those motorcycles are going to stand out. You two will take up wing formations. Calvin will be on the left, David on the right. We'll keep your positions keyed into the program."

Both men signaled acknowledgment.

"Calvin," Encizo called, "I have the target now."

"I'm backing out, Rafael. He's all yours."

Katz gave directions for McCarter and James.

The Briton could tell from following along with the map that the Israeli was attempting to anticipate Cota's moves. The Kawasakis would allow the team rapid hit-and-git capacities to cover an attack or a tactical retreat if necessary. But only if they were in position. If Cota and his men saw them coming, it would turn the hit-and-git strikes into kamikaze rushes.

The SPAS-15 was folded and tucked along the frame of the dirt bike, covered by black leather. It wouldn't fool anyone on close inspection, but the color blended the combat shotgun into the machinery. McCarter wore his Browning Hi-Power under his bomber jacket in a shoulder rig. Other munitions were strung out along his combat harness.

He downshifted into first gear and twisted the accelerator. The motorcycle responded smoothly, and he followed the tunnel of illumination his headlight carved into the shadowed street.

Fourteen minutes passed as the caravan crept through the night. Katz switched off with Encizo, and they brought Manning farther into the net.

"Definitely headed downtown," the Cuban said.

Headlights flared to life in McCarter's rearview mirrors and closed rapidly. He leaned the bike to the outside, letting it wheel him to the outer limits of the road.

A long black Lincoln Continental shot by him, followed by another. Both vehicles carried at least a half-dozen men.

"I just picked up a couple of bogeys," McCarter said into the radio mike. "Two black Lincoln town cars, local plates, carrying wrecking crews or a group of gents late for the local bingo action."

Brake lights glared in the distance, then the cars broke left without warning, disappearing around the corner behind a hardware store.

"The game's afoot, mate," McCarter said tersely. "Those blokes just broke back into our field of operations."

"I see them," Manning called out. "And I got two more coming from the opposite side."

"Follow them, David," Katz instructed, "but discreetly. It appears that we aren't the only ones tonight who are interested in Cota's movements."

"Something to consider," Encizo said quietly. "Since we didn't get a whisper of these guys earlier while we were watching Cota, they must have known in advance where he was going."

"True," Katz said. "Provided these people aren't connected with the Colombian law-enforcement agencies, it would be better to take them out of the action as soon as possible."

"On my way," McCarter said. He twisted the accelerator, then reached forward and unplugged the headlight. The dark night closed over the rough street in front of him. The 125 cc engine revved, the blatting noise trapped between the rows of buildings. He reached for the SPAS-15, pulled it free, then slid it through the loose leather thong in the center of the handlebars, which would help stabilize the shotgun if he had to use it from the bike.

He dropped a foot to help balance the tire-eating turn he made at the corner. The Kawasaki slid, drifted momentarily, then the off-road knobby tires regained traction. He geared down, not using the clutch now, listening instead to the engine's roar. Then he geared back up, shedding the distance between himself and the suspect vehicles.

At the next intersection Manning cut the wheels of the ten-wheeler they'd liberated to use as a heavy vehicle for the operation against Cota. As soon as the truck fell into line, the big Canadian cut the lights.

McCarter slipped a gloved hand more tightly around the folded stock of his combat shotgun. It was loaded with double-aught pellets and choked out to give him a full spread. Accuracy wouldn't be a problem.

The distance dropped to thirty feet. Then two of the shadows at the rear window of the vehicle moved. Hairs rose on McCarter's neck an instant before the windows sprouted gun muzzles.

"You're made!" Manning yelled. "Clear the way!"

Cursing, McCarter released his hold on the SPAS-15 and used both hands to control the Kawasaki. The rear tire slid as he brought it around. His booted foot touched the concrete, slipped, then helped him reverse directions.

Bullets flamed when they struck the pavement around him. At least two ricocheted from the Kawasaki's metal frame, and he felt the vibrations through the handlebars. Manning ground the truck's gears, then the big engine kicked into full throttle.

The rear car slewed around as the driver fought it to a halt. The gunners kept up their barrage of fire.

Streaking from the street, McCarter popped the clutch and brought the front tire up in a wheelie as he accelerated toward the curb. He rose slightly and kept his knees bent to cushion the impact as the Kawasaki shivered across the curbing. He surprised himself by keeping it upright, then dispensed with the congratulatory thoughts when the shop window beside him evaporated into a thousand gleaming shards that raked at his bomber jacket and helmet.

He halted at the corner of the building and saw Manning bearing down on the town car. The ten-wheeler took up the center of the street, effectively blocking the sedan's passage. Bullets rattled off the front of the truck.

McCarter hit the transmit button on his headset. "Katz."

"Go."

"We're going to be delayed, mate, so don't count on us for anything quick."

"Understood, David."

"Give me a twenty when you figure out where Cota's making for." McCarter cleared the channel and roared down the alley coming off the street. He needed to back Manning's play, and he had damn little time to figure out exactly how.

A WAVERING LINE of 5.56 mm tumblers whacked out the double windshields of the ten-wheeler. Broken glass blew back over Gary Manning as he struggled to take cover.

"Son of a bitch," Manning growled. He kept the accelerator pegged to the floor and grabbed another gear. The ten-wheeler surged forward with the transmission whining in protest.

He'd planned on pulling McCarter from the fire, not ending up as the sacrificial lamb himself.

He reached for the Squad Automatic Weapon lying on the opposite floorboard and made sure the 100-round box was flush with the rifle's feeding system. A

Beretta 9 mm pistol rode in shoulder leather under his left arm. The metal box containing his combustibles sat on the passenger seat.

A fresh wave of hostile fire chewed into the front of the truck and eroded the top of the cab without coming in at him. The angle was all wrong for the shooters.

The driver of the Lincoln was backing up the vehicle in a desperate attempt to get clear of Manning's path. An unlighted lamppost on the curb blocked it, crunching into the rear bumper. Before the driver could reverse directions, Manning was on top of him.

The ten-wheeler was loaded with sand and rock and rode sluggishly over the rough places in the street, with only a light hand necessary at the wheel. At forty-plus miles an hour it was an unstoppable juggernaut.

The ten-wheeler's front end covered the nose of the Lincoln, the tortured screech of rending metal slamming hollowly along the street. Manning came up from his defensive crouch, trying to manhandle the steering wheel as it bucked in his hands. Forward momentum seemed stalled for just an instant, then the ten-wheeler popped up on the right side and rolled over the stalled vehicle.

The truck came down hard, weaving for just a moment while Manning fought with the wheel. He reached for the shift, geared down and built up speed again. A glance in the rearview mirrors revealed the smashed town car. Two figures were struggling out, pulling at a third. Muzzle-flashes sparked in his wake, but Manning knew the bullets would never penetrate the load to reach the cab. The knowledge didn't keep his shoulder blades from tightening expectantly.

The second town car slowed. The brake lights flared three times as the driver moved to block Manning's progress. Whomever they ultimately proved to be, the big Canadian realized they were playing for keeps.

The driver matched his speed, remaining thirty yards in the lead. Gunfire erupted from the rear windows and the front passenger side of the car.

Manning jerked up the SAW and mashed his foot on the accelerator. He squeezed the trigger and sent a spray of 5.56 mm hardball rounds through the empty windshield and across the rear of the town car. The gunners ducked, and the driver accelerated away before the tires could be hit.

Manning shifted gears again, then cursed violently when a radiator hose blew under the hood. Hot steam swept back into the open cab and bathed him in perspiration. In moments the engine would overheat and render him as helpless as a sitting duck.

When he glanced in the rearview mirror to examine his options, he saw another Lincoln closing in on him, sweeping around the wreckage of the last one. Bullets slapped into the rear and side of the ten-wheeler. Evidently the mystery teams were using a radio network of their own.

"You seem to be in a bit of a pickle, mate," McCarter called over the headset.

"Yeah," Manning grunted, recharging the SAW. "I was just about to ask for suggestions."

"See the side street coming up on your left? Boot shop on the corner?"

Manning looked and saw the darkened mouth of the street sandwiched between two multistory buildings. A sign held a large cowboy boot with a silver spur. "Yeah."

"Take it."

Pulling hard, Manning steered the ten-wheeler onto the street. The heavy load kept the tires from slipping, but didn't prevent the inside tires from coming up from the pavement for one heart-stopping moment. It clunked back down solidly, and he dropped gears to attempt to gather speed again.

Katz broke into the connection, sounding calm. "Cota just made his destination. He's pulled into the underground parking garage of the Hotel Galeno." He added the address.

Manning remembered it from the mapping sessions. The hotel was only a few blocks away in the opposite direction.

"Copy," McCarter responded. "We'll be there as soon as we can shake the competition."

Manning glanced in the rearview mirror. The town car that had circled around behind him was hot on his tail. Even as he saw it he caught sight of the second car—the one he'd been following—swinging into position, as well.

He keyed the transmitter, coughing against the thick burning vapor of the escaping radiator steam as it scalded his throat. "David, I got two—count 'em, two—bogeys on my tail, and we're coming in hard. Whatever you got in mind, it's going to have to come damn quick."

The truck's engine sneezed, lost power for a moment, then struggled valiantly to regain it as Manning put his foot down hard on the pedal. Steam continued to pour from the holed radiator, thick enough now to obscure the Canadian's vision of the darkened street.

"Keep coming straight," McCarter instructed.

Manning held to the center of the thoroughfare. An oncoming car honked at him in frustration, then the driver gave up and went over the curb, ran over the awning supports in front of an outdoor restaurant and brought the striped material down.

"You still got that little nasty rigged?" McCarter asked.

Glancing down, Manning scooped the radio-controlled detonator from his combat vest. "Yeah, but we were planning to use this as a backup just to buy us some time if things got tight, and we definitely hadn't considered using it from a moving vehicle."

"Necessity is the mother of invention, mate, and risk is her bastard child. You take out the first car and I'll help with the second."

Manning surveyed the rear action through the mirrors. The first car was almost at his bumper, jockeying for position as they raced down the street. The second vehicle was three car lengths back, waiting for a target of opportunity.

He armed the detonator, then was occupied for an instant in blocking the first car's attempt to come up alongside. When it floated back behind him, less than six yards away, he pressed the detonator button.

A double series of explosions shivered through the ten-wheeler, followed immediately by the shriek of twisted and torn metal. The truck's front end swerved across the road. Manning controlled the vehicle with difficulty, his mind cataloging the demolitions as they occurred.

The first charge of C-4 plastique had been light, just enough to shear the rear axle pins holding the dump bed to the truck. The others had gone off a heartbeat later and were heavier, designed to use the ground surface beneath to accumulate the necessary force. Propelled by the carefully positioned explosives, the dump bed came up off the ten-wheeler without being blown apart and came down hard on the lead pursuit car.

Sand and rock brought the Lincoln to a sudden stop as it covered the front end. The dump bed slithered off the mountain of dirt and automobile and rolled into a nearby building. Nobody appeared to be moving.

"Hell, yes!" Manning shouted. "Couldn't have worked any better."

"Nice piece of work, chum," McCarter said, "but you had two of those rascals nipping at your heels."

Before his teammate's words ended Manning saw the second car. Bullets struck the back of the truck and smashed through the sheet metal of the cab. The rear section sagged suddenly, letting Manning know at least one of the tires had been holed.

Keeping his head low, the Canadian weaved the truck from side to side in an effort to prevent the town car from coming up beside him. The truck's engine coughed, then added a decidedly sick metallic clattering to its repertoire of noises.

"Come on, David," he whispered to the mirrors. The truck lugged down another five miles per hour.

McCARTER TWISTED the motorcycle's accelerator and aimed the vehicle at the pile of sand and rock that had buried the pursuit vehicle, sped up the loose incline, then shot over the top. He sailed into empty space for nearly twenty feet, then came down hard at street level.

Glancing ahead, McCarter saw the other Lincoln closing the gap on the ten-wheeler. Sparks flared from the cab and the rear axle and wheels. He moved the SPAS-15 around on its sling until it pressed across his chest with the muzzle pointing to his right. He reached under his helmet and pressed the transmitter button. "Look alive, mate, I'm burning up your backtrail."

"I wasn't exactly feeling lonely."

McCarter grinned tightly. "Yeah, well, we get one shot at this, then all element of surprise is out the window."

"Terrific."

"Feeling pessimistic?" McCarter studied the back windshield of the Lincoln. The Kawasaki's headlight was still extinguished, and he doubted they could hear the double stroke of the snarling engine through the sound of gunfire trapped inside the vehicle.

"Getting shot at from any distance does that to me," Manning replied.

"Let's put the shoe on the other foot then, mate." McCarter closed the distance, readied the motorcycle for quick acceleration and chose his spot. He could tell Manning's ten-wheeler was dying even as they spoke.

A warehouse on the left loomed in the distance. It looked durable, made of stone and steel, exactly what McCarter had been searching for.

"Let them come up alongside," the Briton said, "then be ready to move."

"Roger." Manning allowed the truck to slide from center position on the street.

The Lincoln driver didn't hesitate. He rushed up on the left side, gunfire sporadic now as the shooters quieted down in predatory anticipation.

Gearing up, McCarter leaned over the Kawasaki's handlebars, then fisted the pistol grip of the combat shotgun. The fire selector was already set on full-auto. The magazine held ten rounds of double-aught buckshot.

The Lincoln's acceleration was no match for the 125 cc engine. Even as the driver was drawing abreast of the truck, McCarter slid up beside the town car like a wraith. His combat senses took over, allowing his professional self to scan the situation. He saw a black reflection of himself and the bike in the Lincoln's polished finish, then one of the men in the back seat pointed at him.

He tightened his finger on the SPAS-15, and the autofire took out the side windows and the driver in a single burst. He reserved the last two or three rounds for the left front tire. The double-aught pellets ripped the rubber to shreds.

At least two men inside the Lincoln grabbed for the wheel above the driver's corpse. The vehicle lunged to the left, veering at McCarter.

Dropping the SPAS-15 to hang by its sling, McCarter clutched the handlebars and leaned out wide to avoid the swooning car. The Lincoln's bumper rubbed his rear tire for an instant, almost making him lose control. He twisted the accelerator and shot away from the car, seeing the factory wall coming up. He tapped the accelerator. ''Manning.''

''Go.''

''Nail the bleeding bastard and let's finish it.''

Manning smashed his vehicle into the town car. As the Lincoln shuddered, the big Canadian drew back for another attempt.

McCarter noticed they were quickly running out of factory wall. When the ten-wheeler smashed into the Lincoln the second time, the heavy sedan gave up the ghost. Manning muscled the attack car over, grinding into it steadily until it smacked into the factory wall. No one had time to shoot at him.

The Lincoln's front end caught on the factory wall and held. The rear section swung around in an arc that carried the ten-wheeler before it. Truck and car came to a sudden stop only a few feet from the factory.

Applying the brake, McCarter dropped his foot and brought the Kawasaki around. He doubled back and roared onto the scene just as Manning was leaping clear of the truck with the SAW in his arms.

"That was your plan?" Manning asked in obvious derision.

"Worked, didn't it?" McCarter parked the motorcycle at the rear of the truck and slipped a fresh magazine into the SPAS-15.

Manning ran up the steps to cover the Lincoln from a higher vantage point. Cradling the combat shotgun in his arms, McCarter approached the steaming wreckage of the attack car with caution.

Two bodies had been thrown through the windshield and were spread-eagled across the hood. One of them was the driver. A man on the passenger side struggled weakly to claw the door open. It gave reluctantly with a metallic scream and allowed the man to fall onto the sidewalk.

"Stay down," McCarter ordered. He held the shotgun meaningfully. "Keep your hands where I can see them."

The man remained silent, just stretched his arms and rested his blood-streaked face on a bicep.

One of the men in the back seat was dead. The other was unconscious. With Manning providing cover McCarter reached in and dragged the man clear of the wreck. The unmistakable sweet odor of gasoline had started to pervade the area. Despite their attempt on his and Manning's lives, McCarter didn't like the thought of any man perishing in flames.

"Can you walk?" McCarter asked as he placed the second man in the street.

"Yeah."

"Then get the bloody hell away from that car before it explodes. Slowly."

The man got up with effort, keeping his hands extended above his shoulders.

"On your knees," McCarter directed, "hands behind your head."

The man slumped to his knees as if exhausted.

McCarter skinned the pistol from the unconscious man's shoulder holster, then did the same for his other prisoner. He threw both weapons into the shadows that hugged the factory wall. Both men looked to be American, and professionals in the field of violence and mayhem.

Manning was rummaging inside the truck. Sirens screamed in the distance.

"Don't have time for the full twenty questions," McCarter said, "so suppose we skip the animal, mineral, vegetable part and cut directly to the chase."

"I don't have anything to tell you." The guy tried to sound firm, but there was no conviction behind the words. The sirens continued to wail.

McCarter let a mirthless smile twist his lips. "Like I said, we don't have time for the niceties. So far you appear to have weathered your experiences in fair health. But if you refuse to answer me, or I get the least little feeling that you're having me on, I'm going to kneecap you and leave you limping the rest of your life. We understand each other?"

The man nodded.

"What were you lads about tonight?"

"We were ordered to take out Cota."

Manning came to a halt behind McCarter. The Phoenix commandos exchanged a quick look, and the Briton couldn't help wondering if a DEA operation and their own had overlapped in the confusion of the past few hours. The hit teams had responded like machined parts, obviously used to working together.

"Who gave you those orders?" McCarter asked.

The man appeared hesitant to answer. McCarter took one threatening step forward.

"We were hired by a guy named Webb August and promised a cut of some bigger money if things worked out."

Inwardly McCarter felt some of the tension dissipate. If the men had been hired, they weren't American agents. "What things?"

"There's a guy who's planning on taking over the Medellín cartel action. He's uniting the members.

Cota, Tijerina, Gutierrez and a couple of others have been the only holdouts. August figured if we put Cota down, and maybe the others, there wouldn't be any more problems."

A sickening twinge twisted McCarter's stomach. "Who killed the DEA agents?"

The man looked at the Briton. "Guys August hired."

"Not Cota?"

"No, not Cota."

McCarter put his anger away before it could interfere with his thinking. "Cota was set up to be the fall guy for the hits?"

"Yeah. Most federal agencies wanted to believe Cota was responsible, anyway."

"But Cota was the target?"

"If you people didn't get him, we were supposed to."

"We got to move," Manning said.

McCarter silently agreed. Against the backdrop of the night he could already see the signature light of a helicopter that would be carrying a police tactical unit toward the area. "How did your teams know where Cota was going to be tonight? We had him staked out for hours before he left his estate, and we saw none of your people."

"August figured it would be easier to take Cota if he came to us. We had an agent inside Cota's organization."

"Who?"

"Maria Alfaro. For a while she was his lover and got to know a lot about his business before taking over the administration of a large chunk of it. Today someone let Cota know she was double-crossing him. With the man's mentality it was a cinch he'd go after her."

"One last question," McCarter said. "Where do I find Webb August?"

"French Guiana. In Cayenne somewhere. I don't have an address. I swear it."

McCarter nodded, trying not to think how the rest of Phoenix Force were already caught up in the vicious cross fire engineered by Maria Alfaro.

CHAPTER NINE

Bogotá, Colombia

Rafael Encizo parked across the street from the Hotel Galeno and killed the Chevy's engine as he readied his gear. The hotel was dimly lighted, barely standing out in the dark neighborhood. The entrance to the underground parking garage was a yawning black pit. Two of Cota's hardmen ran interference for anyone who might try to pull inside. They carried their Uzis blatantly.

"Calvin?" Katz called softly.

"I've already got the back door," James replied. "Give me four minutes."

Encizo glanced up at the rooftop eight stories away. James was going to be running on empty by the time he made the top.

"Rafael?" Katz said.

"On my way." The Cuban shrugged into a stylish topcoat that made his jeans seem more affected than casual. Using a handkerchief from the glove compartment, he forged an ascot that he was sure would pass cursory inspection.

"Soft probe only," Katz admonished. "If you can ascertain Alfaro's whereabouts, fine. Don't put yourself at unnecessary risk. Cota is our target here."

"*Sí.* I'll be ten-ten until something breaks." Encizo doffed the headset, dropping it into one coat pocket with the walkie-talkie handset. He screwed a silencer onto his 9 mm Beretta pistol, shoved it into the opposite coat pocket, then snugged his backup piece into shoulder leather. The heavier hardware would have to be left in the car.

He opened the door, got out and pulled on a pair of skintight black leather gloves. His boot heels clicked against the pavement as he trotted for the building. Calvin James's four minutes fell through his mind second by second.

The foyer was filled with dusty glass and chrome, red leather booths and chairs. The elevator cages were to the right, against the opposite wall. To the left, past an atrium filled with artificial flowers and sprawling ivy, was the registration desk. It was manned by a young night clerk in a brown uniform blouse who tried to ignore the two men stationed nearby.

Encizo had his right hand inside his coat pocket. He cringed slightly as he approached the registry desk, almost as if he were intimidated by Cota's men. Both of the hardcases regarded him mutely, obviously feeling in control of the situation. Neither had weapons visible, but the Phoenix Force commando recognized the lumps of shoulder holsters the cut of their suits couldn't quite disguise.

"Good evening," the deskman said. "Can I help you?" The glance he gave to the nearer guard clearly indicated he was trying his best to do everything correctly.

Encizo felt sorry for the guy and felt bad about having to play him in the middle of things. "I need a room." He came to a halt in front of the counter. One of Cota's men was to his left, watching the street through the window while the other stood in the center of the foyer beside the atrium.

"I'm sorry, sir," the clerk replied, "we don't have any vacancies tonight."

Encizo nodded wearily and tapped a credit card with a false identity against the countertop. "I understand, but this was a reservation."

The clerk glanced back at the man standing near the window, then started to walk to the computer only a few steps away.

The guard shook his head.

"I'm sorry for the inconvenience, sir, but I see no reservations for tonight. And I let the last room out an hour ago."

"Tourist season?" Encizo asked doubtfully. "I've never known this hotel to be full up. And my reservations have always been honored. Let me speak to the manager."

"Hey, pal." The guard stepped away from the window and invaded Encizo's personal space in an obvious attempt to be intimidating. "He told you there weren't any more rooms. You don't want to make things difficult for yourself. Understand?''

"Sure," Encizo said with a smile. "I don't want any problems here." He turned toward the man, reached out and seized the guy's jacket before he could move and slid the silenced pistol out of his pocket. The barrel rested against the hardguy's shirt. Encizo squeezed the trigger three times and felt the man's body shake with each impact. Sparks ignited on the cotton material, then went out just as suddenly.

Pulling the dead man toward him, Encizo let the man's slack weight help spin him around to face the remaining guard. He brought the silenced Beretta up in a sideways sweep and fired on the point.

The other man had been caught flat-footed. He was trying to pull his gun when Encizo's first bullet caught him in the thigh. The six that followed caught him in the chest and tipped him over into the atrium.

Encizo let the body he held slump to the floor as he turned back to the clerk. "Where are the others?"

"Sixth floor. God, please don't shoot me." The clerk shrank behind the counter, covering his head with his hands.

"What room number?" Encizo pulled the walkie-talkie from the coat and keyed it to life. He glanced at the elevators. Two were stationary. The one on the right climbed from the fifth floor and halted at the sixth.

"I don't know."

"Alfaro," Encizo said. "Is there a listing for Maria Alfaro in the computer? Come on, man, move."

The clerk made two attempts to access the information from his computer terminal and botched both.

Encizo keyed the walkie-talkie. "Calvin."

"Go."

"Sixth floor. And you've already got company."

"Roger."

Encizo watched the clerk bring the file up on-screen, then start a search for the Alfaro name. "Katz, do you copy?"

"Affirmative, Rafael."

"There's no Alfaro registered."

"Cross-reference it," Encizo instructed.

"I am."

The walkie-talkie burped for attention in Encizo's hand. "Go," he said.

"We've got company," Katz told him.

The harsh bark of autofire sounded distant, and Encizo guessed it was coming from the parking garage. "The players McCarter and Manning turned up?"

"The very same."

"I've got it," the clerk shouted. His forefinger pointed at the gray screen. "Room 629. The reservation was made for a Carlisle Johnson by someone named Alfaro."

"Who is he?"

"It doesn't say. Only that he is en route from Chicago, Illinois. The United States."

"Did he check in?"

"Yes. At three o'clock this afternoon."

"Rafael."

"I hear you, Katz." Encizo waved the pistol at the clerk. "Get the hell out of here. Use the back way. Call the police. And keep your head down."

The clerk nodded and sprinted away.

"Katz."

"Go."

"I'm on the move. Calvin's already inside the building. I'm going to try to link up with him on the upper floors and fade out the way we've discussed."

"Affirmative. There's definitely no way back out onto street level."

Encizo paused long enough to check the dead men. The corpse lying in the atrium yielded a MAC-10 in .45ACP and three extra clips. A hard sprint put the warrior inside one of the elevator cages in record time. The doors closed just as the front entrance was reduced to a thousand gleaming shards of glass. Someone heaved in a smoke canister, which spewed a noxious black cloud over the foyer.

Remembering the computer and the information logged onto the screen, Encizo hit the stop button on the elevator panel, opened the door and took careful aim at the monitor on the desk. The Beretta coughed, and the monitor exploded.

As the cage started up, Encizo reloaded the pistol, then slipped the headset back into place. He hoped James was holding out okay.

BREATHING HARD from his climb up the fire escape, Calvin James cradled his CAR-15, raised a booted foot and kicked the window out of a sixth-floor room. It was dark inside, had the musty smell of being closed up and was silent.

Satisfied that he'd chosen an unoccupied room, he used the barrel of the assault rifle to clear the broken glass from the window frame, then clambered inside. Hoarse shouts rang out in the hallway, followed immediately by bursts of gunfire.

He paused at the door, twisted the handle and eased it back. Bronze numbers gleamed on the door face: 623. Mental calculation figured him to be three doors down from the man Alfaro was meeting. The direction was still a mystery.

Three men flanked Cota as the drug lord strode down the corridor from the elevators.

James briefly debated going for broke and taking Cota out, but his chances for escape afterward were decidedly slim. Phoenix Force had already spread out before the arrival of the unknown shock troops. Every man counted when they all worked together. That was one thing that Katz had drilled into their heads. They survived as a team, or they died as a team.

"Where's the woman?" Cota demanded.

"Room 629, boss," one of the men answered.

"And the man? This American? Johnson?"

"There, as well." The guard held up a radio handset. "And we're under attack."

"The police?"

"No. Our people don't as yet know who they are. But they've managed to kill the men we had assigned to the parking garage, and they've infiltrated the lower levels of the hotel."

"Assassins," Cota announced, "purchased by the goddamn Americans."

None of the men had anything to say to that.

James had the CAR-15 raised and ready to fire, if necessary. He kept the door marginally open and watched.

Two doors down to the Phoenix Force commando's right Cota and his entourage came to a halt. At the drug lord's instruction one of the men stepped forward and kicked the door open.

"No one is here, boss," the man said a moment later when he stuck his head back out of the room.

"Check the bathroom and closet," Cota ordered. "Dammit, they can't have simply vanished."

The three men hurried into the room.

Moving silently, James closed the door and hustled back to the window. If Alfaro and Johnson weren't in the room, and no one had seen them leave by the elevator, that left only one place for them to go. He climbed out onto the fire escape again, but saw nothing except blackness on the side of the building and the dark alley six floors below. When he glanced up, he saw a man's leg disappearing over the rooftop.

"Hey, Mr. Cota," one of the bodyguards said, "this window is open."

"Then get out there and find that woman. Now!"

The man scrambled through the window, eyes flickering across the straggling length of the iron fire escape. He saw James and started to turn and raise his pistol.

With the CAR-15 on semiautomatic James put a 5.56 mm round between the man's eyes. As the corpse tumbled backward and came to a seated position against the building, the Phoenix Force commando fired four more rounds into the building frame for good measure.

Blind fire ricocheted off the iron railings and sent sparks out over the alley. None of them came close to their target.

James tugged a smoke canister from his combat vest, pulled the pin, counted down and heaved it in front of the window. In the open it would last only a few seconds, but he planned to make full use of those seconds. The rest of the team had Cota's escape route to the ground cut off. If Cota wanted the Alfaro woman badly enough, James figured to make use of that to draw the man out into the open. Katz's original plan had gone awry from the git-go.

The landing leading to the seventh story was behind him. James ran, his booted feet making clanging noises against the metal. The ladder was completely vertical, narrow, the rungs made of thin metal spokes that seemed on the verge of bending as he put his weight on them.

Gunfire tore into the black smoke cloud hovering in front of the window. Several more bullets struck the corpse, which finally fell over. At the eighth floor James reached for the rooftop and began pulling himself up. Below him the hotel's lights were suddenly extinguished.

"They've cut the power to the building," Katz said over the headset. "Calvin, Rafael? Are you all right?"

"Yeah," James replied. He pulled himself over the roof's parapet, then rolled into a prone position while he scouted the terrain.

"Yes," Encizo said. "However, for the moment, I'm trapped in the elevator."

"Can you get free?" Katz asked.

"A matter of moments," the Cuban replied.

"Where are you?"

"The fourth, maybe the fifth floor."

James pushed himself into a crouch. The eerie keening of police sirens blasted through the night. Dark clouds scudded over the pale yellow profile of the moon. He heard scurrying, frantic movements across the rooftop, bits and pieces of voices that allowed him to piece together the conversation.

"Lying bitch!" an American voice said in guttural tones. "Get me out here to get my ass killed."

"No. You're making a mistake."

"The only mistake I made was in listening to you in the first place. If you wasn't such a good-looking bitch, and the money hadn't sounded so right, you'd already be dead and your momma'd be whining over your grave."

"It's no trick," the woman insisted. "The offer is there and the money is everything I said it would be."

"Your words be falling on deaf ears, babe. You ain't nothing but DEA lunch meat now. You better hope your friend Cota be in a negotiating mood if he catches us."

"Calvin?" Katz called in James's ear.

"Rooftop." James exchanged the CAR-15 for his pistol, then slung the assault rifle over his shoulder. He darted a quick glance over the side of the building and saw Cota and his two surviving bodyguards coming up the fire escape.

"Cota?"

"On my ass."

"Don't lose him," Katz said.

"Don't worry." James worked his way around the air-conditioning and HVAC units as quickly as he dared, zeroing in on the voices. He kept the moon in front of him, using it to skyline the rooftop.

"Cota won't stop to negotiate with you," the woman said. "He'll kill us both as soon as he sees us."

"You gotta try harder than that, babe. I had you checked out. You been Cota's main squeeze for months, and you been pulling the wool over his eyes that whole time. You honestly think he's gonna kill me for checking out the action down here and sacrifice all the personal time he could have with the bitch that's betrayed him?" The man laughed. "I don't think so. Cota, he's gonna want you all to himself."

"You're crazy."

"Crazy like a fox, babe."

"Cota will never deal with you. You're not in his league."

"We'll have to wait and see, won't we?"

Pistol leading him, James rounded a final corner and found the woman struggling with her captor. Maria Alfaro was a head shorter than the black man holding her. She wore dark slacks and dress boots, and drops of blood from small scratches on her face dotted her white blouse. A necklace glinted at her throat, only inches below the hard gleam of the switchblade pressed against her jawline. Johnson was a skinny piece of work dressed in a light-colored suit that made him stand out on the rooftop. Gold rings adorned most of his fingers, and a bracelet and watch encircled his wrists, diminishing the flash of his cuff links. A pencil-thin mustache lined his upper lip, flowing into the short-cropped beard staining his chin and cheeks.

James eased back the Beretta's hammer. The noise attracted Alfaro's and Johnson's attention. The man raised the knife to the woman's throat.

"Let her go," James ordered as he stepped away from the air-conditioning unit he'd crept up to. "Let her go and you walk."

Alfaro turned her head desperately away from the knife blade. Her flesh peeked over its edge, and fresh drops of blood ran down her throat.

"Man, you take me for a fool?"

"Not if you want to live." James kept the threat of the Beretta's muzzle steady and silent.

"I release her, you shoot me. No dice."

James showed the man the barest hint of a smile. "You don't release her, I shoot you, anyway."

"That sounds like a bluff to me."

"Play it out if you want," James said, "but you're putting all of your chips in the pot to stick if that's what you decide to do."

A gold tooth gleamed in Johnson's grin. "Man, you want this bitch. You know that. I know that. Who you think you're fooling?"

Voices drifted to James, letting him know Cota and his group had made the climb and that time was definitely running out.

"You need be alive to keep her alive."

James shifted the Beretta slightly. "Wrong." He stroked the trigger gently, monitored the recoil and set up for his second shot.

The bullet struck Johnson in the elbow of the knife-wielding arm. Bone crunched with a sickening sound as the 9 mm hardball cored into the joint. Blood spattered Alfaro's face, and she turned from it instinctively. Moonlight sparkled the length of the blade as it tumbled to the rooftop.

Screaming in pain, Johnson spun around, caught himself and made a grab for the switchblade. Instead of running when she was able, Alfaro had stepped in closer to the man, reaching for him protectively.

For a moment James was puzzled, frozen by the incongruity of what was happening in front of him. Alfaro should have made a clean break, not stepped back into the danger zone. The Phoenix Force commando was barely aware of David McCarter calling for him over the headset.

Johnson didn't hesitate once he had the knife in his uninjured hand. He lunged and drove the point toward Alfaro's midsection.

James reacted immediately, firing without aiming, totally on the point in combat mode. The Beretta bucked in his fist three times.

All three Parabellums took Johnson in the chest, punched through his heart and knocked him backward. The knife halted before it could touch Alfaro, then the man crumpled to the rooftop, unmoving.

Gunfire from Cota's position rattled through the HVAC units. None of it came close to James or Alfaro. Hitting the transmit button on the headset, James said, "Go."

"Have a care up there, mate," McCarter said. "Have you found Alfaro?"

"Yeah. She's here with me now."

"Well, watch your bloody arse," McCarter warned. "She might not be DEA anymore. Chances are, she's doubled herself in this operation and cut herself a piece of the pie.''

Alfaro turned and leveled her arm straight out before her. The stubby barrel of an Intratec Protec-25 poked out from her fist. "Don't move."

James froze. The woman had him cold, and he could hear Cota and the bodyguards creeping closer.

CHAPTER TEN

Stony Man Farm, Virginia

Hal Brognola stared out the Huey's window. He couldn't help thinking how lucky he was to be alive.

After the hit on Ross Melton, the President had insisted that the big Fed accept a small contingent of Secret Service agents as bodyguards until Stony Man could get a handle on what was going down. Brognola gave in gracelessly—but was grateful for the Man's foresight.

The assassination attempt came in the parking garage of the Justice Building with four men in combat black sniping at Brognola and his guards from behind a row of cars. At the end of the battle the four attackers were dead, as were two federal agents.

The big Fed didn't know what was going on, but he was determined to find out.

Second later the helicopter touched down and Brognola disembarked.

"Hey, Hal."

Brognola looked up and saw Jack Grimaldi's face suddenly appear out of the darkness when the pilot switched on a flashlight under his chin. Grimaldi sat behind the wheel of a canopied Jeep.

Taking a cigar from his pocket, Brognola swung into the passenger seat. Grimaldi fired up the vehicle and turned down the road leading to the nerve center of the Farm.

The main house rose out of the shadowed landscape, followed by the two outbuildings and the tractor barn. Standing three stories tall, with a fourth story underground, the main house had a plain exterior that advertised none of the armor-plating underneath. And the satellite dishes hooking up Kurtzman's computer room to the world were carefully hidden in the forests.

Grimaldi hit the coded door opener mounted on the Jeep's dash, and the left garage door swung up easily in spite of the extra weight it carried. The pilot pulled inside and killed the engine while the garage door closed automatically behind them.

Brognola led the way out of the garage and into the kitchen, paused long enough to take a box of raisins from the pantry, then moved on through the dining room to Kurtzman's office. Grimaldi was behind him, opening a can of smoked almonds. The steel door was ajar, so both men could enter without keying in an access code.

Kurtzman was at his desk, and Price was standing at his side. Both of them were studying scenes being relayed on the monitor between them.

Brognola poured himself a cup of coffee and offered some to Grimaldi, who shook his head vehemently and took a canned soft drink from the ice tray. "Anything?" he asked Price as he crossed the floor.

"Maybe. We'll know in just a moment." She glanced at him as he tore the raisins open. "Miss dinner?"

"Among other things."

"Don't get too involved with the raisins. You and Jack are going to have a man-size dinner in ten minutes. I don't want you giving out on me for lack of nutrition when I need you most."

"Yes, ma'am," Grimaldi replied. "Now there's a commanding officer I can respect."

Brognola shook out two antacid tablets, chewed them and washed them down with the coffee. "What are you working on?"

"We're profiling the guys who tried to whack you."

"And?"

"And I don't think either of us is going to be too happy about the results."

"I got them," Kurtzman said. His fingers dashed across the keyboard while the modem purred like a contented cat. Hard copy spewed out of a printer with an almost audible hiss. As each sheet came out, he glanced at it, then passed it on to Price.

Brognola got them next. He recognized the official seal at once and knew the documents had come from CIA headquarters in Langley, Virginia. There were two of them. The big Fed couldn't remember any of the faces from the firefight. He held them up when he was finished scanning them. "We got their finger-prints?"

"One of Kissinger's people did," Price said.

"So two guys out of the team were ex-CIA?"

"Right." Price passed across more data sheets. "We got these, too."

Brognola took them and saw that one was from Interpol and another had been requisitioned from an intelligence network that had once been affiliated with Germany's GSG-9 antiterrorist groups.

"Certainly is a mixed bag," Brognola commented when he put the papers on the desk.

"I'm sure whoever put them onto you," Price said, "assembled them that way so that if they were put down or somehow captured it would be more confusing than anything. At this point we don't know where the hell to look for the answers. And you can feel the time slipping away from us."

"For right now we're still in the ball game," Brognola said. "Where do you plan to look first?"

"At home."

Brognola glanced at the wall screens and saw television news stories and newspaper hard copy being rifled through at amazing speeds. "Why at home?" He had his own reasons and agreed with her completely, but being the devil's advocate would allow him to try to poke holes in his own theories as she worked on hers.

"Basically a hunch," Price admitted. "For the string of hits that took down so many of the drug enforcement agents around the world someone would have to have access to a hell of a lot of information. I don't know of any country that processes more international facts, figures and gossip concerning the drug trade than us."

"The Russian's have an enormous amount of intelligence, too."

"Not on drug agencies and suppliers. They've only recently started dealing with those kids of crimes."

"There are always Britain and France."

Price shook her head. "They don't have the kind of problems that we do with drug abuse. Trafficking is more prevalent here, the distribution systems more in place."

Brognola sipped his coffee. "I happen to agree with you. You're looking at the situation from the point of how these people would get the tools to pull off what they've been doing. Flip it over and you may have the motive, as well. Besides being the most capable of dissemination regarding international drug trafficking, the United States is also the largest marketplace for them."

"Meaning we're looking for people who know their way around U.S. intelligence circles."

"As well as somebody who knows the inner working of the drug organizations." Brognola sighed. "Yeah."

"Once a can of worms like this is opened," Price said, "there's no telling what will turn up. Covert agencies in this country and operating abroad have a long history of using drug kingpins for their own purposes."

"Nobody says they've stopped doing that, either."

Price nodded.

Brognola looked down at the collection of faces spread before them, knowing that only a few of the questions they had had been answered. Unless something broke damn quick it was going to be a matter of waiting for the other shoe to drop. And when it did, he was sure it would be heard internationally.

Bogotá, Colombia

MARIA ALFARO REMAINED professional as she held the pistol on Calvin James. The barrel of the Intratec Protec-25, chambered for .45ACP, looked like a cavern to the Phoenix Force commando. The woman's hand shook and her eyes were bloodshot. James could tell at once that her deep-cover assignment had included using drugs. She'd become one of the casualties she'd signed on to stop. It made sense that Cota wouldn't have let her into his inner circle without knowing that she was hooked as badly as any of his other people.

The headset chirped in James's ear. "Calvin."

He didn't dare reach for the transmitter. "Look, lady," he said, "Cota has two men, and they're on this rooftop with us. If you keep screwing around, you're going to get us both killed."

"Why did you have to shoot him?" Alfaro asked. "If I'd wanted him dead, I'd have shot him myself. Now you've fucked up everything."

"He was out of control."

"I could have gotten him back, cooled him down, if you'd just stayed back. You pushed him over the edge."

"No," James stated calmly, "you couldn't have. That man had checked common sense at the door. He was wired directly to fear."

Alfaro looked at the corpse and said, "You dumb son of a bitch."

Balanced on the tips of his toes, James waited for the proper moment to throw himself forward and try to take the gun from the woman. The Beretta was a heavy weight in his right hand, but he didn't want to have to shoot her if he didn't have to.

"Who are you?" Alfaro asked.

"You don't know me."

"DEA?"

"Yes."

"Give me a name."

"Eddie Cates. The password is Glass Slipper."

"And little Cinderella is supposed to change right back into what she was before?" Alfaro's smile was strained and sad.

James felt sorry for her and almost forgot about Cota and his approaching pet goon squad.

"It's come too far for that to happen," Alfaro said hollowly. "Much too far."

"Calvin," Katz radioed again.

James started to reach for the headset.

"No," Alfaro ordered. "Don't answer. And put down the gun."

Moving carefully, noticing the insane gleam behind the woman's eyes, James put the Beretta on the rooftop. "Cota's going to be here any second."

"Cota's the least of my worries. Now take off the radio and put it down, too."

James did as she ordered, waiting for his chance to move on her. But it didn't come.

"Move back." Alfaro kept the pocket pistol leveled at his chest.

James stepped back. All around him he could hear the gunfire in the streets surrounding the building. Police sirens shrilled their warnings as they neared.

Without wasting movement Alfaro stepped forward, lifted her foot and smashed the radio transmitter. "Now, my friend, it's you and me alone up here. And, if you listen very closely to me, I'll get you out of this alive." She bent, retrieved the Beretta, clicked the safety on and tossed the weapon to James.

He caught it, totally lost as to what to expect or what to do next. While he stood there trying to get a bearing on Cota and his bodyguards, Alfaro looted the dead man's body.

She looked up at him. "Help me." The Protec-25 had disappeared somewhere inside her clothing. She had both hands in the dead man's jacket and was tugging but getting nowhere.

James reached down with his free hand and leaned back with the corpse's weight. With the electricity cut off to the building the rooftop was almost as quiet as a graveyard. "Where are we going?"

"The edge of the roof." Alfaro dragged the body after her, James keeping it mobile.

Certain he was keeping company with a madwoman but unwilling to desert her, James helped her get the body to the roof's edge. Once they had it there, he asked, "Now what?"

"Throw him over." Alfaro made the effort, straining against the deadweight.

"You're kidding."

"No. Push."

A line of 9 mm rounds tore fist-size holes in the parapet beside Alfaro.

Moving instinctively, James grabbed the woman and pulled her down behind a HVAC unit. The corpse dropped into a prone position. More bullets slammed into the sheet metal covering the machinery.

When James glanced around the cover, he saw one of Cota's men break from hiding, angling to get position on them. The Beretta bucked in James's hand as he emptied the magazine. Most of the rounds were hits. The bodyguard stumbled in midstride, then pirouetted and fell over behind a thick length of pipe.

James changed magazines and scanned the rooftop again. At least four other men were scrambling over the rooftop from the fire escape. Cota was bellowing orders to the new arrivals, who fanned out in response.

"Reinforcements," James said when he turned to look at Alfaro. "We can't hold this position." He leathered the Beretta and unslung the CAR-15. "And we don't have anywhere to go."

"Yet," the woman replied, scanning the skies expectantly.

Crouching with the assault rifle on semiauto, James lined up his shot. He squeezed the trigger and put a round through the exposed knee of another of Cota's men. When the guy fell to the rooftop screaming in agony, he placed three more 5.56 mm tumblers into the man's head. The screaming died away a heartbeat before a new fusillade of bullets assailed the sheet metal.

The whirling of helicopter rotors sounded directly above them. James glanced up and saw a small Bell helicopter homing in on them. He brought up the muzzle of the CAR-15, targeting the pilot's window.

"No." Alfaro dropped her hand onto the assault rifle and pushed it down. "He's on our side."

James felt like pointing out that he wasn't exactly sure of what side she was on but passed. He waited because there was nothing else to do and returned the fire from Cota's wrecking crew to let them know he was still alive and dangerous.

"Quickly," Alfaro said. "We have to get that body thrown over the side."

"Why?"

"Because they can't know he's dead. The fall should keep the local police from identifying him. They don't have any records on him here."

"Suppose you tell me what's going on?" James suggested.

The helicopter came closer and the firing decreased. Evidently Cota and his people were confused as well about who might be piloting the craft.

"There isn't time." Alfaro glanced at him imploringly. "You must trust me."

"Lady, stranded up on this rooftop, cut off from my team, with a half-dozen hostile guns at my back and nowhere in hell to fall back to, believe me when I say there's nothing I'd like to do more."

"This is bigger than Cota," Alfaro insisted. "While I was in deep I turned up things I couldn't pass on to the agency."

"Why?"

"Because I couldn't be sure how deeply the corruption goes. If I tried to pass on the information too early and it fell into the wrong hands, I would have been dead and no one would know until it was too late. I've been monitoring the news and I've seen the reports of the drug enforcement agents' deaths around the world. Believe me when I say that's only the tip of the iceberg of what's yet to come."

Shouldering the CAR-15, James spaced a line of bullets across the hiding places Cota and his men had chosen. "They think you're rogue."

"They're wrong. I've been working Cota for over a year. My partner was killed, and as a female operative I don't have to tell you everything I've had to give up to make this case."

"No."

"And I'm going to make it. Not just for my partner or myself, but for the people who're going to be hurt if this operation is allowed to succeed. You have no idea of the ramifications involved." Her pain and conviction showed in her eyes.

"Okay," James said, "let's do it."

Alfaro clasped his wrist. "Wait." She looked up at the hovering Bell helicopter and took a small flashlight from her pocket. She flashed it three times, then twice.

Inside the darkened cockpit a light flared twice, then three times. Then the helicopter shifted, coming around to bear on Cota's position. A pair of high-intensity spotlights flared to life on both sides of the chopper. The harsh, rattling bark of an M-60 machine gun followed immediately. Metal spheres arced over James and Alfaro's position. Dulled explosions sounded heartbeats later, and vibrations from the grenades trembled across the rooftop. Waves of black smoke mixed with the shadows to cut down visibility.

"Now!" Alfaro yelled. She moved out like an uncoiling spring.

James was on her heels. Together they grabbed the clothing of the corpse, then levered it over the side.

The dead man pinwheeled as he fell, arms and legs moving in a semblance of life by the rushing air. The body landed on top of a marked police cruiser below, caved in the roof and scared the hell out of the two men crouched on either side of it.

Dropping back into a defensive posture with Alfaro, James watched the helicopter float down closer to the rooftop. The yammer of the M-60 was a constant, and the gunner never let up.

A bay door opened, and a rope ladder tumbled free and unfolded. It wavered just over the edge of the rooftop, then crept closer.

Alfaro pulled James to her and cupped a hand over his ear to be heard above the gunfire and rotor wash. "You've got two choices. You can stay up here and die, or you can get on that helicopter and do everything I tell you or you'll just as surely die."

"Some choice."

She pressed the dead man's ID into his hand. "Once we board that craft, you're Carlisle Johnson, a syndicate drug liaison from Chicago. If you let them think you're anybody else—*anybody else*—they'll kill us both."

James would have preferred staying on the rooftop and taking his chances. He knew Katz and the rest of the team were out there somewhere, and that they wouldn't leave him willingly. But if the woman was on to something that might help the efforts of the Stony Man teams and save lives in the process, he couldn't back away. Maria Alfaro was in bad shape, looked as if she were running on empty, yet he knew she wouldn't back away willingly. All things considered, there were no good choices. But there still remained only the one he could make. "Just say when."

The rope ladder drifted over onto the rooftop.

Alfaro pulled at James. "Now, amigo, and don't look back. I need you alive."

James ran, grabbed the rope ladder at almost the same time the woman did and stepped up onto the lowest rung. Alfaro followed suit on the other side. They stood pressed together, and he could feel the heat of her against him.

A head poked out the open bay above them. The features were American or European. The accent was pure Texas twang. "Hang on. We're going for a ride."

Abruptly the helicopter swung away from the hotel, over the confusion parked in the street. James held on tightly, his stomach fluttering slightly as he looked down eight stories. Bullets sparked off the helicopter's body but did no disabling damage. Within seconds they were out of range of the hostile fire.

"Now climb," the Texan yelled down. "We only got a few minutes to make the landing strip before the *federales* are on top of us."

"When we get up there," Alfaro said, "you talk to no one. You're above them. They're only the hired help. I don't give a goddamn if they don't like you. I'll brief you on Johnson's personal history during the flight. I know everything they know about the man. Understand?"

"Yeah."

Alfaro started climbing, obviously ill at ease about hanging from a rope ladder while the city whizzed by below her.

James waited at the bottom of the ladder to help provide stability until she reached the top, then started up after her. "Man, oh, man, brother Calvin," he whispered to himself, "what *have* you let yourself in for now?"

CHAPTER ELEVEN

Bogotá, Colombia

"Calvin, come in." Katz waited for a reply, but none was forthcoming. His mind worked frantically, played with all the new variables that had been introduced into the scenario. According to their initial plans, the team should have already been under way, out of reach for the local law-enforcement people. Instead, they were still looking to confirm the hit on Cota and were minus Calvin James. He called to the rest of Phoenix Force as he used the powered window washer's stand to climb the outside of the apartment building across from the Hotel Galeno. The motor popped and snapped fitfully, and the unit lurched awkwardly at times as it trundled up the brick skin of the building.

From his rising vantage point, tucked securely in the shadows of the apartment building on the alley side, he could see the grim flurry of battles taking place in the street in front of the hotel. Everything was in confusion down there. The police, Cota's men and the people McCarter had identified as ex-American agents formed three sides of a very deadly triangle.

"Yeah, Katz," Gary Manning responded.

"Has there been any sign of Calvin?"

"No." The Canadian's own worry about their missing comrade was evident in his voice. "But I haven't given up on him. He has a way of turning up."

Neither Encizo nor McCarter had seen or heard from James, either.

The apartment building went up twelve stories. Katz halted the window scaffold at the ninth floor as the little Bell helicopter swung in toward the hotel's rooftop. At that distance the men working their way across the pebble-and-tarred surface looked only slightly larger than ants.

He lifted the Galil 308 ARM assault rifle to his shoulder and used the StarTron scope to bring greater clarity to the scene. Sweeping the rifle from right to left, he deduced that the men scattered across the rooftop belonged to Cota. Then machine gun fire ripped into the area, followed swiftly by explosive and smoke grenades.

Activity at the other end of the building drew Katz's attention, and he focused the scope on James and Alfaro in time to see them pitch a body from the roof. Moments later the pair was running for the rope ladder trailing from the helicopter. It carried them away easily.

Katz pushed away the questions hurtling pell-mell through his mind away. They'd have to wait for a time when he had more information. He played the scope over the men remaining on the rooftop.

Unconsciously they came together in a group surrounding their leader. The Israeli had seen it happen a number of times before when dealing with people who weren't versed in military special forces techniques. All the pawns returned to the king during a disaster to find out their orders.

A professional tactician made sure the pawns had their orders before going into combat, plans that covered every eventuality. A professional fighting man was trained not to give away any intelligence by his actions out on the battlefield.

Katz followed the gathering men to Cota. The drug lord spent his last few breaths on earth screaming obvious imprecations at his men.

Then, cross hairs settled firmly on Cota's left temple, Katz caressed the Galil's trigger and absorbed the recoil the 7.62 mm bullet made as it screamed across the street. The impact drove Cota to the rooftop.

Katz confirmed the kill through the scope and lowered the rifle. There was no need to take out anyone else. With the head of the monster cut off the Colombian police and F-2 squads could deal with the body that remained. For the moment Cota's organization would drift back into the bastardized groups it had once been.

He tapped the transmitter as he engaged the scaffolding's motor to take him to the ground. "Break off the attack," he said. "Our target's been eliminated."

"What about Calvin?" Encizo asked.

Dropping down the side of the building, Katz gazed after the helicopter disappearing against the dark horizon. "For the moment he's lost to us."

Tarpon Springs, Florida

THE PRIVATE FLIGHT Leo Turrin had chartered from Dulles Airport put him down at the Clearwater Executive Airpark on Hercules Avenue in Clearwater, Florida. He took a cab to the nearest car rental agency and paid for a year-old tricked-out luxury edition Mercury Cougar painted a two-tone dark blue with a lot of chrome. He didn't figure anything less would have suited Parrella's parking accommodations.

Twenty minutes after that he'd penetrated the Tarpon Springs city limits.

Liborio Parrella's estate was north of the city, butted up against the coastline with a mass of orchards behind and around it. The old man might have been forced out of the business, but he hadn't been forced out of it penniless. All that had been gleaned from his contact within Mob circles, along with the warning that if Turrin had any smarts at all, he'd be better off just leaving Packy the hell alone.

Once he'd scanned a map and had the directions figured out Turrin stopped at a convenience store and bought two big foam cups of coffee and a package of white powdered minidoughnuts because he'd missed dinner.

He hadn't missed the news. Things were definitely heating up in South America and California with the retaliations reported. Things hadn't slowed for the rest of the world, either. The undeclared war was still on.

Turrin had a gut feeling that they were just experiencing the calm before the storm.

Before getting back into the Cougar he took the time to unlimber his weapons from his suitcases. The .38 Airweight Bodyguard slid into the paddle holster at his back. The Colt Government .45 long-slide went under the seat. He considered calling the Farm but decided not to. He had nothing to report, and all he'd end up doing was wasting somebody's time.

Instead, he climbed back into the Cougar and put the wheels to the road. Twenty minutes later he topped the last rise leading to Parella's home.

The main house looked like a starlet's dream home from old Hollywood, all paint and gingerbread trim from a time fifty years past. It faced the coastline some two hundred yards distant from atop a gently rolling hill. A widow's walk jutted from the second floor on the seaward side. It didn't take much stretch of the imagination to picture a worried wife pacing the hardwood floor waiting for her sailor husband to return.

Behind the house neat and trim orchards stretched into the near distance. A security fence at least ten feet high enclosed the estate, with guardhouses at the front and rear entrances. The garage was a long, squat building that matched the house, fully capable of sheltering at least a dozen cars. The circle drive in front of the house linked it with the garage. The gardner's shed was a two-story affair that Turrin figured was home to the extra muscle Parrella kept around for protection.

Turrin put the transmission in drive and pulled back onto the road. A long sedan eased through the front gates of Parrella's estate like a shark cutting through dark waters, and his sixth sense nudged the needle over into the danger zone.

He wasn't surprised when the car cut sideways in front of him fifty yards from the house and blocked the road. A mercury vapor spotlight splashed across his windshield and blinded him. His gut tightened up into an ice-cold ball. No matter how many times he'd stepped into it he wasn't used to the gleaming and serrated edge of the threat of sudden death. He put his foot on the brake and left his hands on the steering wheel, hoping to hell he was dealing with professionals instead of guys who shot first and asked questions later.

Two men got out of the car and became walking black cutouts against the blinding light as they came toward him. "Out of the car," one of them ordered in a gruff voice.

Turrin climbed out slowly, posing no threat. Without being asked he turned, placed his palms on the rental's hood and leaned against the car with his feet out behind him and spread.

Both of the men were young and cocksure of themselves. They carried Mossberg pump shotguns on slings and dressed in dark clothes.

"Smart guy," the one with the thick mustache said. He kept his shotgun centered on Turrin's chest. "Are you a cop?"

"No."

The other man left his weapon beside his partner, then knelt quickly and began to frisk the little Fed.

"I've got a .38 in a paddle holster by my right kidney," Turrin said. "There's a .45 tucked under the driver's seat. They're both clean. When I get them back, I expect them to be in the same condition."

"Maybe you're not so smart," the first man said. "You're not exactly in a position to be handing out orders."

"And you don't exactly know who you're holding on the other end of that shotgun, do you?" Turrin asked.

The second man removed the .38, the two Speedloaders and Turrin's wallet, then got the .45. He flipped the wallet open and went through the ID. "Name's Turrin. Leo Turrin. From out of D.C."

"You're Leo Turrin?" the first man asked.

"Yeah."

"I was expecting somebody taller, bigger."

The second man nodded, then began another comparison with the wallet's ID as if checking for a mistake.

"I mean, you got a big rep," the first man said. "No offense, Mr. Turrin. The Old Man spoke highly of you when he said you were coming."

Ignoring the feeble attempt at an apology, Turrin asked, "What's your name, soldier?"

"Dion Saluri."

The second man passed Turrin's personal effects back to him. "Sorry. I'm going to have to keep the guns for now. Boss's orders."

"Keep them clean like I said."

The man nodded, stepped away and took up his shotgun.

"You mind if I stop leaning on the car, Dion?" Turrin asked.

"Yeah. Sure." He acted nervous.

Turrin wanted to keep the guy that way. As long as Saluri was nervous, he wouldn't notice Turrin's own anxiety if it showed. "Who's the head rooster on the yard?"

"Dan the Man," Saluri said. "Come on with me. We'll drive you in."

Turrin went along, knowing it would provide the security teams with a chance to go over the Cougar for any unwelcome surprises. "Does Dan have a last name? I might know him."

"Canary. Dan Canary."

"He ain't no *paisano* with a name like that."

Saluri smiled knowingly. "No, he ain't, but the bastard knows his job like nobody's business. You'll get to meet him real soon. Anybody wants to see Mr. Parrella, they got to go through Dan the Man first."

Turrin sat in the back seat of the car, mugged by the thick smell of men's bay-scented after-shave and stale cigarettes. He used his peripheral vision as they drove through the main gates and up to the big house. He noticed a number of men in the shadows, standing guard professionally but with enough boredom in their postures to let him know they'd been doing it for a while.

The numbers he came up with, figuring for a four-shift day for optimum performance, were staggering. Even with all the money Parrella had socked away in the Caribbean banks, an operation this size would bleed him heavily if it lasted more than a few months. Nobody had been around Parrella to instill this kind of paranoia for years.

When the car halted in front of the house, Saluri got out and escorted Turrin inside. They picked up another bodyguard at the door.

Turrin automatically logged the home's design, part of an undercover cop's natural survival skills if he was going to live deep. They paused for a moment in the entrance hall while Saluri took his coat. A flight of stairs ahead and on the right led to the second floor. Straight through the entrance hall was the family room, filled with elegant furniture that matched the house. To the right was a dining room, long table and chairs spaced carefully under a gleaming chandelier. On Turrin's left was a closed blank door with an electronic key card reader.

Saluri walked to the door and pressed a hidden buzzer that echoed inside. Gazing at the reinforced hinges, Turrin figured the door to have an armor-plated core. A quick glance around let him know the other doors were the same. Any room in the house could be turned into a minifortress. The thing that bothered the stocky little Fed most was that the work looked new.

"Come in," a deep voice called from the other side of the door. A metallic chuckle sounded as an electronic bolt slid free.

Saluri went in first, followed by Turrin, who was sandwiched by the second man. The Justice man gazed around the room openly. They'd expect him to at this point.

The room was large, spacious, easily fitting the large desk and chair at the opposite end. Bookshelves filled one wall, and most of the titles had to do with legal matters and weaponry. Another wall was lined with computer hardware.

The wall behind the desk had a dozen security monitors mounted into it. Most of the views were from outside the main house and covered much of the surrounding grounds. The others focused on the interior of the house. At least one was keeping surveillance over the boat docks.

Turrin reached inside his suit coat, took out a pack of cigarettes and lit up. He breathed out smoke, saying, "I guess Mr. Parrella has gone for the new technology in a big way."

The man sitting in the swivel chair behind the desk looked like no bodycock Turrin had ever seen before. He was too young for the job to begin with, maybe late twenties or early thirties. Only made men, men with kills under their belts and years in service generally made the cut. His blond hair was neatly trimmed, almost military, and added a certain boyish charm to his good looks. He wore a kelly green turtleneck, black slacks and a casual sport jacket that had been tailored to hide a shoulder rig. The rimless glasses made him look enthusiastic and honest. The blue eyes behind the lenses held no warmth at all. Turrin knew he was looking into a killer's eyes.

"Dan the Man," Saluri said, "I'd like you to meet Leo Turrin."

Turrin didn't move. "I don't generally speak with the help when I've got an appointment."

If the remark bothered Canary, it didn't show. The man gestured to a chair in front of the desk. His fingers stroked a remote control panel on the desktop and some of the security cameras changed viewpoints. Then all but the center one winked out, leaving a gray film flowing across the screen.

"Times have changed," Canary replied. "You're retired. Mr. Parrella's retired. There's no need for formalities anymore."

Turrin crossed his knees. "You're not Family, Dan the Man, so I don't expect you to understand. There's some things you got to be Family to know. These things, they don't go away just because of a little thing like retirement. Things like respect and hospitality."

A nerve twitched high on Canary's face, but the white-toothed smile never lost its wattage. He glanced back at the solitary screen lighted on the wall and pressed a button on the control panel.

A frontal shot of Turrin filled the screen, faded quickly into a profile shot, then into a montage of newspaper pictures and video stills that had come from another life.

Turrin's stomach tightened. Canary wasn't Family. The man figured to be ex-military or ex-Agency of some sort. The OrgCrime Division file on Leo Turrin as an undercover agent was supposed to be dead and gone, but sometimes paperwork got hung up in the system.

"Leopold Turrin," Canary intoned. "Called Leo the Pussy. Worked for Sergio Frenchi in the good old days, running cathouses and escort services. Then came the bad old days when Executioner Mack Bolan dropped into Pittsfield and started shooting holes in the Mafia Families. You were a lucky one, though. Lots of promotions after that. You have a wife, Angelina, and three children, all grown, though none of them seem to have followed in your footsteps in the Family business. You retired from an active role in Family affairs a few years back and now maintain some sort of public relations angle for Family members. That right?"

"You forgot about the mole on the left cheek of my ass."

The monitor screen winked out. "I'm assuming your presence here has something to do with Family concerns over Mr. Parrella's current business."

Turrin flicked ashes into a paper cup sitting on the desktop. "Truth to tell, college boy, the Family wasn't sure if Mr. Parrella even had any current business." He stood up abruptly and walked back to the entrance hall. "When you get through tinkering with your gadgets there and impressing the hell out of yourself with how smart you are, tell Mr. Parrella I'm here to see him."

Canary's eyes looked like blue ice marbles behind his glasses. A slow flush colored his face. He reached for a house phone.

Saluri walked out of the room and closed the door behind him. "You really shouldn't have done that, Mr. Turrin," the bodyguard said. "Dan the Man's really not somebody you want gunning for your ass. The Old Man's taken a real shine to him."

"Couldn't be helped." Turrin shrugged. "Man's not Family. He doesn't know how to act, and I don't have time for his bullshit. And, anyway, I'm here to see Mr. Parrella. As long as I'm under his roof by his invitation, nothing's going to happen to me."

Turrin hoped that held true. From the looks of things Liborio Parrella was involved up to his eyeballs in whatever was going on.

Victoria, Hong Kong

THE BUSINESS WAS a combination bookie joint and loan-sharking operation in a third-floor office suite just out of the Queensway district. The public that didn't have business dealings with it thought the office housed a factory labor temp service, and most of the people who did place bets or make loans didn't know the main offices were located there. Shoebox business fronts all channeled their funds back to the main office, and the money scooted back into Keran Tat's financial holdings legally. Business for the temp service was booming.

The main building doors opened at 8:30, and the businesses followed shortly thereafter. According to the map in the foyer, the latest opening business was a bookstore at 10:00.

Mack Bolan walked in the main entrance and went directly to the elevators. He carried a box that had once contained a dozen long-stemmed roses. The roses had been left at the first convenient street corner, and the box carefully repacked with equipment necessary for the plan he was about to carry out.

Inside the elevator he punched the button for the fifth floor and went up. Executive office suites covered most of that floor, and it wouldn't look out of place for a boss or lover to send a secretary flowers.

At the fifth floor he found the nearest public rest room and went inside. A guy in a three-piece suit was cleaning his hands at the wash basin. "Hey, guy," he said congenially, "it looks like you're going to make somebody's day."

"I certainly hope to," Bolan replied.

The man pulled some paper towels from the dispenser and worked on drying his hands. "That's the kind of job I could go for right about now. Nothing depressing about delivering flowers. Nobody tries to look the other way when they see you coming.'' The man nodded and left.

Bolan stepped inside a stall, opened the flower box and took out the gray coverall he'd stashed inside. Underneath was his 9 mm Makarov pistol.

A small dented red toolbox had been stashed at the other end of the flower container. The warrior had taken it from the back of a truck parked in an apartment garage in the wee hours. The MAC-10 he'd recovered at the site of the cocaine lab was nestled in the toolbox with three spare clips, as were the two Mason jar bombs he'd whipped up from diesel fuel and gardening chemicals. He took out the roll of electrical wire he'd already outfitted with a plug, stuffed it into the top pocket of the coverall, then wrapped the belt of tools around his hips on his left side. The Makarov went into his right-hand pocket, and the extra clips went into his hip pocket.

In less than five minutes he'd completed his gear check, folded the gift box into the big trash bin and was out in the corridor. He slipped on a ball cap as he headed for the service stairs. Building security might pick up on an unauthorized utility worker coming in, but he didn't think they'd notice someone who was already inside.

He descended to the third floor and stepped into the hallway. The maid who met him on the way up didn't even give him a second glance.

He made a show of checking the output of the air-conditioning duct in front of the factory labor temp office. The front walls were all glass and revealed a casual waiting room, a bored secretary reading a romance novel and nearly a dozen artificial plants. Stieglar Factory Temp Service was printed on the glass door in silver letters along with the office hours. Business didn't appear to be booming today.

Putting a dissatisfied frown on his face, Bolan gripped his toolbox and walked into the office. The woman put down her novel long enough to look up at him. "Does the AC in here seem okay to you?" he asked with a note of exasperation.

"Seems fine to me," the woman replied, "but then people tell me I'm cold-natured."

Bolan nodded, pulled the cash register receipt for the gardening supplies from his pocket and studied it. "Guys down in 306 and 309 are complaining about it. The duct work to their offices runs through here. Mind if I take a quick look? Won't be but a moment."

"I'll have to buzz you through first," the secretary said as she reached for a phone.

"Naw," Bolan said. "It's okay. I won't be a bother." He walked to the door, opened it and stepped through.

"Hey, asshole, what the hell do you think you're doing back here?" The voice belonged to a big security man who was slowly turning to fat. He looked Oriental, but his accent was European.

Without bothering to answer Bolan swung the toolbox at the guard and trusted in his wrapping to keep the Mason jars safe. The toolbox bounced off the big man's jaw with a resounding thunk, and he dropped like a poleaxed steer. Before anyone else in the room could move the warrior had the Chinese pistol in his fist.

Eight men sat at desks covered with computers and telephones that seemed to ring constantly. "Get away from the desks and telephones," Bolan ordered. "If you don't act stupid, you don't have to die."

Slowly at first, then with gathering speed, the eight men moved away from their work areas.

"Hands up where I can see them," Bolan said, "and keep them there." He set the toolbox on the nearest desk.

The telephones kept ringing stridently. He figured the room had to be soundproofed, otherwise the avalanche of calls would be distracting. It would definitely make his work easier.

"You must be a madman," one of the men said.

"Keep quiet unless you're spoken to," Bolan warned in a graveyard voice. "And line up against the wall with your palms reaching for the ceiling and your backs to me. If you turn around, I'll shoot you where you stand."

They moved into position like a chorus line on opening night.

"Who's in charge?" Bolan asked.

As one, the other seven men pointed to the guy who'd offered his opinion regarding the Executioner's sanity.

"Get over here."

Trembling, the man did as he was told, trying to keep his eyes on the toes of his shoes so that he wouldn't look like a man who'd remember a face.

"Open the cash vault," Bolan ordered.

"Keran Tat will kill me."

"At least you'll get a chance to run from him. With me you get no chance at all. Open it."

The man walked around the fallen guard and removed a lithograph from the wall. He slid a panel free and exposed a heavy safe with an electronic readout instead of a combination lock on a door slightly smaller than a manhole cover. "The keypad to unlock it is in my desk."

"Move slowly." Bolan kept the man at little over arm's reach so that he couldn't complicate things, and watched the other seven men.

When he had the digital keypad, the man aimed it at the vault.

"One word of warning," Bolan advised. "If security should come through that door before I'm out of here, I'm going to put the first bullet in your head."

The man nodded, his hands shaking as he pressed the buttons.

Across the room moving components snicked and clicked, then the vault door slid silently open.

"Open it the rest of the way," Bolan said. He watched the man for effects of any kind of gas that might have been released inside the vault along with the lock.

When the man pulled the heavy steel door open, color-coded plastic racks of money—in several foreign currencies as well as domestic bills—were neatly stacked inside. Other containers held computer floppy and hard disks, and Bolan guessed they were backup copy for what was contained in the filing cabinets.

"Move away slowly and get back in line with the others." Once the man was back against the wall, Bolan opened the toolbox and took out one of the Mason jars. He reached deep into the vault and set the jar against the back wall with a satisfied smile. The cylindrical shape of the vault hadn't been expected, but it certainly promised to liven up the events he had in mind.

He moved to the filing cabinets next and tipped them over in a big pile around and over the eight desks, unmindful of the noise. Some of the phones were knocked to the floor, which cut down the constant ringing. Papers scattered as folders fell out. He put the second bomb on top of the mess.

Reaching into the top pocket of the coveralls, the warrior took out the electrical wiring, added a roll of black electrical tape from the toolbox and set to work on the bombs. He wired the one in the vault first, taping the leads to the detonating device he'd rigged using guncotton as the primer. Finished with that one, he cut the wire, then rigged a second wire to the other bomb. He spliced them together, shook out the extra footage and closed the toolbox.

"All right, gentlemen," Bolan said, "we're going out of here together. Slowly. When you hit the hallway, you're on your own. Starting on your left, move out. The first two men in line take the security guard."

"We can't carry him," one of the men protested.

"Drag him. Get it done."

The first two men grabbed the unconscious guard by the feet and pulled him through the door when Bolan opened it. He pinned a Texas Ranger badge on each of them before letting them go. The secretary looked up in alarm, the romance novel in her hand forgotten.

"You've got the rest of the day off," the warrior said. "Scram."

Blood from the guard's broken nose tracked the carpet. The woman hesitated for only a moment before racing the two men for the main door. The remaining five men moved out, as well. By the time the last one cleared the entrance, the first two men had dropped the security guard and were screaming for help as they raced down the corridor.

Bolan shot out the glass wall fronting the hallway to add to the general confusion, then pulled the fire alarm inside the office. Warning bells clanged and drowned out most of the noise the men and secretary made.

Crossing to the window, the Executioner picked up a chair and knocked the glass out. Some of the shards landed out on the busy street, but most of them were caught in the red-and-white-striped canvas awning of the deli below.

He pulled the collapsible grappling hook from his pocket, hooked it to the nylon rope he had wrapped around his waist and secured it to the windowsill. Another piece of cord he cut from the rope was used to tie the toolbox to his coverall. He shoved the Makarov into his pocket. With the electrical cord in his teeth he climbed over the side of the building and lowered himself to the second floor.

His feet braced on the side of the building, his weight leaned back on the cord, he glanced through the window of the music store directly below the office he was leaving. No one was in front of it.

He shifted, kicked the glass out and scrambled inside. Racks in the center of the store held CDs and cassette tapes. A long-haired Chinese youth stood alone behind the counter with an incredulous expression on his face.

Taking the electrical cord from his teeth, Bolan asked, "Where's the nearest electrical outlet?" Mentally he was still counting down from the time he'd released the men, knowing he was going to be cutting it close if he didn't want innocents hurt.

The clerk pointed at the wall.

Bolan shoved a rack of tapes aside and plugged in the electrical cord. It took a moment. Even with the guncotton primer the fertilizer explosives were slow to detonate. Then a double thunderclap shook the building and rattled the shelving.

Looking out over the street, Bolan watched burning money and flaming computer disks belch out through the broken window. The money looked like confetti raining down onto the traffic, quickly attracting the attention of pedestrians and motorists alike. Judging from the traffic snarl below, it would be some time before the local law could descend on the area, must less seal it off. He planned on being long gone by then.

The clerk was staring through a window of his own as Bolan passed him. "Outrageous, dude. Did you do that?"

"Yep." Bolan took a sack from the counter, found out it had the store's logo on it and put it back. "Do you have any unmarked bags about this big?" He showed the guy with his hands.

"Sure." The clerk reached under the counter and came up with a brown plastic bag.

Bolan took it, shoved it into his pocket and turned for the door. Once he ditched the toolbox and coveralls, the bag could conceal the MAC-10 and other ordnance.

"Uh, you don't have a thing about record stores, do you?" the clerk asked.

"No." Bolan gave him a small smile of reassurance. He used a longpick to let himself into the first empty office he found, changed out of the coveralls and put everything in the bag. With the bag cinched tight he looked like a lot of the other shoppers who were gathering out in the hallways of the mall area.

Five minutes later he was out on the street and walking east to where he'd left his car. Before he covered the first block he knew he had a tail. A dark blue sedan trailed him sedately through the stalled traffic. None of its occupants tried to get out to make a grab for the falling money.

Halfway through the second block he picked up the two guys on foot behind him and knew he wasn't going to make the car before they overtook him.

CHAPTER TWELVE

Santa Monica, California

George Russell, attorney-at-law and representative of downtrodden Rastafarian drug dealers in L.A., was a hard man to find. He hadn't been at the large house he maintained outside L.A. or at the spacious apartment he kept downtown. No one at his office had heard from him since that morning. He hadn't been at the courthouse since noon to represent three clients who were now threatening civil suits against him. Two of the judges, Lyons discovered, had pronounced Russell guilty of contempt of court. He wasn't answering his car phone, his cellular phone or his pager.

Lyons was beginning to believe someone had already paid a visit to Russell when Price turned up the beach house on Ocean Avenue in Santa Monica through a connection at the IRS. Apparently the lawyer had been so busily engaged trafficking drug money that he neglected to be as careful with his own hidden assets.

The sun was beginning to drop into the sea when they reached the address. Lyons killed the lights and pulled into the parking area overlooking the beach homes and hotels.

Hermann Schwarz was riding shotgun. He lifted the night glasses from the dash and scanned the beach houses below, saying the addresses in a quiet whisper.

Lyons listened to the tick of the van's cooling engine and tried to be patient. Having Merripen turn up dead under his nose hadn't sat well with him, especially when he figured the assassination was done because the Rastafarian had had information they could have used.

"Got it," Schwarz said. A moment later he added, "Bingo. Our boy's home."

"You're sure?" Lyons asked.

"Plates on the Jeep Renegade parked out front jibe with what I've got showing on the printout Bear sent." Schwarz passed the binoculars across.

Lyons refocused the lenses and swept the area methodically.

Russell's beach house was built on stilts. A narrow stairway led from the deck overlooking the ocean to the sand. The whitecapped waves were curling up on shore less than fifty feet away. A solitary light was on in the living room, but Lyons couldn't see into the house.

"How do you know he's there?" Lyons asked.

"Elementary, my dear Lyons," Schwarz said in an atrocious British accent. "Take a look at the wet spot under the Jeep beside the right front tire and you'll see where the air conditioner's been sweating. It isn't dry in this weather, so it means the vehicle hasn't been there long. I thought you were the detective."

"Anybody could have driven the Jeep," Lyons pointed out.

"Plus," Schwarz added, "I saw our guy stick his head outside the door a minute ago."

"I'm convinced," Blancanales said from the back seat. "Let's go get him. You're just mad because you didn't see the air-conditioning sweat spot first, Ironman."

"I'd have felt the hood when we got down there," Lyons said defensively.

Blancanales passed over an ear-throat headset. "I'm impressed. Still remember that one from the official Hardy Boys detective manual?"

"Cereal boxes," Schwarz said. "Carl gets his best stuff from cereal boxes."

Ignoring the habitual ribbing at his expense, Lyons stepped outside the van and pulled his gear into place. The .357 wheelgun rode his hip, and the .45 went into shoulder leather. He dropped two grenades into his pockets to tip the scales of Lady Luck in his behalf and slid an M-16/M-203 combo from the racks in the back for good measure. Then he headed out, leading the way down the sandy incline where the shadows provided the thickest cover.

Blancanales and Schwarz spread out around him, securing the perimeters as they closed in on the beach house. Music and bits of conversation drifted up from the beach area. Dirt bike and quad-runner engines blatted loudly, echoing in the distance.

The sand crunched under Lyons's feet. He held the M-16 steady and searched for shadows that didn't belong, certain that Russell wouldn't have come out here without some kind of backup.

He paused at the side of the house, looked up the incline and saw Blancanales standing guard to monitor the area and provide coverage in case of a hasty retreat. Lyons knew most people wouldn't have been able to spot Politician if their lives depended on it. The only reason he did was because Blancanales tipped him a nod.

"I got the back door," Schwarz called over the headset.

Lyons paused under the house at the foot of the stairs. "Say when."

"When."

Effortlessly Lyons moved up the stairs, careful with his weight. Even though he was a big man, he'd learned to move silently. Big men who didn't learn in his business didn't live. He made it without squeaking any of the wooden rungs.

The front door slowed him for only a moment. He got past the lock with a plastic rectangle he carried just for that purpose and let himself inside. The warm glow of the floor lamp by the wall splashed over the cozy living-room furnishings and made the burnished luster of the coffee table come through the fine layer of sandy dust.

An orange glowing dot in the kitchen belonged to a coffeemaker. A white sack containing leftover Mexican takeout was on the table. The Irish whiskey bottle beside the coffeepot was uncapped, letting him know Russell was having trouble with his nerves.

"I've got him," Schwarz called out through the house.

"Where?" Lyons moved carefully on point, making sure the bedroom was empty.

"Family room at the back," Schwarz said.

Lyons walked into the room, M-16 leading the way.

"I demand to see some ID," Russell said. "You people have violated my civil rights by coming here. You've trespassed in my home."

"Shut up," Lyons said.

Russell did.

"Is he clean?" Lyons asked Schwarz.

"Beats me."

Lyons turned to Russell. "We've got some questions and you're going to answer them."

"I've got a right to see my attorney."

"Funny. That's what your clients were saying earlier today when you didn't show up for court." Lyons waited a beat for the aggressive posture to drain out of the man. "We know how you've been skimming off the tops of the accounts you've been handling for the drug people. We know you're the reason Merripen got dead so quick in the L.A. County Sheriff's Office. I want the name of the guy you're working for, and I want to know the scope of this thing."

"You can't make me talk," Russell said quietly. "I know my Miranda rights."

"Let me clue you in, fat man," Lyons said, stepping into the man's personal space. "I'm not a cop. I am, however, the guy who's going to kick your ass if I don't get some answers in the next couple of minutes."

"Besides," Schwarz said levelly, "do you really want us to be cops?"

Russell looked at Gadgets.

"Your employer didn't seem to have any trouble taking down Merripen once they had him caged. And I figure you're more dangerous walking around talking than Merripen was."

Desperation fired Russell's small eyes. "You can't let him get to me. If he does, I'm a dead man."

"You'll talk," Lyons said, "or I'll put up the neon arrow over your head and draw the map myself."

"Immunity. You've got to grant me immunity. Witness Protection."

"You'll get it," Lyons said, "provided what you say is good."

The headset crackled in warning. Blancanales yelled, "Gadgets! Ironman! Get out of the house! Now!"

A roaring like distant thunder settled over the house. Windowpanes rattled in their moorings.

"Back way," Schwarz said. He reached out and grabbed Russell, pulling the man after him as he ran through the house.

As Lyons followed, he heard the scream of air brakes and unhurried rifle fire coming from Ocean

Avenue. He came to a stop on the rear deck and looked up the steep incline behind the beach house. A tunnel of lights coming over the edge turned into a narrowing cone that got brighter and brighter. The air brakes squeaked again, followed by screaming rubber.

"Ironman," Blancanales broadcast.

"We're out." Lyons grabbed Russell by the shoulder and swung him over the deck railing, ignoring the man's screams. "Jump, Gadgets, and get up running."

Schwarz didn't hesitate. The ground was a dozen feet below, but the Able Team warrior hit the railing and flipped over expertly.

Lyons was dimly aware of the eighteen-wheeler coming over the top of the incline like a metallic avalanche as he jumped to the railing and pushed himself into free-fall. Sand sprayed down over him, and the steady fire from Blancanales's rifle sounded like a slow drumroll to his adrenaline-fired senses.

He hit the ground and rolled, aware that Schwarz already had the lawyer up and was streaking for the waterline. He dug for traction, hurled himself forward and watched as the truck slammed into the beach house.

The structure was knocked off its stilts and punched sideways by the incredible tonnage backing the eighteen-wheeler. Then the truck ended up in the middle of the rubble and the walls exploded outward. The trailer came loose when the tractor hit bottom and spun end over end until it tore apart and scattered across the beach.

Lyons came to a halt thirty feet from the tractor as it clunked over on its side and died. He hit his transmitter. "Pol?"

"I'm okay," Blancanales responded, "but we've got company."

Before the words died away in Lyons's ears he saw the headlights of three vehicles spilling down the side of the incline from Ocean Avenue. He lifted the M-16/M-203 to his shoulder and put his finger on the grenade launcher's trigger.

Schwarz was pulling Russell out to sea. Once in the waist-high water, any chance at land pursuit was over.

The three vehicles were tricked-out dune buggies, colorful fiberglass shells over Volkswagen chassis. Their mufflers stuck out behind them like trumpets.

Lyons squeezed the trigger as autofire tracked down on his position and rounds kicked into the sand toward him. The 40 mm grenade leaped from the launcher and impacted squarely on the nose of the lead craft. The concussion lifted the dune buggy and the three men inside into the air like a child's play toy filled with puppets. It flipped backward and crashed to the ground in flames.

The Able Team warrior threw himself down as they shot past. He pushed himself to his feet, fumbled for another grenade and charged his weapon as the remaining two dune buggies chewed around in circles for another pass.

The driver of the buggy on the left shuddered suddenly and fell out of his seat as the high-powered crack of Blancanales's target rifle rent the air. The other buggy roared forward, straight at Lyons.

Keeping cool, the big ex-cop aimed the M-203 again and squeezed the trigger. At the last minute the driver locked the brakes. The 40 mm round landed only feet in front of the skidding vehicle and blew a pit in the sand. The buggy went into it nose-first and flipped.

On the move, Lyons sprayed the area with 5.56 mm slugs, taking out the two men who tried to shoot him as they stumbled from the wreckage. He used the spilled dune buggy for cover as he closed in on the last attack craft.

Blancanales had already moved down the hill and taken up a new covering position. Only a short distance away most of the beach parties had broken up as the people stood in fascination, trying to figure out what was going on.

The two men in the dune buggy had removed the corpse from behind the wheel. One of them slid into the seat and gunned the engine. Lyons calmly reloaded the grenade launcher.

"Ironman," Blancanales called.

"I got him." Lyons sighted down the barrel and waited until the off-road vehicle tried to climb the incline back to Ocean Avenue. It lost speed and struggled like a bug trying to get up a wall. When Lyons touched the trigger, the 40 mm round slammed into the vehicle and blew it apart. Nobody got up to walk away.

Before the sand settled Able Team was hustling their prisoner toward the waiting van.

CHAPTER THIRTEEN

Stony Man Farm, Virginia

Kurtzman's voice over the desk intercom interrupted the steady whirl of thoughts inside Barbara Price's tired mind. "I've got Yakov on line two. There's been a problem in Bogotá."

"Secure line?" Price asked.

"Yeah."

She picked up the phone. "Price."

"We've lost Calvin," Katz said without preamble.

Price's stomach twisted in knots, and the sour taste of bile rose in her throat. She'd lost operatives before, at agencies before taking on the Stony Man Farm assignment. She'd seen their bodies afterward, made apologies to the families. Steeling herself, she made her voice steady. "How did it happen?"

"He's alive. It came out more blunt than I'd anticipated." He quickly explained about the helicopter that had flown James and Alfaro from the rooftop.

"He never contacted you?" Price asked when the Phoenix Force leader was finished.

"No. But neither he nor the woman appeared to be under any duress, and both seemed to know the helicopter was going to be a friendly."

"Alfaro knew. There's no way Calvin could have known."

"That's what I was thinking, as well."

"Did the local police overtake the helicopter?"

"No. According to police reports that Rafael and Gary monitored, the helicopter made a rendezvous at the airport and they took off in a plane that falsely filed a flight plan to Mexico City."

"What kind of plane?"

Katz gave the particulars. "The registration has also proved to be false."

"I'll give this to Aaron. With as much satellite surveillance as we already have in place on this operation, we might get lucky. What about Cota?"

"The man is down. However, we did pick up a third party of players. And a name. Most of them were ex-CIA agents and mercenaries."

"That correlates with the information we've received on the team that tried to kill Hal." She brought Katz up-to-date on Brognola's experience with terse sentences.

"The man who hired these people," Katz said, "is named Webb August."

"Just a minute." Price called Kurtzman on the intercom. "See if we can find a file on a guy named August, Webb. No known middle initial. Katz says the guy's supposed to have CIA contacts, maybe a contract player subsidized by the Agency. If you don't turn up anything direct, try accessing the Air America files. The guy has a line on mercs, so it might play that way, too."

"I'm on it. Back to you as soon as I have something."

Katz went on. "We also have an address on August in Cayenne, French Guiana."

"Do you need transport to get there?"

"No. David's handling that now. But there's another unexplained thread. Cota was very upset tonight. To the point that he was trying to kill Alfaro."

"Her cover broke?"

"I don't think so, but it's possible. The man David talked to said that Alfaro was an agent working for them, that she was part of a trap designed to snare Cota. They knew about us, but if we didn't take Cota down, they were supposed to."

"Alfaro might be working a triple-cross."

"It gets complicated."

Price silently agreed. "And Calvin has worked his way into the eye of the storm."

"Or been lulled into it, yes. Since we're operating with so little information pointing in any certain direction, Calvin might have seen this as the chance to make a breakthrough."

"If Alfaro doesn't betray him."

"Yes." Katz paused. "There was a man Alfaro was meeting. An American who came in on a flight today. His name was Carlisle Johnson. He hasn't turned up in any of the police reports. In the last few minutes that I saw Calvin he and Alfaro were shoving the body of a black man off the rooftop. The police haven't been able to identify the man.''

''He didn't have any ID on him?''

''No.''

''And you think Calvin and Alfaro lifted it.''

''It's a possible scenario that would explain part of the puzzle.''

''Hold on.'' Price stabbed a finger at the intercom button again.

''Yeah,'' Kurtzman said.

''I need somebody who can take time to run a quick trace.''

''I'm switching you over to Akira.''

The intercom buzzed.

''What's up, mama-san?'' Akira Tokaido's youthful voice asked. Thrash metal music leaked into the connection from the ever-present personal cassette player he wore.

''I've got a name,'' Price said. ''Johnson, Carlisle. Spell it any way you have to. He arrived in Bogotá, Colombia, today. Find out where he's from and who he is, then get back to me.''

''You got it.''

Price returned her attention to the phone and punched up the information she had on the contacts she had in French Guiana. Katz estimated the time it would take Phoenix to reach the country, and she plotted the arrival of whatever ordnance they might need. In the end she was able to beat Katz's time by almost half an hour. She put the call through on another line.

Kurtzman beeped for her attention. "Let me have your screen."

Price switched the monitor over to Bear's control, slaved it to his board, then dumped the telephone conversation into three-way mode on the speaker phone.

"I'll walk you through it," Kurtzman said. "I'm sending copy through to Katz on the fax line."

A picture of a high-browed, white-haired man with seamed features chugged onto the monitor. A ragged scar bisected an eyebrow that looked like a fuzzy ivory caterpillar. He wore an open-throated denim shirt and a low-crowned black Stetson.

"First frame, Jonathan Webb August. His friends call him Webb. He's not, and never has been, CIA. But he has been involved in contract work for nearly forty years. He started out doing it himself, worked mostly for the United States against Communist countries. Then in the early seventies he retired from an active role except on special occasions." A series of color and black-and-white stills followed. Webb August aged quickly in them, and several years seemed to be skipped entirely. "By the time he stepped out of the hands-on side of the business, he knew a lot of the independent players on both sides of the iron curtain. If you needed someone to make a hit, steal computer information or infiltrate a terrorist unit, August could give you the name of the man or woman who could do the job. For a price. During the last years of the cold war, our boy was scabbing money from both sides of the wall."

"Evidently he was no longer as enthusiastic about his patriotism," Katz said.

"It wasn't paying as well. August has learned to love money."

Price scanned through the information quickly. "I don't see anything in there to indicate that August could design an elaborate scheme like the one that's taking place now."

"He's not," Kurtzman said. "The guy's a mechanic. You give him a blueprint that's feasible and he can get it done. But he's not inventive."

"So he's working for someone."

"That's my guess."

"There were ex-CIA agents at the strike against Hal, and in Bogotá," Price said. "I'm not willing to write that off as just a mere coincidence. Who handled August at the Agency?"

"A lot of people. August wasn't anyone's pet."

"We'll ask the man when we see him," Katz promised.

"Be careful down there," Kurtzman advised. "From what I've been able to put together from news footage and Agency reports, August maintains a well-staffed little army. You guys may be in for a rough ride."

Price leaned back in her chair and studied the man again, trying to see the drop of truth in the well of suspicions.

"I came up with something else that bothered me, Barb," Kurtzman said. "In reviewing August's files I discovered that the DEA has been using him for information about the Medellín cartels a lot lately."

"That fits," Katz said. "In order to play the games August has been playing with Cota and the other cartel members he'd have to be well versed on all of them."

"Yeah," Kurtzman agreed, "but it turns out that a lot of August's snitches were where we got the information we used to take down Luis Costanza and our little Panamanian dictator friend last year."

A cold feeling twisted through Price's stomach and sat there like a stone toad. "If that's true, we were used and never even knew it."

"Costanza posed a large threat," Katz said. "That's why we went after him. But McCarter's intel also suggested that the man August is representing is after control of the cartel."

"If that's true, that means they've had over a year to prepare for this."

"I'd believe it," Kurtzman replied. "This thing's been falling like an international avalanche ever since it started. The way it's been put together, with a piece nudged here, another turned there, you wouldn't even notice it until the domino effect had started."

Price wondered how the hell she could plan to stop it if she still wasn't sure exactly where it was headed.

The intercom beeped. "Yo," Tokaido called. "I found Carlisle Johnson."

"Who is he?" Price asked.

"Chicago Mob affiliate. I'm putting together a file now. Have it to you soonest. As a thumbnail sketch, though, Johnson's been heavily involved in the drug action in the mid- and northeastern sectors of the United States. OrgCrime, the DEA and the FBI have been after him for years, trying to flip him. Johnson is a guy who knows where the bodies are buried. And he's also a guy local drug gangs go through to settle territorial grievances. He's got some pull with people behind the scenes who can make little troublemakers vanish. Word is, you don't go into business in a big way in those areas without approval from Johnson and his backers unless you want some heavy trouble. Still doesn't stop people from trying, though, and the files I glanced through suggest that Johnson has been indirectly responsible for deaths well into three figures."

"Another networker," Price mused. Her mind tugged at the possibilities, appalled at where they might eventually lead. She thanked Tokaido and cut him out of the communications link. "Yakov, taking your scenario for Calvin one step farther, in light of this new information, he could intend to pass himself off as Johnson and find out who's pulling the strings on this operation."

"It's possible. When it comes to the drug problem, you know he sometimes gets emotionally involved."

Price knew. James had lost family to drugs, recognized the potential for disaster from a personal perspective. "Keep me posted on the French Guiana end of things."

"You do the same."

Price hung up. At the moment there was nothing else she could do. And she hated it.

Victoria, Hong Kong

THE MEN FOLLOWING Mack Bolan had good moves. Even when he let them know he was on to them, they didn't panic.

The pair on the sidewalk broke into a trot and closed the distance. So far there was no sign of weapons. The warrior didn't figure on it staying that way. They'd been too close to Keran Tat's operation. If they weren't working for Tat, they were working for someone else monitoring Tat's operations.

Bolan ducked into the underground parking garage and broke into a sprint. By the time he reached the two elevators set into the plain concrete block wall to his left, the two guys on foot had made the corner and paused for protection. The dark sedan wheeled into the garage with shrilling rubber, halting at the ticket booth.

An elderly Chinese couple stepped out of the cage on the right. Catching the door and seeing that the cage was empty, Bolan stepped inside and hit the button for the first floor, then rapidly hit the buttons for the other five. The stairs were at the opposite end of the building. Provided some of the men split off to cover the stairwell, the Executioner assumed at least one of them would come up the elevator after him.

The car stopped at the first floor and he got out while a small group of people boarded. Three young men in business suits were waiting for the second cage as it descended. When the doors opened, they started to get on.

Bolan held the door with his foot, smiled ruefully and flashed one of the Texas Ranger badges on his open wallet quickly enough that none of them got to see it plainly. "Sorry, guys," he said. "Security. I'm afraid I'm going to have to have that elevator."

The three men nodded and moved back. None of them appeared happy about it.

Once inside, Bolan tapped the emergency stop button, opened the escape hatch and crawled on top. The air inside the shaft was muggy and hot, and only dim light filtered in. He reached down, managed to get the restart button on the panel with effort, then replaced the hatch. The elevator started to descend.

The two men got on at the garage level. Bolan peered at them through the crack he'd left in the hatch. Both were very polite but insistent while they kept two other men from boarding, as well.

As the doors closed, the Executioner slid the hatch to one side and covered them with the Makarov.

"What do you want?" one of them said in Russian.

Bolan replied in the same language. "Stop the elevator before anyone can get on. Do it now."

The one who'd spoken pressed the emergency stop button and the cage rocked to a halt. Both men lifted their hands above their shoulders.

"On the floor," Bolan ordered. "Hands behind your heads."

They did as they were told.

The warrior slithered back through the opening and dropped the bag containing the MAC-10 and extra ordnance into the corner out of their reach. When he searched them, Bolan found two Makarov 9 mm PMs in concealed leather. He tossed both pistols through the open hatch on top of the elevator, then closed the hatch. Removing a multipurpose tool from a pocket, he opened the elevator's control panel, erased the previous programming the unit had received, then restarted the cage and hit the garage-level button. The cage dropped with a sickening lurch.

Both men watched him closely.

"Up," Bolan said, motioning with his pistol before he tucked it under his jacket and picked up the bag. The numbers were going crazy inside his head. There was no way to figure a wild-card play like this, but he was hoping the other side would be just as confused.

The men managed to get to their feet just as the elevator came to a stop and the doors opened. The Executioner went through first, found no one waiting and waved them outside. They followed wordlessly. He pointed to the car he'd rented during the night and had them lead the way. He didn't see the dark sedan that had been tailing him and figured maybe the driver had raced around to the other side of the building.

A bit of plastic glinted behind one of the men's ears. Bolan plucked it off, ready in case the guy tried to turn on him. The plastic housed a tiny speaker attached to a small walkie-talkie in his shirt pocket. Someone was calling for someone else to respond. He dropped the walkie-talkie into a trash receptacle. Things were already starting to heat up, because now the other teams knew something had happened to the first one.

There was no time for a question-and-answer session. The men knew that. They'd remain silent, or lie to him in the minutes that were left.

Bolan opened the trunk of the rental and removed the spare, jack and jack handle. "Get in."

The men weren't happy about it, but they did. It was a tight fit.

Bolan slammed the trunk lid and slid behind the steering wheel. He dropped the MAC-10 onto the passenger seat and pulled out onto the street. The memorized streets and businesses flipped through his mind as he drove. He checked the rearview mirrors constantly. When he remembered a place he knew would serve his needs, he made a left-hand turn and cut into traffic.

Three more turns and eight blocks later he stopped the car in front of a small photocopy store. Only a tired old man reading the morning paper was inside.

Bolan opened the trunk. "Get out," he said.

The two men climbed out, brushing at their clothing and glancing suspiciously at their surroundings. They were obviously puzzled about their destination.

Herding them inside the photocopy shop, Bolan halted them beside a copier and lifted the cover. "Take your jacket off and stick your face on the glass."

The man started to protest and looked at his partner for support.

Bolan showed him the pistol without letting the old man see it. Evidently the clerk thought it was a joke, because he shook his head, grinning big enough to show pink gums and went back to his paper.

"Your choice," the Executioner said menacingly. "I don't care if I get the before or after shot. Bullet holes will make it harder, but not impossible."

Grimacing, the man stuck his face to the photocopier glass. Bolan threw the jacket across the back of the man's head and thumbed the button twice. Both prints came out clear. "Now the left profile."

The man moved under the jacket.

Bolan took two more pictures, then did the second man. When they finished, he gathered the prints, paid the clerk, passed on a receipt and moved his captives back outside. He left them standing on the street corner as he drove away.

Tarpon Springs, Florida

LIBORIO PARRELLA LOOKED like hell. Both his hands, looking like skeletal models wrapped in blue-veined, fleshy spiderwebbing, were piled on top of the wooden walking stick that had long ago lost whatever gloss it might have once had.

Leo Turrin felt as if he were interviewing a corpse that hadn't been given the bad news yet. But in spite of his appearance a definite spark of life glowed in Parrella's eyes.

"So, Leo the Pussy," Parrella asked in a whiskey-hoarse voice, "what brings you out to see me? I know you didn't come all this way to see the Mouse and EPCOT Center. You ain't in the right town." He laughed, and the effort sounded as if it hurt.

Dan the Man stood in the corner with his arms folded across his chest. His expression was deadpan.

"I came out to see how you were enjoying your retirement, Mr. Parrella," Turrin said. "Then I see you got your house looking like Fort Knox, or prepared for the next world war."

"The next world war is a long, long way off, Leo." Parrella walked to the bar and looked at the man standing behind it. "You and I won't live to see it. Your children won't live to see it. Maybe the next world war, one side will have spiked tails and the other will have halos." He laughed again. "Make us a couple of drinks, Mike. What are you drinking, Leo?"

"You got beer?"

"Beer I got. You sure you don't want anything stronger?"

"I'm sure." Turrin yawned to show it. "It's been a long day. And maybe I'm getting older."

The bartender uncapped a bottle of Rolling Rock and poured it into a chilled glass. Parrella handed the glass over and raised his own. *"Salute."*

"Salute." Turrin took a deep draft of the beer.

"So, Leo, who sent you?" Parrella leaned heavily on his cane.

Turrin started to shrug the question away, say something polite to deflect the interrogation.

"Don't bullshit me, Leo," Parrella said. "I still keep an ear out to the rest of the world. Don't let this old husk of a body fool you. Officially you've semi-retired, living the life of Riley. Unofficially the Commission calls you in to smooth over troubles between Family members because you're nonpartisan. Is there anyone in the north who thinks they have trouble with me?"

"No, sir," Turrin replied. "Back there you've still got a lot of respect, Mr. Parrella. People remember you and what you've done."

"Bullshit." Parrella stumped over to the window, stayed out of the line of fire and at an angle so he wouldn't be easily seen by anyone outside. "Those old men up there, the ones who are left, they've lost their balls. Or their knowledge of how to act. You ask them, Leo, if they know what inflation is, what the stock market does. Hell, most of them probably get the shits every time the economy in this country has gas. There was a time, and you remember it, when we took what we wanted, held on to only what we were strong enough to hold. There's no Cosa Nostra like I remember it. Just a bunch of old men and young pups trying to be goddamn yuppies.''

Turrin let the old man talk. Parrella was on a tirade, so evidently the guy had something to compare what had been lost to what could be gained.

Dan the Man seemed antsy and shifted uneasily against the wall.

"They sent you to find out what I was into, didn't they?" Parrella's bony stare was penetrating. "Somebody up there smelled the scent of new money."

"Some of the Family members are worried about you," Turrin said honestly. He'd been asked by some of the Commission's top people to talk to Parrella after the old man's name came up associated with the drug hits. "They don't want to see you spend the last few years of your life in a federal prison."

Parrella laughed until he choked down a coughing spell. "They're just worried that I might bring them inside with me. Big Ears Palumbo, Sal Maneri, others. They know I remember where some bodies are buried. Even after all these years I could bring them down with me."

Turrin realized the old man was feeling his oats. If word got back to some of the Family heads about how loosely Parrella was talking, a quiet contract would be issued, executed and never mentioned again. And if there was time, the stocky little Fed would have let the Families take care of Parrella. But now there was the question presented by Dan the Man and the electronic Pandora's box in the study below.

"They shut me out," Parrella said bitterly. "All those years ago they shut me out. Left me to fight those damn Colombians and Rastafarians all by myself. The police, FBI and DEA would have been picking over my bleached bones if I'd waited for my friends to help me." He glanced at Turrin. "But that's the thing about life, you know, Leo—you make new friends. Friends you never even thought about having before."

"Mr. Parrella," Dan the Man said with a sour look on his face, "it's getting late and you're under a doctor's care."

Parrella smiled broadly. "Dan the Man. Looks just like a Boy Scout, doesn't he, Leo?"

Turrin grinned and noticed the tic was back on the guy's face.

"I like to listen to him worry," Parrella said. "Cross my heart and swear to God, he sounds like a Jewish mother at times. You know the kind I'm talking about."

"I know," Turrin said.

"For the first time in a lot of years," Parrella went on, "I've cut myself a sweetheart of a deal. And all I had to do was introduce a few of my new friends to a few of my old friends. Soon it's going to be like the old days around here. Parties, women. And respect, Leo. Respect like I had when I was a younger man.''

''Mr. Parrella,'' Dan the Man cautioned.

Parrella waved the man's objections away. ''He's right, Leo. I really should get my rest. We'll talk more tomorrow. You'll be staying here the night?''

''If it's no bother.''

''It's no bother. Dan the Man, see to it Leo has a place to sleep tonight. I find it enjoyable talking to someone from the old school.''

The headcock nodded, but Turrin could tell the man wasn't happy.

Victoria, Hong Kong

MACK BOLAN DROPPED change into the pay phone and dialed. It was picked up on the second ring.

''Hello.''

''You just lost a hell of a lot of cash and accounts receivable,'' the warrior said to Keran Tat.

''So I've heard.'' Tat's voice held a hostile edge to it that was barely restrained. ''I have a name for you.''

''I'm waiting.''

''Dean Chantre.''

''Spell it.''

Tat did.

''And what's his story?''

''He's a Briton, and he's supposed to have under-world connections that spread across the globe. He works for himself, and he works for others if the price is right. Until now he's been strictly small-time, nothing too big or too risky.''

"And now?''

"Of late I've discovered he's been enticing my smaller competitors to join against me and force me out of Hong Kong and the mainland. I'd known of this before, but I'd been unable to retrieve a name until now. Last night was very costly to me, not only for the damage you did, but in terms of what I had to do to get that information.''

Bolan didn't sympathize. "Where do I find Chantre?''

Tat sighed. "That I can't tell you. My sources indicate that he might be in London, but I can't be sure.''

"Chantre moved on before things got hot.''

"Yes. I've also been informed that Chantre is largely responsible for the recent DEA killings I've been unjustly accused of masterminding. I've been told he's even done some information gathering for that agency.''

Bolan passed on commenting on the man's guilt or innocence. Tat had been responsible for a lot of other deaths that had gone unavenged. "Where do the Russians fit in?''

"They're working with the same group Chantre represents.''

"Which is?''

"I haven't been able to determine that." Tat paused. "Is this information enough to send you on your way?"

"Yeah. But I'll get back this way soon. Bet on it."

"I hope so," Tat said tightly, "because we have unfinished business. And I can assure you, the next time you come through, things will be very different."

Bolan took out one of the Texas Ranger badges from his pocket and grinned slightly. "I don't think so. In case you haven't got the message I've been sending you all night, there's a new sheriff in town." He broke the connection.

Above the Caribbean Sea

CALVIN JAMES LOOKED OUT the window of the Lear jet at the dark water below. It appeared black and cold, as smooth as ice, and unending. The interior of the jet seemed to reflect that. The men running the transportation end of things had relieved him of his weapons except for the Beretta and the Randall survival knife sheathed under his pant legs.

Beside him Maria Alfaro opened a small bottle, took out the tiny spoon inside and inhaled a spoonful of cocaine into each nostril. She slipped it back into her purse without looking at him. Leaning her head back against the seat rest, she was silent for a few minutes.

James could almost see the drug working inside her body.

"Don't stare at me," she said.

"Sorry." James turned away and studied the blank bulkhead separating them from the pilot and copilot. They were alone in the body of the jet.

Alfaro smoothed back her hair self-consciously. "I know your opinion of me isn't very high right now, but I'm a good cop. I always have been. It's just that this is a very dirty job."

"I couldn't do it," James agreed.

"Most people can't," Alfaro said with a hint of pride. "And the work I do saves lives."

"Who's going to save you?"

She faced him and laughed, but it sounded pained. "I'll save myself. I always do." She gestured toward the purse. "I've kicked the drugs before, and I will this time. It's just that I need them right now for part of my cover. They help me hold it together. If I tried to go cold turkey right now in deference to you and your feelings, I'd fall apart."

James didn't say anything.

"It bothers you, doesn't it? Having to place your life in the hands of somebody who's wired?"

"Yeah."

She nodded. "That's a good sign. If you can be honest with me, it means you can be honest with yourself. Do you trust me?"

"No. Not completely."

Her eyes hardened and she glanced away from him. "Then what are you doing up here with me?"

"I took a chance on you."

She was quiet for a moment. "Do you do that often?"

"Not if I can help it. And only then if I get a good feeling about the person I'm relying on."

"That's supposed to make me feel better?"

"No. It's just an answer. What you do with it is your business."

"You're very sure of yourself."

"Sometimes. Right now I don't feel like I've gotten in totally over my head."

"You think you could take the two men up there?"

"If I had to."

"And land the plane?"

James nodded.

"My, my, you are a self-reliant kind of guy."

Anger burned inside James at her sarcasm, but he pushed the emotion away, knew it was only the drugs and her own fears that made her speak like that.

"I don't have all that talent," Alfaro said. "I've got this body and my wits, and those are the only things that have kept this wolf pack from devouring me."

James waited a moment, then asked, "You still haven't told me what this is all about."

"This is about control," Alfara said. "This guy we're going to meet wants to talk to Carlisle Johnson about the drug trafficking in the northeastern United States. I've handled the dialogue so far from both ends."

"Why you?"

"Because Johnson was dealing heavily with Cota, which meant lately he was dealing heavily with me. I stole Johnson from under Cota's nose. Johnson had a thing for Latino women, so it was easy."

"Who is this guy?"

"I don't know. I've been stonewalled the whole time. The guy likes his privacy."

"Where are we supposed to meet him?"

"In London. Our first stop is in Jamaica for refueling, then we're going to leapfrog up the eastern coast and make the hop over to London."

"Who's been your contact?"

"Different people. I've never seen any of them three times running. I think I'm working directly for the head guy, but I won't know until I talk to him. I'll recognize his voice."

"So what does he want?"

"The drug trade," Alfaro said solemnly. "Every last bit of it. At least that's my opinion based on what I've seen, heard and been a part of. This guy has sources and people all the way around the world."

"There's no way he can hope to control that much territory," James said. "There are too many groups willing to hit the streets and cut themselves any part of the action they can."

"He has men, like the ones you saw back there. And he has other, more devious ways." She looked at him and shook her head. "You think this is impossible, don't you?"

"Sounds like science fiction," James replied. "I've been up against the drug people plenty of times. It's an ego trip for most of them. Fast cars, easy money..."

"Easy women?" She arched an eyebrow.

"I wasn't going to say that."

"But it went through your mind. I saw it on your face. It's okay. I'm not that thin-skinned. I've learned not to be." But she lowered her eyes.

James wished he could think of something to say that didn't sound patronizing.

"This guy is setting things up like a business," Alfaro continued. "Everybody who works for him gets a piece of the pie. And those things you listed, they're still there. Executive perks."

"What about the people who want to remain independent?"

"Remember the independent gas stations? My father owned one of them until the corporations forced him out and into early retirement. There are ways of squeezing out the people who don't want to go along, either physically or economically. There'll always be the cowboys, of course. No business is entirely free of those, but the percentage of the trade they handle is going to be infinitesimal compared to what he'll ultimately control."

"You talk like this could happen."

"I think it's so close to happening right now that it scares the hell out of me. The reason I went AWOL was to get close to this guy. He picked me to rat Cota out and get to Johnson. I did it, and in the process I made myself valuable to him. How valuable, I don't know. But enough that he wanted me here when he met with Johnson. If I can get a name, something solid, maybe the agency can track him down and stop him before he gets the organization into the driver's seat."

"But getting that done would take time."

Alfaro shook her head. "Denial isn't going to help. I've tried. Cota tried. He's had time. Remember Luis Costanza last year?"

"I read about it."

"This guy set up Costanza's bloody exit, worked it through some intelligence people he had on the payroll. Cota told me all about it. Costanza was really close to consolidating the Medellín cartels. Can you imagine what that would have been like?"

"Yeah." James had, the whole time he'd been involved with the Stony Man operation that had put Costanza down.

"This is going to be even worse. We live in strange times these days. The Berlin wall has fallen. The cold war no longer exists. The Soviet Union no longer exists. And the Communists have embraced democracy and capitalism."

"There are still a few holdouts."

"For how long? Cuba's Communist government rests on the sloped shoulders of a tottering Fidel Castro. The Chinese are still struggling through the fallout from Tiananmen Square. Even if it takes years, drugs are filtering into Europe faster than ever, and the Commonwealth of Independent States is now a wide-open market. Try to put a price tag on the potential growth out there. It's staggering."

James agreed.

"He's got to be stopped."

"Why didn't you go to the DEA with this?"

She forced a laugh. "I look at you, see me through your eyes. You see a burned-out wreck of a human being wired so tight she might explode. You're having trouble believing me now, and you've got more of an inside track than most of my supervisors." She shook her head. "No one would believe me. No one. But if I get the bastard's name and fade before it goes down, then find a safe place with a neutral agency and start yelling my head off about it, somebody has to listen." She paused. "I have to worry about the people I work with. I know for a fact that some of them are on this guy's payroll, too."

As they fell silent, James thought about that, wondered how far into domestic intelligence circles the corruption had spread. There was never a shortage of money in drug trafficking, only in how much a guy wanted to pay out to stay in business. He also thought about the woman beside him, wondered what it must be like to be so far out of the system, so very alone. It was depressing, and as scary as hell wondering which way she was going to bounce if everything turned into a busted play.

"Break's over," Alfaro said a few minutes later. "Let's go through the background on Johnson again. Tell me what you remember."

"This has got to be the longest shot I've ever played. There's no way in hell I can hope to remember enough about this guy to play him even for five minutes. There might even be someone there who's met him."

"Not in England," Alfaro said. "Johnson talked to me about that. Except for Mexico, Canada and Colombia, he'd never been out of the Unites States."

"What if I forget something?"

"Look, you're not going to be there playing twenty questions. Come on hard. Don't let anyone play games with you. You're a businessman waiting to do business. Money talks, bullshit walks. You only have to maintain the cover long enough to let us know who's calling the shots. Then we're out of there."

"We could go in with what we know now."

"To your agency?"

James didn't say anything.

"Come on," Alfaro said. "I knew you weren't DEA the first minute I laid eyes on you. You're a spook, probably DIA or NSA. You don't have to worry about the law. You *are* the law."

James didn't bother to correct her. Stony Man Farm was a totally covert operation, and he didn't want to help narrow her field of speculation.

"As to sinking into Johnson's character, don't worry about it. People can read whatever they want to in reports concerning Johnson, but if you can project an image that's close to what they're expecting and hold to it, they're going to buy you." She paused. "It's easy to become someone else, but if you do it long enough, it gets hard to figure out who you really are." Tears glinted in her eyes as she turned away.

James reached out, took her hand and squeezed it reassuringly. "We can do this," he said softly. "No problem."

CHAPTER FOURTEEN

Stony Man Farm, Virginia

"Our new buddy, George Russell, has become real cooperative," Carl Lyons said, his voice coming through the telephone speaker box on Kurtzman's desk.

Barbara Price thought that Lyons sounded tired, but up for the conversation. Blancanales and Schwarz could be heard in the background, talking with another man.

"We heard about the hit at the beach house," Price said. "How's everybody at that end?"

"We made it through with nothing to complain about. Though if the locals catch up with us, there could be hell to pay. We left a lot of worried civilians behind. We could have a problem getting Russell out of here if anybody figures out who the beach house belongs to."

"That's been taken care of," Price replied. "For the moment the IRS records concerning that house have been conveniently misplaced."

"Old George is showing his appreciation," Lyons went on. "As soon as you guys are ready there, we'll transmit the computer files he has on the drug-trafficking skims. Someone hit his office with fire-bombs at about the same time they tried to take us out at the beach house, but Russell kept a couple of spare copies of everything he did. I figure he was covering his own ass in case things got too sticky.''

"Did he say who he was working for?"

"Local Mob action," Lyons replied. "Small-timers looking to go big. He did a lot of the legwork for us. The trail he followed took him to some of the guys in Las Vegas, then moved on to Florida. A guy named Liborio—''

"Parrella."

"You already had him?"

"Leo did. But he was just playing out a maybe."

"Yea, well, no more maybes. Russell says Parrella has been playing banker for the operation."

"Where are the accounts the money is going into?"

"The Cayman Islands."

Price nodded. At the other end of the room the wall screen was tuned to local news channels, flipping through them on scan mode as computers sucked up the various stories for later retrieval and consolidation. Not quite fourteen hours after the initial strikes against the various drug enforcement agencies had begun, a new wave of murder was spreading across the globe. Besides the activities undertaken by the Stony Man teams and the Executioner, and the legal vengeance being extracted by the world's police agencies, drug gangs had started killing off rival gang leaders and narcotics heads with frightening regularity. Price could almost see the balance of power shifting across the globe as the unidentified organization wiped out the competition through efforts started by the law-enforcement teams. The assassinations of the key individuals heading up the international crimebusters scene hadn't stopped, either, merely slowing as targets were ferreted out with greater skill.

"Why did they choose Parrella?" Price asked.

"Russell says it was because Parrella already had the machinery in place to collect and move the money. Besides the California and Las Vegas connections, as well as some of the other major U.S. cities, Parrella knows a lot of the bankers in the Caymans on a first-name basis. He greased the wheels."

Price reflected on that, sorting through the pieces of the mafioso's past that she remembered from Kurtzman's debriefs. "Aaron?"

The big man looked up.

"A sidebar for investigation," Price said. "Parrella was one of the Mob people covertly involved in the Bay of Pigs attempt in 1961 sponsored by the CIA. We'll cross-reference him with Webb August concerning Company handlers when we get the chance."

Kurtzman opened a window on the screen and made the necessary addition to the Webb August file. "We're ready to receive here."

"Carl," Price said.

"On its way," Lyons replied. "Gadgets, do your stuff."

The big modem on Kurtzman's desk lit up and chugged as the cybernetic systems absorbed everything coming from Lyons's end.

Price watched numbers and stats blur by, occasionally picking out a name or seeing an amount that she could verify.

"Nice," Kurtzman said after the files had been copied and he was spot-checking them. "What you've got here, Barb, are the actual amounts involved from the different operations Russell handled, and where some of those monies ended up. If I can't sort through this and get two and two to equal four, you can give my job to Carl."

"Can't see it happening," Schwarz said in the background. "I mean, think about Ironman trying to crack a computer file for a moment. Holding a .357 Magnum on a VGA screen and shouting, 'Give up or die, scum,' just isn't gonna cut it."

Despite the seriousness of the moment and the situation, Price couldn't suppress the smile that lifted her lips.

Lyons sounded remarkably unperturbed. "Something else Russell volunteered, boss lady."

"I'm listening."

"While he was trying to scratch the itch his curiosity had developed, Russell backtracked a few of the records the cash flow had generated. Seems some of the money went for the purchase of a freighter from San Francisco."

"A freighter?"

"Affirmative. She's called the *'Bama Town Lady*, and she was sailed down to Houston four months ago to get reoutfitted."

"Reoutfitted for what?"

"I figured when we got down to the shipyards, we'd ask," Lyons said. "We've about done all the damage at this end that we can do, and that's the only lead I can see to follow. Unless you have something else for us."

"No. Follow the ship. It hasn't turned up on any of our other investigations. The money that was involved in purchasing and reoutfitting her warrants our attention."

Kurtzman was already talking to Hunt Wethers, setting the man into motion tracking the freighter.

"Let me know what you find," Price said.

Lyons agreed and broke the connection.

Price flipped off the intercom phone and watched the financial documents sliding across Kurtzman's screen.

"Damn it," Kurtzman growled. "This gives us part of a lever, but not everything we need. I can trail the money so far, but then it disappears. We're missing other files that we need to tie it all together. It's been moved around a lot, if this account is any example, but once it moves off the continental U.S., I lose it."

"Will Parrella have the information?"

"Maybe. Somebody does. That's for damn sure. I can see where disbursements have been made, which I assume are payoffs for domestic personnel, but the bulk of it is gone."

She put a hand on Kurtzman's shoulder. "If anybody can find it, I'd put my money on you."

Kurtzman only nodded, lost in the programming he was initiating.

Price wandered back to her office for another dose of pain relievers. She knew the headache she had now was from stress and fatigue rather than frustration. They were getting close; she could feel it.

She took a container of orange juice from the ice bin, tore the cover off and sipped. The cold, sweet taste was refreshing. She glanced at her watch and realized Brognola and the President would be wanting an update soon. Brognola had been with the Man for a few hours now, weaving together a tapestry of truth and defensive supposition. The White House was already getting heat from the other countries for possible heavy American intelligence involvement in the current world crisis. If it turned out that American agents were largely responsible for the conspiracy in the drug-trafficking groups, there was no guessing what kinds of adverse effects it would have on the world situation. The closer things got to peace, the more unstable everything seemed.

The intercom beeped for her attention.

She pressed the button. "Price."

"I've got Striker on the horn," Kurtzman said. "He's got some pictures he wants us to look at."

"I'll be right there." Price picked up her orange juice and crossed the room.

Kurtzman was scanning a lean, ascetic face done in a black-and-white photocopy and plastered across the computer monitor.

She clipped a phone headset on and watched as Kurtzman's hands zipped across the keyboard. Color was added to the black-and-white frame. The hair turned brown, the eyes blue. In seconds it was starting to look more warm and strangely cruel.

"Price," she said.

"Hello, Barb," Bolan said tiredly. The warmth in his voice was unmistakable.

Despite her worries concerning the man and his recent activities, Price kept her voice light. "You've been busy."

"Places to go, people to see."

"Is this one of your appointments?"

"A recent drop-in. I didn't have time to quiz him, but he speaks Russian and was running loose security on one of Keran Tat's operations."

The picture on the screen came into clear focus, then moved to one side while a second window started flipping through a series of head shots.

Price was aware of Tat, knew the crime lord's history and had known the Exectioner was chipping away at his organization in Hong Kong in a bid for information. "Tat doesn't have a history of working with the Russians. The Communist government tried to close him up a number of times."

"That's what I remembered, too. Tat says they aren't his, and he gave me a name."

Kurtzman picked up a pencil and held it poised over a note-covered legal pad.

"Go ahead," Price instructed.

The pictures on the monitor kept screaming through in flashes of color that got faster and faster.

"Dean Chantre," Bolan said.

"He's a networker," Price said. She'd worked tangently around the man in her pre-Stony Man Farm days. Intelligence circles were very incestuous when it came to people ready, willing and able to do any necessary dirty work. "His name fits in with the others we've turned up so far." Quickly she gave him a thumbnail sketch of the information turned up by Able Team, Phoenix Force and Leo Turrin.

"So what we've got here is a collection of guys who're used to working behind the scenes to make things happen," Bolan concluded when she finished.

"We've got the arms and legs, but we're still looking for the head."

"I've got a name on your first guy," Kurtzman said. A military ID picture of the man in an army uniform filled the window to the right of the retouched fax photo Kurtzman had had to start with. "Demyan Litvinov. He was a field operative for the KGB before the USSR went belly up."

"The KGB?" Bolan repeated.

"Yeah." Kurtzman consulted the computer document. "Did a lot of overseas work and has been tagged with a number of executions, though it's never been proved.''

"We're searching for a Russian link, too," the warrior said.

"I'd say so," Price agreed. "But that makes sense because that part of the world is going to be up for grabs in the next few years. Whoever our guy is, he definitely takes his empire-building seriously."

"Sergei Belenkov," Kurtzman interrupted. "Also of the KGB, also a field operative."

"Who was their commanding officer?" Price asked.

Kurtzman tapped the keyboard. "A man named Yuri Zuberov."

"Where is he now?" Bolan asked.

"According to the CIA files and Military Intelligence," Kurtzman said, "the colonel disappeared two, maybe three years ago."

"This was already in motion then," Price commented.

"Zuberov could be one of the new guys on the block," Bolan said. "It's possible his involvement could be more easily traced than that of Chantre, August, Parrella or Johnson."

"Good point," Price conceded. "We'll give that angle some play first."

"I've got an address on Chantre," Bolan said. He quickly gave it.

Kurtzman's computer screened an answer in seconds. "It's good, Striker. According to the MI5 files,

Chantre has lived there for the past six years when he's been in-country.''

"I'm finished here for now," the warrior said. "The streets are getting tight for any kind of continued engagement with Keran Tat's forces, and I don't think I'd find anything more regarding Chantre or the people he's allied with. I'm convinced Tat is on the outside looking in with this operation."

"Agreed," Price said. "Tat doesn't fit the profile of the players we're turning up. The man is too greedy to work with others."

"How soon can I get a plane to London?" Bolan asked.

"Make your way to Singapore," Price replied, "and there'll be one waiting for you." She glanced at the computer monitor, and saw Kurtzman accessing the available information on Dean J. Chantre from National Security Agency files. "And I'm having Kissinger and Grimaldi meet you at Heathrow. I'm getting a definite feeling that the other shoe is about to drop."

"Yeah, I've got the same itch. Tell them I'll see them there. Stay hard, Barb."

"You do the same, guy." Price broke the connection, then lifted the receiver again to put the wheels in motion in Singapore. When she was finished a handful of minutes later, she noticed the excitement in Kurtzman's eyes when the big man regarded the screen.

"I've got a name that links the people we've turned up," Kurtman said.

Price looked at the screen.

CHURCHILL, SWAINE M.

The name looked small in block letters centered on the monitor, not large enough to have caused all the trouble the Stony Man forces suspected him of.

"Who is he?" Price asked.

"I've got a query running through the CIA files now." Kurtzman sat with his elbows resting on the wheelchair arms, his fingers steepled under his chin.

Suddenly the monitor flickered, and ACCESS DENIED printed across the screen.

"Damn," Price said.

Heathrow Airport, England

THE SIGHT of the two hardmen in three-piece suits making their way through the crowded airport terminal toward Maria Alfaro and himself banished all thoughts of jet lag from Calvin James's mind. He felt naked without weapons. Even the Randall combat knife had been left inside the Lear because there was no way to get it through customs.

"It's all right," Alfaro said. She was at his side, her eyes hidden by dark sunglasses. They'd stopped over in Atlanta long enough for clothing purchases to be made while they waited at the jet. The DEA agent wore a navy blue dress with white trim, and had taken hours of fatigue and worry from her features with makeup.

James was dressed in slacks, a dark turtleneck and a sport jacket. He'd salvaged the strings from his boots before throwing them away and now had a pair of knotted garrotes in his pocket that didn't leave him entirely defenseless.

"Miss Alvarez," the man on the right said.

James picked up the telltale bulge under the man's left arm despite the special tailoring.

"Yes."

"You will come with us, please."

"Of course."

James stayed close to the woman. Once they left the shelter of the airport terminal and walked into the parking lot out front, the noonday sun beat down on them. The passports had been another surprise and had appeared without photos with the clothing. The copilot had taken their pictures and developed them on board while they flew to La Guardia, then slipped them expertly into the passports that were already prepared for them. New York and British customs people hadn't blinked an eye at them.

The first man led the way to a black limousine double-parked in front of a row of cars. The second man brought up the rear.

James walked beside Alfaro, trying to read their current situation from her face. She was a confused lady, he knew that, but whether she was clever enough to pull off her present scam was another matter.

The lead man opened the rear door.

"Get in, get in," a man said from the back seat. A fringe of white hair encircled his bald head. "Traffic is going to be terrible at this time of day."

Alfaro got in first, taking a seat beside the old man, who patted her hand affectionately.

"It's really good to see you again, my dear."

She brushed her lips across his cheek.

One of the hardmen got in first, taking a seat on the bench opposite the old man and Alfaro. James took the unspoken hint and crawled in after. The other man sat like a bookend beside him. Their shoulders touched.

The old man lifted a phone and said, "Let's go." The car's transmission engaged smoothly, and they coasted toward the front entrance to the airport. Jets cracked thunder as they passed overhead. Alfaro's contact turned his attention to James.

The Phoenix Force member tried a tentative smile and sorted through everything he'd been briefed about Carlisle Johnson.

"I'd heard there was an unfortunate accident. I was told Mr. Johnson wouldn't be joining us."

"He isn't," Alfaro replied.

"So this is one of the people who have been covertly working against us?"

"Yes."

"Marvelous." The old man rubbed his hands together in sinister anticipation.

Before James could do more than slightly shift his weight, readying for the coil of reflex that would aid him in his attempted escape, the men leaned in on either side of him.

"At ease, mate," the man on James's right said. He thrust the barrel of a small automatic against James's neck. "Don't want to get your bloody head shot off now, do you?"

James froze.

"Something to help you sleep," the other man said. "Don't want you getting all flustered on us later."

A sharp, jabbing sensation bit into James's left arm. He never saw the needle. Whatever was in the hypo worked quickly. His vision began to blur in less than a minute. The last thing he saw before slipping into unconsciousness was Alfaro's face swimming before him. There was no trace of remorse.

Tarpon Springs, Florida

LEO TURRIN WASN'T a morning person, and he'd skipped a lot of breakfasts over the years by choice. Liborio Parrella, on the other hand, was very much a morning person and had already read the newspaper and drunk a pot of coffee before Turrin heaved himself out of bed at what he considered to be the ungodly hour of 6:00 a.m.

Personal conversation relating directly to Turrin's reason for being there was sparse. Evidently the old man had lost none of his caginess about his current operation and was satisfied enough with his part in it that he didn't feel it necessary to brag.

Turrin had contented himself with an assortment of fruits and skipped the breads and meats. Parrella spread a good table and didn't mind sharing. It was served outside on a large deck overlooking the Gulf of Mexico and the boat house. His men came in and ate with him on shifts, exchanging pleasantries, sports speculations and gossip the way any family would. As long as they showed the proper amount of respect, of course.

Besides Parrella and Turrin, Dan the Man Canary was the only person to sit through the entire meal. The headcock came and went, though, constantly with a cup of hot chocolate in his hand. The beeper attached to Canary's belt went off frequently and drew him away for several minutes at a time. After each return, he neglected to ask Parrella's forgiveness, which offended the old mafioso.

Turrin noticed Parrella's cold stares toward the younger man, as did several of the longtime associates of the old man's organization. That Parrella didn't chastise Canary was silent testimony to the fact that Canary was a highly prized asset.

Turrin was also intrigued by the concern that visibly darkened Canary's features. The headcock had developed a habit of repeatedly cleaning his glasses while staring into the distance.

During breakfast, while listening to Parrella regale his listeners with stories from the Mafia's early days in Cuba, Turrin learned that two other men—computer technicians and operators—had access to the electronically coded cards that allowed entrance to Canary's cybernetic fortress. Neither of them truly fitted in with Parrella's people, either, and Turrin figured them for strictly a support group for Canary's computer hardware.

When Canary excused himself and left the house on some unspecified business, Turrin waited patiently and kept an eye on Harvey Minter, a soft-looking man in a white lab coat who obviously would rather have taken breakfast by himself.

The computer technician sat hunched defensively in his seat and shuddered twice during Parrella's graphic description of a face-to-face contract killing he'd done in New Orleans. Minter had trouble keeping his meal down.

The technician was finished eating in fifteen minutes. As the guy left the table, Turrin excused himself to Parrella and followed.

"Hey," Turrin called as Minter headed out the front door.

He turned around in the doorway, his shoulders hunching even more as he tensed.

"Minter, right?"

The man nodded.

Turrin put on a smile, turned up the kilowatts behind it and dropped an arm across the other man's shoulders. He could feel Minter squirm at his touch, but the man didn't try to get away. "I saw that system Dan the Man has in his office. I figured you helped him set it up."

"Yes."

Turrin led the guy out onto the landscaped lawn, toward the outbuilding where he was evidently housed. "I've been talking to some of the families back home, telling them they should get with the times, you know. Computers are really where it's at. You push a button, those things do the work of nine hundred men."

"It's really not that easy," Minter said.

Turrin hugged the guy and laughed, as if he thought everything Minter had to say was one big joke. "Jeez, sure it's not that easy for guys like me. I'm all thumbs. But the Families, they'd be interested in a guy like you who knows his way around this computer-whacking stuff."

"Uh, you mean hacking."

Turrin nodded. "Yeah, right, that's what I said. Hacking. Anyway, I was thinking, when I get back home, I'd like to mention your name to a few of the old men. Maybe you could do some referrals for us. You know, guys who'd be good enough to do the work that needs to be done. You'd be well paid for your time."

A gleam of avarice entered Minter's eyes. "Consultation work is very expensive, Mr.—"

Turrin waved the thought away. "Money's no object when we're getting quality stuff, right?"

Minter nodded. "Very few people understand that."

"When I get back, I'm going to be in touch with you." Turrin shook hands with the man and turned back to the main house. He had Minter's door card in his left palm. Besides playing cops and robbers while he'd been in deep, there had been all kinds of opportunities to learn other skills.

Parrella was still out on the deck when he went back in. The breakfast crowd had thinned, and house security was more concerned with the outside perimeters than with the inside ones.

Turrin got to Canary's door without being seen and slid the plastic card through the electronic reader. The lock clicked and the door opened. He went inside and closed it behind him.

Kurtzman had given him courses over the years, and his own experience as Leonard Justice in the Justice Department had schooled him in various aspects of computer systems. He flipped on the machines, listened to the hums they made, then booted up the files.

His heart was beating like a trip-hammer. "You're getting too old for this shit, Leo," he chided himself.

Picking up the phone, he switched on the modem and dialed one of the numbers he had for Stony Man Farm. Even later, when Parrella got the phone bill, he wouldn't be able to trace the call to its destination.

Kurtzman answered.

"Me," Turrin said. "I broke into the computer systems here. Don't know what's available to you, but get in there and find out. Don't stop to window-shop. I'm working on borrowed time here."

"I'm on it," Kurtzman said.

Screen after screen of warped images flashed across the computer monitor. Turrin couldn't keep up with it, didn't try.

While he was sitting on the edge of the desk, the door flew open and Dan the Man Canary followed it in with a .45 clenched in a white-knuckled fist. "You're one dead son of a bitch."

And Turrin believed him.

CHAPTER FIFTEEN

Solitaire Island, French Guiana

David McCarter came out of the sea on the island's eastern side with the sun at his back. Three members of the SEAL team strike force Barbarba Price had arranged through Brognola and the President followed him.

Despite using the Swimmer Delivery Vehicle to push in from the submarine six miles out, they'd still had to swim the last mile while towing gear. McCarter was winded from the unfamiliar activity, but tried not to show it.

Two more SEALs ran in from the shoreline, making their way easily through the short rocky beach that managed a brief existence before the jungle reclaimed the land. They dragged a plastic sled behind them, piled with tied-down gear. Two of the SEALs with McCarter split off and helped their teammates drag the ordnance into the brush and conceal it.

As McCarter scanned the tree-filled horizon, he reflected that Calvin James would have felt right at home about now. The thought brought morbid speculation to his mind. James was still out there among the missing.

"Sir," one of the SEALs called.

McCarter looked up and saw Forbes—his second in this unit—holding a bundle in one hand. "Sir" was all they'd call him. Aboard the USS *Spearfish* during the briefing on the tactical op designed by Price and Katz, "Sir" was the only title assigned to McCarter, Encizo and Manning. Used to covert operations around the globe, the SEAL team commanders and their warriors hadn't had any questions. The mission bore the presidential seal of approval.

"Throw it here, mate," McCarter said.

Forbes tossed the bundle.

McCarter caught it easily, dropped it long enough to strip out of his wet suit and tanks, then crept with it to the top of the hill. Forbes gathered McCarter's discarded attire and hauled it to the community burial pit two of the men were digging with combat knives.

At the top of the hill McCarter sat naked for a few minutes, letting the wind dry him.

In the distance he could just make out the blue-tiled tops of Webb August's private compound. Sounds of automobile engines and machinery drifted in on the breezes.

He looked north and saw part of the crescent-shaped harbor fronting the house. Two pleasure crafts were in motion, streaming whitecapped waves in their wake. McCarter took the Bausch & Lomb binoculars from his bundle and scanned the turquoise waters. Manning was out there somewhere, he knew, backed by another SEAL team. They'd be using rebreathers so they wouldn't be noticed as they mined the area. Kurtzman had sent a collection of geographical and topographical maps, as well as dozens of satellite pictures taken of Webb August's little island kingdom. While reviewing those Manning had chanced upon a discovery that would be a definite surprise to August and his people.

Sweeping the field glasses southward, McCarter locked in on the large sheet-metal hangar that housed at least two helicopters, a Lear jet, and possibly the F/A-18 Hornet that had shot down the DEA agents off the coast of Florida.

The small warehouse well back of the main house was a puzzle. Constant surveillance seemed to be kept over the structure, but there were no clues as to what it held. Rafael Encizo and his team would be removing the mystery there, though. McCarter's part of the operation would be to knock down the aerial arm of August's defenses before it could be brought into play.

Satisfied with the prelim recon, he dressed quickly. The team was outfitted with jungle camous, streaked their faces and hands with green and black combat cosmetics and wore jungle hats. He pulled on the tough hiking boots and wiggled his toes in appreciation of being warm and dry again.

By the time he draped the military webbing over his body, slid the spare Browning Hi-Power into his shoulder holster and took up the H&K MP-5 SD-3 he'd chosen as his lead weapon, the five SEALs were waiting behind him. He slipped on his aviator sunglasses, looked at the collection of hard young faces around him and grinned. "I've got no locker room speech for you, lads. We're here to kick some ass, so let's get it done."

"Yes, sir," Forbes replied.

McCarter took the lead, and they came down off the hill as smooth as oil sitting on water and as deadly as an avalanche.

SITTING IN THE passenger seat of the SH-3 Sea King, Katz compared the notes he'd made on the topographical map of the island with what he saw. It was his first personal look at the area. In his estimate it was too chancy to try for a flyby until they were ready to act. Webb August was no one's fool, and Katz was certain the man knew at least something of what had transpired in Bogotá. August would be expecting at least some kind of retaliation.

The pilot took an indirect flyby, from east to west, as if headed into Cayenne. Katz held the clipboard in his lap between the pinchers of his prosthetic right hand, kept a pen in his teeth and held a pair of binoculars to his eyes.

The island was roughly nine square miles. It sprouted up from the seabed with no real beach areas. The lagoon area where the harbor had been built was roughly forty feet deep.

Katz checked, but there was no sign of Manning or his small demolitions force. He moved on.

The main house was a two-story affair that literally sprawled across almost fifteen hundred square yards. A half-dozen outbuildings encircled the house. Beneath the white paint were cinder-block walls that would withstand a fair amount of shelling. Nine-foot-high electrified fences with coiled barbed wire set in rows along the top set the compound apart from the jungle that seemed poised in readiness to devour the landscaped area at the slightest show of weakness.

The warehouse was next, almost hidden in the blur of trees and foliage, surrounded by wire fencing. Nothing about it had been mentioned in any of the data they'd received.

An eerie feeling crept along Katz's spine. August had gone to pains to ensure that his little empire was defensible and together. The only reason the Israeli could think of why August would move the warehouse away from the main buildings was that the man was afraid of what was inside it.

Katz lowered the field glasses as the island's civilized area drifted out of view. From the facts and figures they had access to, including the discreet computer inquiries Kurtzman had directed through the supply companies in Cayenne that August made his monthly purchases from, the compound housed about a hundred fifty men.

The SEAL ground teams in the area had been limited to thirty men, five teams of six. They were there to soften up the compound's defensive structure and pave the way for an amphibious assault group culled from the ranks of an American Marine Amphibious Force from the Landing Craft Utility stationed in hiding at another island twenty klicks away. Katz would lead those troops into the open throat of the harbor when the time was right.

Once free of the island perimeters, the chopper pilot started a lazy circle that would take them back to the *Spearfish* and the LCU.

Langley, Virginia

BARBARA PRICE pulled her yellow Fiat to a halt in front of the tall gate at the end of the curving road leading to CIA headquarters. Sunlight gleamed on the razored wire loops crowning the ten-foot chain-link fence.

The sentry inside the guardhouse on the other side of the gate was garbed in a military uniform, but Price knew enough about Company operations to know the man wasn't military. He peered at her through the gate and waved to a companion to cover him as he approached the sports car.

"Your name, ma'am," he asked.

"Price," she replied. "I'm here to see Ronald Jefferies."

He spoke into his walkie-talkie, found her name on the schedule, then waved her on through and asked her to halt just inside the gate. She stopped, and he crawled into the passenger seat while the gate rolled closed behind the Fiat.

"Sorry about the inconvenience, ma'am," the young guard said, "but—"

"It's policy to let no one from another agency onto the grounds without an escort. I've been here before."

"Yes, ma'am."

Price drove with both hands on the wheel. The past few hours had limped by as the players had moved into position. The whole time the Stony Man teams had been in transit she'd expected Swaine Churchill to implement another wave of whatever operation he'd concocted that would threaten their effectiveness. Timing was critical now, and things could very easily slide either way.

As she drove through the wooded hills leading to the CIA's main buildings, she thought about Calvin James, wondering if he was skirting the outer perimeters of danger or had slid down into the depths. Kurtzman's call regarding Leo Turrin's capture and perhaps his death had reached her en route to Langley. Even with Charlie Mott and his team in the area, she'd resisted the impulse to send in the Stony Man storm troopers. If a rescue attempt was launched, Churchill and his forces would know how quickly and quietly Stony Man was slipping the noose into place.

She hoped Turrin and James were all right, hoped that she wouldn't be wrong in thinking that if Churchill or his people wanted them dead, it would already be too late to save them. It was hard putting the operation above the lives of those men, especially since they were her friends. But she felt she had no choice. Churchill and his operation had to be deep-sixed all at once—not fragmented, but completely destroyed so that it couldn't rise up from its own ashes at a later date.

It hadn't helped that Brognola had agreed with her call. Every one of those warriors knew a time might come when they had to give up their lives in the name of freedom.

The parking lot covered more than twenty acres. The main building was seven stories tall, grim and forbidding, with wire-mesh-covered windows recessed into the concrete walls. On the building's right was an auditorium under a domed roof.

When she saw Jefferies standing beside a gunmetal-gray sedan at the opposite end of the executive parking lot, Price stopped the Fiat. "You can get out here," she told the guard.

He nodded and got out without a word.

Price cruised forward and pulled to a halt with Jefferies on the passenger side of the car.

Jefferies was a long, lean man, sporting outdated sideburns the color of burnished copper under a dark salt-and-pepper mop of hair that covered the tops of his ears. He wore glasses that slightly magnified his lizard-green eyes. The brown suit was off the rack, but it hung on him well. His cowboy boots tapped on the concrete as he approached the car.

Price reached to her console and thumbed down the window on the passenger side.

"Long time no see, Barb," Jefferies said with a sardonic smile.

"I could have lasted a few more years without this little reunion."

"Ouch." Jefferies made a pained expression. "The lady never forgives."

"Never."

Jefferies leaned in through the window. "So what do you want?"

"The private file on Swaine Churchill."

Jefferies took a deep breath, held it for a moment, then shook his head. "I don't know what you're talking about."

Price switched off the Fiat's engine. "Bullshit," she said coldly. "You might have those files sewn up, but I've got some contacts who have let me know you were the guy responsible for Churchill's operations while he was with the Company."

Jefferies raised his hands defensively. "Me and about a dozen other people."

"No." Price leveled an accusing finger. "You."

Jefferies didn't say anything.

"Those other people were pawns in your games," Price said. "Cannon fodder you used to keep suspicion from yourself while you played with Panama and the *contras* and toyed with the arms-for-hostage trade-off in the Middle East."

"We'll handle Churchill," Jefferies said. "You've got my word on that."

"Your word's not good enough. It never was. I learned the hard way."

"You still hold that against me, Barb? Christ, that was years ago."

"And Hoskins and Delamer are just as dead. I was responsible for them. I had to tell Hoskins's wife he wasn't coming home, had to know his three children had lost their father because I trusted you. You betrayed me on that mission, opened up graves for those two men and poured them right in."

"'Betrayed' is a strong word."

"Not nearly strong enough. If it was me, I'd have it engraved on your headstone."

Jefferies shook his head. "You were always one stone-cold bitch."

"Gotten colder and harder these past few years," Price assured him. "You fuck with me now, you're going to look as if you ended up on the wrong end of an argument with an eighteen-wheeler."

The green eyes behind the lenses were marble-hard and gleamed with inner fires. "You think you're big enough to take me, Barb?"

"With one arm tied behind my back and my dress on fire." Price reached into her purse. Jefferies didn't flinch. He knew she didn't carry a gun, and he knew why. She passed him a letter. "Read it and weep, you son of a bitch."

Taking the envelope, Jefferies opened it and read it quickly. The presidential seal showed dark through the paper. He glared at her over the top of the sheet. "You've got this kind of pull?"

"You sealed Churchill's files when he left the Company," Price said, "and you've deflected every attempt I've made to access those files since last night. Now, you either play ball with me, or I'm going to break your bat, send you home and take what I want, anyway."

Jefferie's features were a study in cold rage. "Go inside. My office." He flipped a plastic ID badge onto the passenger seat. "Ask for Paige Bass. She can access the files for you."

Price restarted the Fiat.

"Who the hell are you working for?" Jefferies asked. "I didn't believe it when I was told you dropped out of intelligence circles, but I never expected you to come up with this kind of clout."

Price put a sweet smile on her face. "I can't tell you, Ronald. If I did, I'd have to kill you." She popped the clutch and sped away from him, nearly knocking him off his feet.

"SWAINE CHURCHILL was released from Agency employment in 1977 during the Carter administration cutbacks under Admiral Stansfield Turner."

Barbara Price nodded. The so-called "Halloween Massacre" had reduced the Agency's covert operations directorate by two-thirds. Churchill hadn't been the only agent to be turned out onto the street, nor had he been the only one to go bad afterward.

Special Agent Paige Bass was a petite brunette who was dwarfed by Ronald Jefferies's massive desk. She adjusted her glasses, then returned her attention to the monitor in front of her while her hands moved confidently across the keyboard. She was dressed conservatively in a gray business suit and maroon blouse. There was something about her behavior and stance that made Price think she'd once been military.

"Of course," Bass said, "unemployment didn't sit well with Chruchill. And he knew a lot of people and even a lot more secrets."

"I assume there was no corporate security job in his future," Price said.

"No. According to Agent Jefferies's field reports, Churchill moved directly into free-lancing his skills."

A face materialized on the monitor and Price studied it. "This is Churchill?"

Bass nodded.

The man was in his early fifties. Iron-gray hair framed a once-square face that was beginning to sag. Personal stats put Churchill at six-four, two hundred seventy pounds.

"Of course," Bass added, "the Agency didn't completely cut Churchill loose at once. For a time most of his free-lance operations were geared around CIA missions. He was a good person to contact for help in or out of a dozen countries."

"He was networking," Price stated.

"Yes." Bass's hands entered fresh commands into the computer. "I'm backing up a disk for your later use. Agent Jefferies wasn't too happy about that."

"He didn't hide it well, either."

"Yes, well, that's understandable. Agent Jefferies became a large target for departmental blame when it appeared that Churchill had gone rogue."

"Jefferies closed the files off?"

Bass nodded. "And he was given the assignment of terminating Churchill back in 1985 because he was believed to have known the man better than anyone else here. In 1987 Jefferies caught up with Churchill in Buenos Aires. There was a brief gun battle that left Jefferies's partner dead and Jefferies himself wounded."

"How did Jefferies find Churchill?"

"Churchill was involved with the cartels at that time. At first it was just security operations, but by 1987 it was Jefferies's opinion that Churchill was organizing some of the drug distribution routes and hamstringing DEA and U.S. Customs operations through contacts he had on the payroll in the CIA."

"You know for sure that Churchill was buying off agents from the Company?"

"Yes." Bass regarded her frankly. "We aren't the only organization that's been corrupted by Churchill's machinations, Ms. Price. There have been documented cases involving the FBI, Dade County and Metro law-enforcement personnel, the U.S. military during Operation Just Cause and a number of others. The files are all available in the materials I'm giving you today."

"Understood," Price said. "I didn't mean to ruffle any feathers here."

Bass glanced back at the screen. "Churchill is a sensitive topic inside these walls. The Agency birthed a monster and it's hard to accept."

"I've put together a file on Churchill's operations," Price said. "From the look of things, it's widespread."

"Global," Bass agreed. "We've discovered that, as well. During the past few years, Chruchill has been involved with a number of things. The cartels, of course. He's also designed and contracted executions, as well as brokering for the killers who fulfilled them. He's well-known in smuggling circles. For a while he was working with Khaddafi, supplying arms and trainers for the Libyan military. There was even some talk that he was arranging the sale of a nuclear weapon to Khaddafi. We've got other trace intelligence that Churchill and his organization have been involved in African affairs. Wherever there's been money to be made by turning a dirty deal, Churchill seems to have been there."

The woman paused. "He's a devious man, very clever. The fact that he's been able to put together everything he has, depending on whether he really is the man you're looking for regarding the global drug-trafficking action, tells you volumes about the man's abilities and desires. Moral judgment isn't something you look for in an agent involved constantly in ballistic involvements. In Churchill's case his sense of morality may be so low as to be practically nonexistent."

"Do you know where Churchill is now?"

"No." Bass leaned back from the computer console. "Jefferies hasn't been close to Churchill since 1987. But there are rumors that he may have recently moved his home operations to England. He seems to have preferred a European theater during his Agency days, and England is one country where he could blend in. Between his college days and his early hitch with the Agency, he spent a dozen years there."

Price thought about Dean Chantre and the England connection the Stony Man teams had already turned up. They had Webb August and Parrella and the banking systems—thanks to Leo—but the missing freighter, *'Bama Town Lady,* remained a mystery. As well as the whereabouts of Swaine Churchill. She wanted to make a clean sweep of things, but the operation might have to run ragged, after all. She didn't try to delude herself into thinking Churchill wasn't aware of the covert force breathing down his neck.

No matter what the man's own plans were he'd have to start kicking numbers into play himself to buy himself some running room. And Price knew that yardage was going to be measured in lives.

Near London, England

SEATED IN THE RESERVED section of the racetrack, Swaine Churchill glanced at the electronic tote board, then at his companion. Yuri Zuberov, ex-general of the defunct Soviet war machine, was familiar with democracy and free enterprise. Lately he was firmly entrenched in learning about the excesses permitted under both systems. Today's lesson was being attended at Epsom Downs.

"I have received a tip," Zuberov was saying as he watched the line of horses and jockeys clad in colorful silks. He pointed. "See the four horse?"

Churchill looked. He had more on his mind than a damn horse race, but he couldn't let that show to the Russian. He preferred that things go quietly to hell while he still had a chance to recoup some of the potential losses. After all, he'd seen nothing to suggest that the situation wasn't salvageable—provided he found out where all the pressure was coming from and neutralized it damn quick. He'd worked too long and too hard to lose it all at this point.

Zuberov was easily seventy pounds overweight. He hadn't been in such shape while in Soviet employ, but he'd discovered another excess early on, which hadn't agreed with his physique. The man's double chins quivered in excitement as he spoke. "There is some speculation," he said, "that the four horse—Cannon Shot—has been held back in her last three races, nudging into second or third, but not going for the win. Her owners want her to take her first checkered flag here. Today."

The horse looked brown and hairy to Churchill, like all the other animals walking into the starting gate. The only things that set her apart were the pink-and-green riding silks on her saddle and jockey. The odds on the tote board showed Cannon Shot at four to one. Churchill didn't think that many of the other track enthusiasts had heard the same rumor, and if they had, they were apparently discounting it.

"At those odds," Zuberov said, "it will take quite an investment to make any real money."

"That's why you wanted the cash brought," Churchill said.

"Yes. You have your connections here. If I were to move around the amount of money I plan to invest here today, I would be noticed. My monies come from outside the United Kingdom. Yours don't. I thought it would be no trouble arranging a loan while I am here."

Churchill put a smile on his face. "No trouble at all." He wiggled a finger at one of the four bodyguards who'd followed them into the stands. The man passed over a briefcase. Opening the briefcase in his lap, Churchill displayed the neatly ranked bundles of money inside. "Will you want to count it?"

Zuberov touched the money with the hand of a man who has learned to take pleasure in physical contact. "No, my friend, I trust you. If I did not, we wouldn't have been associates all these years."

A trumpet sounded out on the racetrack, the notes echoing hollowly over the gathered crowd and bringing a hush.

"I must go," Zuberov said, getting to his feet and taking the handle of the briefcase. "They will be closing the betting windows for this race soon."

Standing and offering his hand, Churchill said, "I wish you luck, General."

"Are you sure you will not stay?"

"I've got things to do. Another time perhaps."

"Of course. I will see you later, then. This evening at your home for the strategies meeting."

"I'll be looking forward to it." Churchill watched Zuberov waddle away, then made his own way toward the exit. His bodyguards accompanied him while the Russian's stayed behind.

He was hot inside the bulletproof vest. The suit itself would have been uncomfortable in today's heat. The soaked leather of his shoulder holster bit into his flesh. Women noticed him as he passed, and he felt their lingering gazes after he could no longer see them.

Females were the first to sense power in a male. Churchill was well acquainted with that rule of nature. There was something in their genetic makeup that attuned them to power in ways men couldn't even begin to fathom. They sought out power—in one form or another—as surely as a compass needle floated toward magnetic north.

He'd first noticed it while still with the Agency. Female counterparts had succumbed to his wiles and charms around the globe. Two of them he'd left for dead after extracting the information he'd been assigned to recover. One of them had died in his arms, never knowing he'd taken her life. The other had left him with a knife scar from a hidden blade that had raked him from right hipbone to midpelvis.

He let out a tight breath as he kept walking. Those were the days he missed, putting his life on the line for his country, surviving only by his wits and skill.

Then his country had deserted him, left him with a burning need for vengeance. Now he wanted his independence of the United States in a way that let them know he no longer needed them, either. He'd been good at his job, and they'd never recognized that worth. As an agent, he knew how to get things done, knew the people to talk to and the kind of deals he could cut before he even went to the table.

The money he'd taken through illicit dealings shouldn't have mattered. His superiors had never had any proof, and most of that cash he'd used as a war chest to further his country's interests.

The deals with the narcobarons had fallen into his lap, and the money involved had been too much to walk away from. When there wasn't a patriotic need throbbing inside him, successes could also be measured in cash. He'd learned to take solace in that. And learned to take pleasure in the amount of power he could wield.

He climbed into the cockpit of the executive Bell helicopter waiting in the airfield and belted himself in.

The interior of the craft was luxurious. It should have been. He'd paid millions for it.

The rotor throbbed and the chopper leaped into the air.

"Mr. Churchill," one of the guards said.

"Yes." Churchill didn't take his eyes from the racetrack.

"Thought you might want to know the general's horse just came in."

Churchill nodded, reflecting on how egotistical the Russian would be tonight. Some days it was a pain handling all of the prima donna personalities in the trafficking empires that he juggled and managed. It had taken years to get the mix right, to bring the drug trade so close to consolidation.

Of course, not everyone had fallen sway to his sales ability. Luis Costanza had been living proof of that. But he had other ways of dealing with those people. Despite the satisfactory strides he'd made in closing the partnerships, there was a list of people he knew he'd begin quietly replacing as the opportunities presented themselves. Once he had key people in all the places that he needed them, the drug conglomerate he'd forged would be unstoppable.

But that lay in the future.

For now he had to look out for the present. The covert teams he'd traced in California, Colombia and China hadn't yet been identified, and they seemed in danger of becoming a full-blown threat. Even Centac, as quiet as that unit's operations were, had been charted. These groups were deadly and unknown. While most of the international law-enforcement agencies were puzzled over what was going on, those groups seemed hell-bent on triangulating him. If he'd had another twenty-four hours, it wouldn't have mattered.

The helicopter swept south, away from the city. The mobile cellular phone in Churchill's pocket rang. He took it out, flipped it open and said, "Yes."

"Is this a secure line?" Ronald Jefferies asked.

"No."

"All right." Jefferies paused. "We've got a problem."

"What is it?"

"Your jacket at the Company got pulled."

"By who?"

"A woman named Barbara Price."

"I don't know her."

"You wouldn't," Jefferies replied. "She worked so deep in the intelligence infrastructure that maybe a dozen people knew what she did a few years ago."

"And who does she work for now?"

"I don't know. I've been digging all morning only to get slapped back out of nowhere. Whoever she's working with, she's got the President's ear in a big, big way."

"Keep looking," Churchill ordered. "If she's connected with the people burning up my backtrail, I want her taken down." He hung up before Jefferies could say anything more.

He seethed inside, on edge because of the lost sleep over the past few days and the tension of not knowing what was coming next. The operation had been planned to the last detail. It had been executed perfectly. Less than twenty-fours had passed since the first aggressive shot had been fired. A number of the necessary people had already been removed from the playing field, and a deadly undercurrent had been starting among the drug traffickers independent of his consortium. He was allowing the next twelve hours for them, aided by police retribution, to weaken one another to the point that his people could walk in easily and take over.

The shipment to Houston was hours too late to be an effective deterrent to the retaliation he was feeling. But he hadn't wanted to risk the freighter's discovery before it was necessary. That would have definitely tipped his hand.

He flipped the cellular phone open again and dialed his own number. Greco answered on the first ring.

"What have you found out about our guest?" Churchill asked. Ever since his arrival the black man had maintained his silence, or given them information that was nothing more than garbage.

Greco sounded young and impatient. "Nothing. Every time I send a computer inquiry about his real identity I get zilch back. The NCIC files confirm him to be Carlisle Johnson. The FBI files say he's Carlisle Johnson. The Illinois Penal Authorities even say he's

Carlisle Johnson. I'm beginning to think we were wrong and he really *is* Carlisle Johnson."

"He's not," Churchill said. "I've met Johnson. The man's a player, and I want him identified."

"All I've got are fingerprints to go on," Greco complained. "I've nearly exhausted all of my stateside contacts."

"Exhaust them. Then take your search farther afield. If this guy's a player, then he might have a record in Russia or Germany that hasn't been covered over with false information. Stay with it. Something will break."

"We could always kill him and toss his body into the open, then wait and see who comes along to claim him," Greco said hopefully.

"No. Not as long as he could be valuable alive." Churchill paused. "Have you been in touch with Canary at Parrella's estate?"

"Yeah. He's still got a big question mark on his guy, too."

"As far as he knows, the guy really is Leo Turrin?"

"Sure. The old guy knows him personally. No trouble with the ID. Canary just can't figure out how the hell Turrin figures into everything."

"Has he had any luck tracing the call Turrin made from the house?"

"No. Canary followed it up, but the trail petered out somewhere in Quincy, Massachusetts. He's sitting on Turrin at the house, keeping him under lock and key. Parrella wants to take Turrin out, give him a pair of concrete overshoes and use him for an underwater decoration in his harbor.''

"Get a message to Parrella from me. Tell him I said to leave Turrin the hell alone until I figure out what I want to do with him.''

"Will do.''

"How is Alfaro acting?''

"She's spent most of the time up in her room with her private cocaine stash. As a precaution, I had her weapons taken away from her.'' Greco hesitated. "Personally I think we should go ahead and deep-six her like we were planning. She's outlived her usefulness, even muffed the Johnson assignment.''

"No,'' Churchill said. "Perhaps she really is as bent as she professes to be. If so, she could still prove valuable. At least for a while.'' He'd seen her shortly after her arrival and had been intrigued by the woman on a number of levels, not the least of which was a sexual nature. She looked like a woman in whose eyes he could see himself, see how powerful he was becoming. As an undercover agent, Alfaro had learned how to see through bluster and ego from petty cartel dictators like Cota. He wanted to know how she saw him.

"She knows who you are now.''

"So she never leaves our sight. I don't see a problem. Do you?''

"No, sir.'' Greco's answer was obviously forced.

London moved off against the horizon as the woodlands took over the ground beneath the helicop-

STONY MAN V 271

ter again. Churchill broke the connection after a few
more words of instruction.

With the freighter still hours from its destination
there was only one thing he could do. And when it
came to bluffing, he considered himself one of the best
in the business. Especially when it was only half a
bluff.

CHAPTER SIXTEEN

The Oval Office, Washington, D.C.

"I knew that bastard," the President said in a voice tight with restrained anger. "I was there when Swaine Churchill was given his walking papers. I knew then we shouldn't have just let him go so easily. There were too many things he knew, too many people he was involved with, too much he had access to."

Unsheathing a cigar, Brognola clamped it between his teeth and waited for the Man's anger to subside. He thought the President looked grayer and waner than he'd ever seen him. It hadn't been an easy year.

"I've talked with a number of other world leaders," the President finally said. "They all view this as an American problem that's threatening them. We're supposed to do something about it."

"We are," Brognola said. He gazed at the silent TV in the recessed wall area. On-screen was a scene from the United Nations floor. It didn't take much effort to deduce what the subject matter was. When news clips of various strikes against international law-enforcement agencies during the past twenty-four hours started flashing across the screen, all mystery was gone.

"I know we are," the President said. "But I can't tell them what we're doing. Your people work best because no one knows about them. I can't very well say, 'Look, you don't have to worry about this anymore because I've unleashed this covert force to find whoever's responsible for all the killings.' And heaven help us if they find out Mack Bolan is involved."

"Striker would have dealt himself in, anyway."

"You know that and I know that."

"They know that, too."

The President sighed and turned to face Brognola. "I'm not trying to make excuses or formulate some sort of denial. I won't give any of those men short shrift, and you know that."

"Yes, sir."

"I just wish there was more we could do."

"We know who we're looking for now," Brognola said. "That's more than we had twenty-four hours ago."

"I know, but I have to ask myself if that's enough."

Brognola took the cigar out of his mouth. "Sir, all respect intended, but you'd have to look damn hard to find anyone who could do the work these people can do. They've been pushing themselves at top speed ever since this can of worms was spilled out onto us."

The President nodded. "I know. But at this point we have to consider that even they may fail. Churchill was always a crude and canny son of a bitch."

"Price is working on some leads. Turrin and Able Team turned up Churchill's banking operations. And wherever the money is, you can always bet you'll find bastards like these close by."

The television set beeped.

The President reached to his desktop and retrieved the remote control. He aimed it at the set and punched a button.

The scene depicting the United Nations cleared, shifting to a pretty brunette wearing an ear-throat headset. "Mr. President."

"Yes."

"There's a satellite communication linkup incoming."

"Who is it?"

"He says his name is Swaine Churchill. He said you'd know him."

A muscle quivered along the President's jaw. "Put him on, Mrs. Chester."

"Yes, sir." She leaned over to make an adjustment to a bank of equipment at her side. "Do you want to return the video portion of the transmission, or the audible only?"

"Both."

Brognola scooped up the phone from the desk, dialed his special Stony Man number and got Kurtzman. "There's an audio and video up-link coming here now from Churchill. Get a trace on it." Kurtzman agreed and Brognola clamped the receiver down.

The television screen cleared. Swaine Churchill, dressed in an expensive suit and looking totally relaxed sitting in a high-backed office chair, looked back at them. "Ah, Harold Brognola," he said. "I'd been wondering whatever became of you."

For the moment Brognola said nothing, hoping Kurtzman's computers were equal to the task of tracing the satellite transmission.

"What do you want?" the President asked abruptly. He stepped toward the video camera mounted on top of the television.

"To bring you up to speed on a few things," Churchill said. He crossed one leg over the other. "I know you've got a headhunting team burning up my backtrail. I want you to call them off."

"Like hell I will."

"Hear me out." Churchill held up both hands, palms facing out. He smiled amiably. "I know by now that you've figured out what I have going on. Consolidation of the drug empires is nothing compared to what's been transpiring around the world in the past few years. Who would have believed the Berlin wall would have fallen? Who would have thought the Soviet Communist government actually would go down? Like the singer says, 'The times they are a-changing.' And the drug trade is changing along with them."

"You won't get away with this," the President said.

"On the contrary." Churchill stood and paced, arms behind his back and his smile locked securely in place. "I've already gotten away with it."

Brognola hung back, mentally counting the number of seconds Kurtzman was getting to work on the trace.

"Let me clue you in on something, pal," Churchill said. "The drug trade isn't something you can get rid of. It's here to stay. I was trying to point that out to the boys at Langley years ago. It's a tool, I told them, and you should learn to use it like one. Now there's all this bullshit about the 'War on Drugs.' Well, if there is, you sanctimonious pricks are setting yourselves up to lose it. No matter what you do, no matter how bad you make the consequences for the people who use them, the drug trade is going to do business. You know what puts businesses into the graveyard? A lack of interest in the product being offered. When was the last time you saw a Captain Marvel Decoder ring?"

"What are you getting out of this?" the President asked.

Churchill shrugged. "Rich. What else is there? I tried that life, liberty and the pursuit of happiness line once before. It didn't work out."

"Do you know the kind of political upheaval you've caused internationally?"

"Sure. That was all planned ahead of time. The noise Japan and the other countries are making about pulling out of their economic ties with the U.S. is rubbish. They'd be nothing without this country. The U.S. has allowed them to define themselves for decades. That's not going to change."

"You sound like a man who's convinced he can start an avalanche, then get in front of it and beat it safely to the ground."

Lifting a hand, Churchill waved the comparison away. "Look. There are untold billions of dollars cycling through the U.S. economy from the drug trade. It provides jobs, housing and upkeep for a number of families. Not to mention a respite from how pathetic and unfulfilling life can be in general. Those people employed in trafficking in turn support other people. Grocers, carpenters, shoe salesmen. The list is infinite. If you could eradicate the drug trade completely, think about the possible economic backlash that could come of it. How would the American economy hold up if all that money was taken out overnight?"

"That's an invalid argument."

"Is it? I don't think so."

"What about the personal losses families incur every day because of drug use?"

"There are losses in every aspect of living. Insurance agents can tell you that. They have little printouts that can tell you exactly how risky your profession, your home life and your hobbies are. People die. It's a fact of life." Churchill paused. "I'm not here to argue semantics with you. Nor am I here to argue over my ability to do what I say I've done. I've done it." He pointed at the President. "I'm talking to you to let you know your options at this point. The people you have assigned to me are good but not undefeatable. You should think about saving them while you still can. I already have two of them in my custody. Say the word and they can die right now."

Brognola felt a chill race across the back of his neck. Turrin shared a history with him, went back years. Calvin James was a friend, a young man with his whole life ahead of him. He didn't want to lose either of them.

"I don't know what you're talking about," the President said.

Churchill smiled. "Of course you don't." He resumed his seat in the high-backed chair. "Are you familiar with a drug called psilocybin?"

"It's a hallucinogen of some sort."

"I'm surprised you remembered." Churchill looked at Brognola. "I can see you've drawn a blank."

Brognola nodded, anything to keep the man talking and buy Kurtzman more time.

"Psilocybin was a by-product of research the Agency paid for in the late 1950s," Churchill said. "It was derived from the seeds of the piule plant. Aztec priests called it *teonanactl*. Loosely translated, it meant God's flesh. Gottlieb did the preliminary studies on psilocybin and found out that it was a hallucinogen that caused extreme paranoia in the people who were subjected to it. I found out about it because an Agency research scientist, Wayne Matthews, had an interest in it. Matthews and I shared similar views on the drug problems of the seventies. To make a long story short, Matthews found a way to make a super-psilocybin in the late eighties. At that time he was working for me."

Brognola jotted the man's name down for quick reference when he contacted Price later.

"Feel free to check it out," Churchill said. "In fact, I'll fax you a file on it—minus incriminating evidence, of course—and you can look over it in your leisure. By the time I had Matthews in my employ, I was already well under way consolidating the various drug-trafficking agencies. And from a business standpoint I wanted to be in the position to offer my clientele something unique, something only we could give them. We thought we had it. Unfortunately that didn't turn out to be the case at all."

"What are you getting at?" the President asked.

"Patience. I can't make it that short." Churchill steepled his fingers over his chest as he leaned back in the chair. "Despite Matthews's repeated efforts the drug was doomed to failure. It's highly potent, sinks right into the nervous system, but it activates an intense fight-or-flight reaction. The subjects became homicidal within minutes after ingesting the drug. Their adrenal systems went into overdrive and they had no concept of reality."

He paused. "I once saw a man take a full clip— thirty rounds—of .308s and remain standing. He was reduced to bloody rags, his heart punched completely out of his body, but he lived long enough to injure seriously the man who'd killed him. Another drawback of the drug was that once it was in the system the effects were lasting. The person subjected to it never quite made it back to reality. Unfortunately we didn't know exactly how lasting. One subject lived for seventeen months before she escaped and we had to kill her. Now, with having to be on the move constantly, we no longer have the luxury of observing what we've wrought."

"I suppose there's some purpose to this little fable," Brognola said.

Churchill shook his head and smiled. "Of course there is. We also discovered Matthews's version of psilocybin could be wedded to cocaine without visible trace."

Brognola's blood ran cold as the ramifications dropped into his mind.

"Yeah." Churchill grinned. "I see Brognola has grasped the possibilities."

The President glanced at Brognola.

"Gentlemen," Churchill said, "call your dogs off. All they'll do is eventually die fighting the machine I've put together and create a certain amount of unpleasantness for me, but they'll do no lasting harm. And if you don't see your way fit to save them, let me add a final trump card." He leaned forward and winked conspiratorially. "At this moment scattered across the United States, there are caches of cocaine laced with psilocybin ready to be put out on the streets when I send out the word. Get those people pulled back now, or I'll make that phone call and by nightfall you're going to be covered over by the first in the worst series of mass slayings you could ever imagine. And it will last for weeks. I'll give you three hours.

Then if I see or hear from those people again, we'll let the shit hit the fan and see what shakes loose."

The transmission ended abruptly and Churchill's face faded from the screen. The brunette came back on, looking troubled. "Mr. President, our fax machines are receiving a transmission now regarding a Dr. Wayne Matthews."

"When it's finished, send it up."

She nodded, then vanished, leaving only the gray television screen. The President switched it off as he sat at his desk.

Brognola was already on the phone.

"Price."

"Me," Brognola said.

"We missed him," the Stony Man mission controller said. "Aaron couldn't make his way through all the cutouts Churchill's programmers had set up."

Brognola took more antacid tablets from the roll in his pocket and chewed them. His thoughts flickered to James and Turrin, as well as the other people who would be hurt by whatever moves they made next.

"I intercepted the fax transmission," Kurtzman said, "and I ran Matthews myself. Churchill was giving it to you straight. Matthews was Agency once, and he did lab work on the mind control drugs experimented with in the fifties. And he was listed as an employee of a company I turned up in the bank records I ransacked from Parrella's files."

"Don't give up on us yet," Price said. "Aaron's got a few moves left. Churchill's people have been trying to ID Calvin. We've got some options open to us."

"I've got my fingers crossed. He's given us an hour to clear the field. Let me know if you turn up anything worthwhile." Hanging up the phone, Brognola turned to face the President and relayed the conversation.

"Three hours," the President said, glancing up at the clock on the wall.

"Games have been won in seconds," Brognola pointed out. "Three hours can be one hundred and eighty hellacious minutes for our side. We're due a break."

"Due one and getting one are two different things."

Brognola nodded. He unknotted his tie and settled in for the long wait.

Solitaire Island, French Guiana

MOVING QUIETLY, knowing a man could pick up movement with his peripheral vision even when his direct stare could see nothing, Rafael Encizo crept through the jungle surrounding the warehouse. Two Navy SEALS flanked him. He couldn't see them, couldn't detect them with any of his physical senses, but he knew they were there.

The hot sun burned down on the back of his neck. The jungle smells reminded him of his early years in

Cuba. He crept on, the Ka-bar fighting knife held tightly in his fist.

A grim watch from hidden ground had let them know only two guards circled the building. After talking with Katz, they'd decided to remove the mystery of the building and maintain a low profile. There seemed to be no exchange of personnel between the warehouse and the main house. Encizo had thought it was safe to assume the operation there was self-contained. Katz had agreed.

He crept to the fence, glanced at his watch as he took wire cutters out of his webbing and waited almost forty seconds before cutting the first strand. In less than a minute he was through.

He jogged to the corner of the building, counting down in his head, and heard the first steps the guard took on his latest round. The man had gotten bored with his assignment, and in the end it cost him his life.

Encizo took the guy before he knew an enemy had penetrated the perimeter. The Ka-bar's blade slid easily between the third and fourth ribs and punctured the heart. He held the guard until all struggling had ceased, then dragged the body into the building with him.

Leaving the corpse slumped in the front entranceway, Encizo stepped inside the building. The Ka-bar was resheathed in his harness and the silenced Beretta was in his fist.

He took cover behind a partition wall and studied the building's interior under the fluorescent track lighting. There were five rooms spread out in a half-moon around him. From his position Encizo could at least partially see into all of them.

Six men were staggered throughout the rooms. Two of them wore white lab coats and lounged around a coffeepot and a computer terminal. The other four were guards, evidently on downtime. They were seated in a room to the left, watching a videotape of last year's Super Bowl on big-screen TV.

One of the SEALs, outfitted in camous, slithered through a window and dropped soundlessly to the floor. The second man dropped through a roof hatch at the opposite end of the building. Both men moved into position and scanned the building until they spotted Encizo.

Using hand signals they'd agreed on for the operation, Encizo exchanged information with them, confirming the number of the building's occupants as six. He waited for a moment, then gave them the signal to move in.

The SEALs took the room with the guards. Short, silenced bursts from their H&K MP-5s pitched the bodies over the folding tables and ruptured the television screen.

Then Encizo lost them as he raced into the room with the white-coated men. He caught the first one by the collar as the guy tried to rise out of his chair. Yanking, he toppled the man to the floor on his face. The other man tried to run, but Encizo tripped him and sent him sprawling hard up against a wall of computer machinery.

He showed them the Beretta, and both men raised their hands immediately.

"Sir?" one of the SEALs called.

"Everything's secure at this end," Encizo replied. "How about you?"

"Got a roomful of dead men here."

"Makes them easier to watch," Encizo said, putting more callousness in his voice than he felt. He glanced at the two men at his feet. "Who's in charge here?"

"Me," the older man said.

"Who are you?" Encizo followed his question with the muzzle of the 9 mm.

"Wayne Matthews."

"Tell me something that's going to make me want to keep you alive."

In a halting, fear-stricken voice Matthews did.

Stony Man Farm, Virginia

"I'VE FOUND the *'Bama Town Lady,"* Akira Tokaido called out.

Barbara Price looked up from the computer monitor she was watching, where four windows were opened on the screen to map out the action going on in the United Kingdom, French Guiana, Florida and Texas. Bolan had been united with Grimaldi and Kissinger in London, as well as a crack SAS unit Price had arranged to be lent to the Stony Man warriors. Phoenix was standing by on Solitaire Island with the SEAL force. Charlie Mott and his people were ready to roll at a moment's notice in Tarpon Springs. And Able Team had linked up with a MACTF—Move Against Crack Task Force—covering the Houston Port Authority in their search for the missing freighter.

"The thing is," Tokaido said, "it's no longer called the *'Bama Town Lady*. It's now registered as the *Jolly Jack*. Using the information Phoenix Force turned up with Dr. Matthews, there's no doubt about the ship's identity. *'Bama Town Lady* disappeared after reoutfitting in Houston, then docked as the *Jolly Jack* in Cayenne, French Guiana."

"Where's the freighter now?" Price asked.

Tokaido referenced his computer intel. "About an hour out of Houston Port Authority."

"Good work, Akira," Price said. "Keep me posted on her movements. If she deviates in the slightest way, I want to know immediately."

"You got it."

A knot uncurled in Price's stomach. When she turned back to Kurtzman, she noticed the slight smile on the big man's face at once. "Aaron?"

"Reeling it in now." Kurtzman's fingers darted over the keyboard. "The last series of false files I slipped into international and domestic intelligence circles under Calvin's name had a virus programmed into it. Took me a while to come up with something most systems wouldn't recognize as threatening. Once the file was pulled and downloaded, the virus programming followed a trail of cybernetic bread crumbs back here. The real risk was that whoever was at the other end might discover it and try to trace it back to us." He paused to scan the results listed on his monitor. "From the looks of things here the virus came home to roost with nary a scratch."

"You know where the queries have been originating?"

"Yeah. Near Dover, along the coastline."

"How about narrowing it down, big guy?"

Kurtzman grinned. "Hell, Barb, I can do better than that. I have the address now."

Without wasted motion Price plugged in the headset telephone jack and punched up the White House number that connected her with Brognola. The big Fed answered on the second ring.

"I think we have Churchill," Price said without preamble. "I'm going to wait for a physical recon from Striker before we move on it definitely, but I want to know what my options are going in, in case there's no time to ask later. We also have another bit of good news. Encizo turned up Dr. Wayne Matthews on Solitaire Island. According to Matthews, the psilocybin-laced cocaine hasn't been distributed in the United States yet. It's due to arrive in Houston within the hour. We beat their timetable."

She studied the four windows on her monitor. "Hal, we've got the whole operation lined out—Churchill, the recruitment arm of the organization, the drugs that were supposed to be used to blackmail the U.S., the schematic of the operation through Parrella's computers and the banking hub down in the Cayman Islands. We know who they are, and we know where to find them. If we move fast enough and hard enough, we can take them all out in one fell swoop."

"Ms. Price," the President said, "at this juncture we can afford no mistakes."

"Duly noted, sir," Price said in a professional voice, "but I can promise you we're only inches away from having this sucker bagged. At this point it's your call whether we wait or we go in."

The Man hesitated for only a few seconds. "Ms. Price, if you have Churchill in your sights, then bring his damn house down."

"Yes, sir." Price broke the connection and turned to Kurtzman. "Notify the teams. We've got a green light."

CHAPTER SEVENTEEN

Near Dover, England

A light rain had blown in from the west two hours earlier and hung on now as spitting mist. Mack Bolan, clad in a skintight blacksuit under a camou poncho, trained his field glasses on Swaine Churchill's manor home. Drops of water landed on the leaves of the tall oak trees around him, occasionally splattering on the upturned collar of the poncho and sliding down his neck. He adjusted the magnification and brought the house into better focus.

The estate was surrounded by a stone wall carefully hewn and fitted together. Wrought-iron decorations hung on the double gates and stood erect over each support post. The foliage was neatly trimmed back from the perimeters of the estate. It helped some, but the sheer thickness of the forest surrounding the dwelling prevented any possibility of being able to see someone determined to approach unobserved. Security cameras moved restlessly, floating along their own arcs and overlapping fields of coverage.

Inside the stone walls the main house occupied center stage, flanked by four outbuildings. Ivy climbed two of the walls, reaching leafy fingers all the way to the third floor. One of the outbuildings appeared to have been built at the same time as the main house. The other three had been added later, with effort made to conform to the estate's overall appearance. Armed guards patrolled the grounds, but a number of them had taken up station around the large parking garage in back of the house.

Tan canvas sheets hung in great canopies in front of the house. Uniformed caterers served the fifty-odd guests from steaming banquet tables set up under the awnings. The weather hadn't been cooperative, but Churchill had evidently decided the party had to go on.

"House wasn't built to hold so many people," Major Sid Adair stated. "Ruddy blokes will have to rough it if they want to continue with their festivities." The SAS commander was squat and powerful-looking, his shoulders broad and thick despite his near sixty years of age. He had white hair, and a neatly cropped mustache that shadowed a stiff upper lip. Like Bolan, he, too, was dressed in a camou poncho over a blacksuit.

"Eating caviar outside and washing it down with a glass of champagne isn't exactly my idea of roughing it," Cowboy John Kissinger said. The big man stood in the shadow of one of the trees, the barrel of his assault rifle pointed at the ground.

Bolan continued his surveillance, marking off the names of people he confirmed from the mental list of suspected players working with Churchill. The numbers inside the estate were about what he figured they'd be from the figures Kurtzman and Price had been able to generate. So far there had been no sign of Churchill.

Forty SAS warriors were hidden in the bush surrounding the estate. They'd been there for the past half hour, lying in readiness. Two roads led to the manor house. Teams had already been stationed there to close them down when the time came.

"It's going to be a tough nut to crack, mate," Adair commented quietly. "What with the regular security crew your man Churchill has in place, his compatriots have added at least fifty percent in their own personal bodyguards."

Bolan lowered his field glasses. "That can be either an advantage or a disadvantage, Major. Fortunately we have the choice of which it will be."

The major cocked an eyebrow. "I'll tell you, you've piqued my interest."

Putting the binoculars away, Bolan slowly pulled back from his position, out of the line of sight of the guards watching the forest. Kissinger followed.

The Executioner paused under the protective shelter of a tree with broad branches. He pulled his map case from a slit pocket of the skinsuit and flipped it open to the terrain maps of the estate area. Once they had the address of Churchill's stronghold, Kurtzman and Price had been able to provide a mass of documentation.

"A change in plans, Striker?" Adair asked, his voice uneasy.

"Not in our plans," Bolan said, "but we're definitely going to adjust Churchill's agenda." He pointed to the map of the estate. "If we attack head-on, the way we've discussed, we're going to have a number of casualties."

"That's nothing we haven't talked about before. My men know the risks involved. This was strictly a volunteer mission."

"Understood, Major." Bolan met the man's steely gaze. "But while I was watching those people I realized there was something we could do to cut down on our losses and their numbers before we even attempt to storm those walls."

Adair folded his arms across his chest.

"We've been looking at this whole exercise from a military standpoint," Bolan said. "We classified two camps here—them and us. We lumped them together as a common enemy with a common goal. Fortunately for us they're not. Each one of those men down there is concerned primarily with one thing only—his own skin."

"I still don't see what you're getting at."

"You will," Bolan said. "Pass the signal along to your troops. We're going to open the ball in about five minutes." He slipped on his headset as Adair and Kissinger did the same. He listened to Adair's professional tone for just a moment as the SAS major checked in with his men, then clicked the headset to the private channel he'd prearranged with Jack Grimaldi. The Stony Man pilot was providing aerial support, and leading the third wave that would break over Churchill's estate.

"Jack?"

"Go, Striker."

"Open a channel for me to Stony Man Farm."

"You got it."

Adair turned back to Bolan and nodded. "They're ready."

"Let's get it done."

Adair gave him a crisp salute and faded into the bush.

Bolan moved out, trailed by Kissinger. His hands passed over the ordnance underneath the poncho. The Desert Eagle .44 rode his right hip, counterbalanced by the Beretta 93-R in shoulder leather under his left arm. He unslung the Mossberg 590 Military 9-shot pump shotgun from his shoulder and gripped it as he took the lead. Military webbing covered the Kevlar body armor he wore, holding grenades of lethal and nonlethal varieties as well as other gear he thought might come in handy during the invasion. A gas mask had been clipped to the web belt at his back.

The ground was soft from the rain, which had helped to soften broken branches that might have cracked and created a sound that would carry. From their recons they knew that none of the estate security people ventured into the forest. The motion detectors and other security devices that didn't rely on constant transmission had already been deactivated.

The headset crackled in Bolan's ear as he moved through the bush with Kissinger flanking him. The handful of men assigned to him picked the warrior up and fell in behind him.

"Stony One, you have Stony Base," Barbara Price said. "Over."

Bolan moved the mouthpiece to the corner of his lips and softened his voice. "Roger, Stony Base. This is Stony One requesting additional assistance. Over."

"How can we help you, Stony One? Over."

"Bear, are you on-line? Over."

"Roger, Stony One," Kurtzman's deep voice rumbled. "Over."

Bolan hunkered down thirty feet from the sagging stone wall that blocked entrance to the estate. He waved the SAS team and Kissinger to ground beside him. "Regarding those financial statements you turned up, how much can you tinker with them? Over."

"The egress I've got into the system is pretty lenient. I've got all the necessary passwords to get inside. What did you have in mind? Over."

"Can you do electronic transfers to all those accounts? Over."

"That's affirmative, Stony One. Thinking of making a withdrawal? Over."

Bolan gave Kissinger a wintery smile when he saw the man's eyes gleaming. The weaponsmith was obviously thinking along the same lines. "Something like that, Stony Base. I don't think our big fish is getting paid well enough. Instead of draining those accounts as we've already discussed, why don't we find a new home for them? At least for a few minutes. Over.''

"You're talking about a mass deposit here, Stony One? Over.''

"Yeah. Right into the primary account." Bolan shifted, shook out the grappling hook and line from the webbing, then dropped the poncho to the ground. "The way I've got it figured, those transfers should be noticed by the other account holders within minutes. I noticed several of their accountants carrying laptop computers. Over.''

"You've got it figured right, Stony One," Price said. "He's working the programming up now. With what we've already arranged it should be ready to run in minutes. Over.''

"I'm holding you to that, Stony Base. Stony One out.''

Kissinger grinned. "I like the twist.''

"Churchill won't," Bolan replied. He switched channels to the SAS frequency. "Major.''

"Here.''

"On my mark.''

"As you will.''

"I've got a surprise working for our targets.'' Briefly he explained the series of money transfers about to take place in the Cayman Island accounts.

"Being the vicious, greedy bastards they are," Adair said when Bolan was finished, "they'll think Churchill managed to rob them blind.''

"That's what I'm hoping," Bolan replied. "That's no enemy force over there, Major. That's a collection of the most ruthless human garbage ever assembled. Every man among them recognizes no allegiance to the other. The only thing holding them together now is the possibility that they could pull this off and turn a profit. Whatever thin strand of trust has existed between them until this point is about to vanish, and they'll be reduced to the cannibals they've always been."

"We're standing by," Adair said. "And I'd like to tell you, Striker, you're a most interesting fellow. Hardly the sort I'd like to take to a civilized party, but you have a certain innate, bloodthirsty charm. Very colonial."

Bolan grinned and switched back to the Stony Man channel. "Stony Base, this is Stony One. Over." From his current position he could watch the movement on the other side of the wall. The banquet was in full swing.

"Stony One, you have Stony Base. The program is ready to run. Please advise. Over."

"Execute the program, Stony Base. Stony One out."

Swaine Churchill finally emerged from the manor house and joined his associates. Six bodyguards formed a perimeter around him, letting people who wished to speak to him through their defenses in ones and twos. As conversations with those were finished, new people were allowed in.

Kissinger touched Bolan's sleeve. "Alfaro." He pointed.

Bolan followed Kissinger's direction and saw the DEA agent hovering on the outskirts of the party. The woman stood erect, her head held high as she surveyed the crowd. She wore jeans and a yellow blouse. Two men trailed her at a discreet distance, obviously assigned to watch her.

"Churchill doesn't appear overly trusting," Bolan stated.

"Maybe the man has reason," Kissinger said.

The Executioner nodded, then hit the transmit button on the headset. "Major."

"Here, mate."

"Be advised that the two friendlies we discussed are possibly on-site."

"Understood, Striker. We'll do everything in our power to get them home to you."

Bolan switched the headset channel. "Jack."

"Go."

"Get a message to Stony Base. Let them know it looks like Phoenix's missing package has turned up here."

"Damn, that's a relief."

"Only a partial relief," Bolan corrected. "We still have to get it out of the fire, and we're going to be turning up the heat."

"I'm on it."

Bolan settled back, lost the woman in the crowd and ticked off the numbers in his mind. Almost five minutes passed before the first reaction set in. It started with a small group of men drawing together around another man operating a laptop computer next to a phone out on the patio. Then other groups formed. The warrior could see the wave starting, moving outward from the patio area as other groups hurried in—unmindful of the spitting mist—to check out things with their own computers.

An angry mob, growing larger by the second, surged toward Churchill. The ex-CIA man's security people rose to meet the challenge and guns appeared like magic. For a moment the tension held and violence seemed uncertain. Then a shot rang out, quickly followed by another. In seconds bodies were strewn across the wet lawn and blood flowed onto the manicured landscape.

The headset clicked and Adair's voice came on. "Certainly seem to be a nasty bunch, don't they?"

"Count on it," Bolan replied.

Lines of demarcation were drawn. Tables were knocked over as gunners went to ground and started returning fire. Windows in the upper stories of the manor house were knocked out, and more of Churchill's guards joined the fray.

"First wave," Bolan called out.

A chorus of "readys" came from the SAS members ringing the house.

"Open fire," Bolan said. He heard the distant whumps of the Smith & Wesson riot guns and saw the impacts of the 37 mm projectiles belch out white clouds of CS gas when they struck the ground. The people staggered across the spacious lawns reacted immediately, recoiling from the gas clouds or being put down by it before they could escape. The Executioner tapped the transmit button. "Now the smoke."

More of the 37 mm grenades arced over the walls from all four sides. Dense smoke poured out, streaming white clouds of black, red and yellow to add to the general confusion.

Tightening his grip on the Mossberg pumpgun, Bolan tapped the transmitter once more. "Okay, hit the walls. Second wave, give us a thirty-second count, then follow us in. Move out!" He leaned into the charge, drumming his feet against the rain-soaked ground with Kissinger a half pace behind him.

Stony Man Farm, Virginia

BARBARA PRICE STOOD behind Kurtzman's desk, watching the three wall screens monitoring national and international news briefs. Each station had its particular section of the overall Stony Man operation to oversee. The tension inside her was a coiling, twisting cobra of uncertainty. Too many things could still go wrong, and she was too damn aware of them.

Kurtzman leaned back in the wheelchair with a big hand supporting his chin as he studied the monitor where his banking program was running. Numbers flickered and changed in the half-dozen accounts he was observing in the space of a single heartbeat.

"Do they know?" Price asked.

"Oh, yeah," Kurtzman said. "I made sure and tripped every bell and whistle I could when I ripped the money out of those accounts. They know."

The radio headset on Price's head beeped for attention. "This is Stony Base," she said. "Over."

"Stony Base, this is G-force," Grimaldi replied. "We have a go at this end. Striker has the area lit up like the Fourth of July. G-force out."

Price switched the communications frequency to the one monitored by Able Team in Houston, Phoenix Force on Solitaire Island and Charlie Mott's team in Tarpon Springs. "Stony teams, this is Stony Base. Over."

"We read you, Stony Base. This is Phoenix One. Over." Katz sounded ready and sure, part of his worry gone with the news that James had probably been located.

Able Team and Mott checked in, as well.

Price hit the transmit button. "Okay, gentlemen, you have your green light. Stony Base will be standing by. Out."

The channel rapidly cleared.

In her mind Price was on all four battle sites, fighting beside the men she'd guided there. Her voice was a harsh whisper as she faced the wall screens. "All right, Swaine Churchill, let's see if you're *really* ready for the big time."

Near Dover, England

SWAINE CHURCHILL RAN for his life. He dodged blindly, pulled by Terril Hedges, his personal bodyguard, toward the open door of the manor house where a trio of his people defended his retreat. Two bodies littered the stone steps, and he had to jump over them to make the entrance. One of the dead men was his. He didn't know who the other one belonged to.

Hedges threw him up against the wall inside the house and shielded him with his own body as a hail of bullets rattled into the stonework and whistled through the foyer. Another man died, a bullet plowing through his face, as they pulled the heavy door shut and locked it.

"Mr. Churchill," Hedges said, his young face tight with anxiety, "you'd better move your ass or someone's going to shoot it off."

"What the hell's going on out there?" Churchill demanded. Plumes of colored smoke stained the sky as he looked through the window to one side of the door.

"We're under attack," Hedges replied. He grabbed Churchill by the upper arm and started forcing him into another room.

"By who?"

"By everyone out there, for starters. And the outer perimeter guards have reported an outside force moving in from the forest."

Churchill freed his arm from Hedges's grip and darted into the library. One of the retreating security team closed the door.

Reaching into his pocket, Churchill produced a key, fitted it into the locked drawer and took out the Government Model .45 inside. He dropped the three extra clips into a jacket pocket, then racked the .45's slide to arm it.

He switched the desk computer on, flipped on the modem and accessed the Cayman Island banking records. The screen displayed the information in seconds. Even when he saw the evidence for himself he couldn't believe it. He tapped the keyboard and checked all the files. As he worked, all of the bank accounts set up in the names of his associates were being drained, feeding directly into his own account. He watched the numbers flip and saw the millions and millions of dollars piling up.

"Goddamn it!" he roared.

Hedges glanced at him. "Sir, those doors aren't going to hold for long."

"We'll move when I'm good and ready," Churchill snapped, "and not one moment before."

Hedges showed him a neutral expression. "Yes, sir. It's your ass they want, not mine."

Ignoring the sarcasm, Churchill seated himself at the computer and pulled out the programming book locked in beside the .45. He flipped it open, studied the encoded information and started to hit the keys.

Everything could still be salvaged. He'd been set up. Surely those people out there would believe him after he returned the money. They couldn't let a business as large as the one they'd formed go down the drain because of this.

His fingers moved so much more slowly than he wanted them to. He made mistakes and had to go back and try again. Abruptly the accounts were drained and the screen focused on Churchill's main account. He stared at the numbers, working frantically, then saw them disappear, leaving the account as bare as old Mother Hubbard's infamous cupboard.

"Damn it!" He shoved the computer onto the floor and the screen winked out in a blaze of sparks.

Someone started to pound on the library door.

"Sir," Hedges said.

Churchill ignored the man, lifted the telephone receiver and punched out the Tarpon Springs number he had for Dan Canary. If there was anyone inside the organization who could have scuttled him so quickly, it was Canary. The telephone rang twelve times and went unanswered. Before the thirteenth ring the line was cut.

He threw the dead handset away and stood. His hand slipped under the desktop and tripped a hidden switch. A section of the library shelving slid away, revealing a dark and narrow corridor. He took the flashlight from another drawer and passed it to

Hedges. The younger man took the lead at once, trotting into the secret exit.

He followed Hedges, trailed by two of his men. There were things he could salvage here once he got away, people who would believe in him after they saw how he'd been set up. He could use them, build again. All he needed was time and space to regroup and re-plan.

HOLDING A LINEN NAPKIN over her nose and mouth to avoid the tear gas and smoke, Maria Alfaro scrambled through the battleground that had formed around her. The men inside the stone walls had fallen into the every-man-for-himself survival theory. Groups took potshots at one another from behind whatever available defensive positions they'd been able to find.

More men, these clad in blacksuits with their faces masked by combat cosmetics, came hurtling over the stone walls in groups of twos and threes. They worked in sync, set up positions of covering fire for the next team working forward and cut through the scattered drug lords and their henchmen like a terrible and swift sword.

Still down on her hands and knees, Alfaro clambered under a banquet table laden with food and reached a hand out long enough to seize a Taurus 9 mm pistol. Hidden by the folds of the tablecloth, she dropped the magazine and checked how many cartridges she had. Eleven shots remained unfired. She wrapped her hand around the large butt of the pistol and screwed up her courage.

The black man she'd conned into following her to Churchill's hidden fortress was in the basement of the manor house. With the intense rain of destruction coming down on the home and the grounds, she was afraid he'd be lost in the confusion, another nameless casualty. With everything she'd had to do to make this case she didn't think she could bear to have his death on her conscience. Enough innocence had been lost or sacrificed.

The cocaine she'd taken earlier still buzzed through her system and she wished it didn't. She took a couple of deep breaths to steady her nerves, then pushed herself into a sprinter's position and ran for the house.

She'd already seen Churchill and his retinue seal themselves in through the main entrance. A small knot of men remained there, trying to force their way through the heavy door.

She avoided them, raced near the hedges surrounding the manor house and kept low until she reached one of the side doors. It was locked, but the window next to it wasn't.

Sliding her finger under the casement, she pushed the window up and heaved herself inside. The room was one of the smaller dining rooms scattered throughout the house. Her heart beat frantically as she carefully made her way toward the basement entrance below the main foyer stairs. Perspiration covered the back of her neck. She tried to make her hands stop trembling but couldn't.

She passed four bodies in the hallways, but didn't look close enough at them to see which side they'd been on. It no longer mattered. The Taurus was in both hands before her, leading every cautious step.

A man stood guard at the doorway under the winding stairway leading to the basement. She recognized him as one of Churchill's crew. He carried a CAR-15 canted across his chest and looked ready to use it.

Two more of Churchill's private security force manned stations on either side of the wall of windows fronting the house. Most of the glass had been shot out and only jagged shards remained. Bullets continued to pound into the room's walls, chewing into the hand-rubbed cherry wood of the stairway banister.

Alfaro ran during a lull in the gunfire, moving straight at the man standing beside the basement door. The guy tried to shift when he saw her, whipping the assault rifle toward her.

She never broke stride. Alfaro held the pistol pointed at the man's chest and squeezed the trigger until she was on top of him. A line of bullet holes stitched through the paneled door after her. It was only after she'd slammed into the wall on the other side of the basement entrance that she realized she'd been hit. There was no pain. Between the cocaine and the shock there was no feeling at all.

She pressed her fingers to her side, checked them and found them covered with blood. Taking a fresh grip on the Taurus, she forced herself to go on.

From down below, where the narrow corridor was dimly lighted, she could hear the sounds of a struggle. She hurried, afraid she might already be too late, or that the wound might be worse than she thought and suck her into unconsciousness before she made it to the bottom of the steps.

CHAPTER EIGHTEEN

Tarpon Springs, Florida

Lying on his back on the bed, Leo Turrin thought the sharp steel glimmer he saw thrust through his ceiling was the work of an overactive imagination. During the last eight hours, he'd had plenty of time to wonder exactly what Liborio Parrella was going to do with him. His mind had been all too fertile in conjuring up images of a slow, painful death.

The steely wink moved slowly. When Turrin saw the fine white powder of acoustic tile and Sheetrock drift down to layer the carpet, he sat up, pushed himself off the bed and held a hand under the stream of white dust. It coated his palm immediately.

Less than a minute later the sharp edge had inscribed a circle in the ceiling. It disappeared, then an Allen wrench poked through the center of the circle and twisted so that the L slid up under the Sheetrock. A muffled thump of impact followed.

The circle popped free of the ceiling, dropped down for an instant, then was reeled back up into the attic. Turrin stepped closer and gazed hard into the black depths of the hole.

Charlie Mott, the Stony Man backup pilot for Grimaldi, poked his head down. "Hey, Leo, you about had all the fun here you can stand?"

Turrin grinned and took the Uzi machine pistol the rugged Canadian passed down. He checked it, found it ready to perform and dropped the extra magazine into his pockets. "I think so. They tell me I've worn out my welcome."

"Well, buddy," Mott said dryly, "you won't exactly be back in good graces when we leave." The pilot lowered himself into the room. He was tan and fit, with a head of dark curly hair. He wore Stony Man black with combat webbing. Two more Stony Man warriors dropped into the room after him, automatically setting up defensive measures on either side of the door.

"So how goes the war?" Turrin asked.

Mott took up a position beside the window. Before shutting Turrin in the room two of Parrella's security squad had dropped a preformed crosshatch of steel bars over the window and locked them into place so that he couldn't escape by that route. The pilot looked over the gently rolling hills that led down to the boat house and hangar. "We're shutting these people down. That's what took us so long to tend to your rescue. Barb didn't want us to tip our hand before we were ready to move on all fronts. Mason and Ellis have been up in that attic with me for the past two hours."

Mason took a hand drill from his leather bag and started working on the door at eye level. Wooden splinters corkscrewed silently back into the room and littered the carpet. Ellis removed a block of plastic explosive from his gear and began working it into the door casement.

"How's that door?" Mott asked.

Mason popped the drill from the door and took a small, shiny cylinder from his shirt pocket, which Turrin recognized as a peephole. The Stony Man fighter inserted it into the augered hole.

"The explosive's ready," Ellis replied. "Say the word and we're out of here."

"I got two guys in the hallway," Mason said. "One on the left and one on the right. The stairway is at twelve o'clock."

"Let's get it done," Mott stated. He unfolded an ear-throat headset and settled it into place, then handed one to Turrin.

The Stony Man blacksuits put on their sets and took up positions on either side of the door, their H&K MP-5 SD-3s up and ready.

Turrin heard Mott's voice crackle in his ears as the pilot transmitted.

"Falcon, this is Hatchling. Over."

"Roger, Hatchling. You have Falcon. Over."

"We're about to have our coming-out party. Over."

"Acknowledged, Hatchling. Falcon standing by. Out."

Mott faced Turrin. "The plan is simple. Once we blow those doors we start moving, and we don't stop moving until we hit that boat house. I've already spent some time with the pontoon plane down there. It's wired, so we don't have to worry about the key. We're going to be really rushed, because we've got to evade these people and try not to get caught by the federal task force Barb has arranged to finish up here.''

Turrin nodded.

Reaching into his pocket again, Mott pulled out a remote control. His thumb hovered over the button, then pressed down. He dropped the control and grinned as a series of explosions took place outside. ''Show time, people.''

A chorus of wild yells sounded from inside the house. Gunfire broke out on the grounds.

''They just lost the garage and parts of their security perimeters,'' Mott explained.

Turrin braced himself when one of the blacksuits took out a detonator and slapped it onto the line of C-4 on the door. He turned his face away and heard the sharp report of the plastic explosive going off.

Dust, smoke and splinters flooded the small room. Peering through the gloom, Turrin caught a brief glimpse of the blacksuits rushing through the ragged doorway. Shots were fired, then Mott was pushing him into motion.

He took a double-fisted grip on the Uzi and ran out into the hall. Mason and Ellis were already securing the stairs, their deadly German subguns burping silenced death.

A door opened to Parrella's sitting room and a hardman Turrin recognized started to step through with a gun in his fist. Lifting the Uzi, the little Fed squeezed off a stream of 9 mm Parabellum rounds that caught the guy in the chest and slapped him backward. Mott followed up with a grenade that blew out the windows seconds later.

A group of men appeared in the double-wide doorway from the dining room. The Stony Man blacksuits dropped into defensive postures on the open floor and settled in for the fight.

Turrin leaned over the stairway railing a heartbeat ahead of Mott and opened fire. He emptied the clip and watched the men fall like tenpins as they were caught in the withering cross fire. The Justice man changed magazines on his way down.

"Take down this door," he said, slapping a palm against the reinforced entrance to Canary's computer room. "Their computer hardware's inside."

Mason and Ellis looked at Mott.

"Do it."

Ellis reached into his pocket for more C-4. Seconds later the plastique detonated, then the reinforced door swung inward, propelled by a kick.

Turrin followed the twisting spiral of smoke inside, but no one was there. He reached out to the harness of the Stony Man warrior, unclipped two grenades, popped the rings and tossed the bombs inside. The explosions came a second apart, hurling plastic and metal fragments out into the foyer.

"Falcon, this is Hatchling," Mott called. "Over."

"Go, Hatchling. Over."

"We're ready for that transport. Over."

"Acknowledged, Hatchling. Transport is en route. Falcon out."

Turrin glanced through the window. Parrella's forces were in disarray. Stony Man snipers were cutting them down from hidden positions.

The main entrance to Parrella's estate blew apart, and a Chevy Blazer 4WD roared through the opening.

"Get ready," Mott advised. "If you don't get the brass ring the first time, you don't get a ticket to ride."

Turrin nodded, wiped his hands on his pants and took a fresh grip on the Uzi. The Blazer braked to a halt in front of the house. A gunner cut loose from the back with a SAW, spitting a stream of 5.56mm rounds across the pockets of resistance formed by Parrella's teams.

"Now!" Mott roared, giving Turrin a push.

The little Fed ran for the rear door of the Blazer and dived inside. Hands seized his clothing and shoved him forcibly onto the far side of the seat as Mott went barreling in after him.

Mason and Ellis jumped into the rear beside the gunner as bullets thunked into the Blazer's body. Fist-size holes punched into the windshield.

"Go!" Mott said, slapping the driver on the shoulder.

The man released the clutch and floored the accelerator. The big 4WD dug in, fishtailed for a moment, then straightened, making for the dirt road that led to the boat house.

The Blazer smashed through the wooden fence and shrieked to a rocking stop on the dock. Mott fired a round from his pistol that tore away the padlock holding the metal gate that closed off the walkway to the pier. The pilot shoved the gate aside and led the rush into the hangar.

Turrin was at his heels. A glance over his shoulder assured him that the rest of the Stony Man blacksuits traveling by Jeeps were joining them. He followed Mott through the hangar's side entrance and caught the man as he suddenly fell back, then realized he'd heard shots. Mott was bleeding on his left side from at least two wounds.

Crouching to support the man, Turrin scanned the interior of the hangar and saw Dan the Man attempting to board the seaplane. Liborio Parrella's dark eyes glared at him from the other side of the plane's windscreen.

As Dan the Man shifted his .45 to cover Turrin, the little Fed cut loose with a one-handed figure eight from the Uzi. The 9 mm rounds chopped into the man and shoved him back over the nose of the seaplane. Blood smeared across the engine cowling as the body dropped into the dark water.

A single round cored through the seaplane's windscreen and blew Parrella's head back as the old mafioso raised an assault rifle.

"Don't hurt the goddamn plane," Mott snarled.

"Are you okay?" Turrin asked.

"Hell, no," the pilot replied, "but help me up, anyway, so I can get us out of here."

Turrin helped support Mott as they made their way to the plane. By the time they boarded, they could hear the scream of sirens surrounding the estate.

Mott fired up the engines while someone threw Parrella's body onto the wooden walkway. The seaplane shuddered with power, blocking out all other noise inside the hangar. "The doors," he said.

"Going now," someone replied.

Sitting in the copilot's seat, Turrin saw the series of small explosions rip around the hangar door hinges. In a sheet, hardly disturbed at all, the two heavy doors plunged straight down into the water and disappeared.

Mott throttled up and sent the seaplane scooting forward into the lighted rectangle of sky and sea. Once they were clear of the hangar, he increased the craft's power unitl they were skimming over the water headed for the open sea.

Turrin watched the ocean drop away as the plane leaped into the air. The ride settled out at once. Within minutes Parrella's estate was fading behind them, swallowed by the distance and the altitude. He reached for the medical kit one of the blacksuits handed him and started working on Mott's wounds. Neither were life-threatening at the moment.

"Looks like we made it," Turrin commented.

"Never had a doubt in my mind," Mott replied.

Turrin carefully placed a gauze bandage over the first of Mott's wounds. "Oh, no, me, neither," he said sarcastically.

London, England

BLOOD FLOWED down Calvin James's left arm from the bite of the steel cuffs. He stood in the center of the basement, arms chained over his head. He was naked from the waist up, his skin dappled by beads of perspiration. His bare feet were cold against the stone floor.

He used the fingers of his right hand to catch the running blood and smear it over his left wrist. The salt from his perspiration stung the rips in his skin but provided a film of lubricant. Satisfied with the coating, he folded his thumb into his palm and began pulling against the cuff again. He grabbed the cuff in his right hand and added his own strength to the combined forces of gravity and his own weight.

He moaned with the pain that ran in electric currents from his wrist and surrounded his brain. His body trembled with the sustained effort. For the past eight hours he'd been questioned repeatedly. In return he'd either remained silent or given nonsense answers dealing with Mother Goose stories.

For his trouble he'd been beaten. His right eye was swollen shut, and the inside of his mouth was cut. Every time he coughed he tasted blood.

He strained against the cuff, pushing the pain away. This was the first time his captors had left him alone. He didn't know when he might get the chance again and wanted to make the most of his present opportunity.

He gasped as his wrist slid another fraction of an inch. Then his left thumb broke, separated from the pressure of being dragged through the cuff. But it gave him more room. James pulled again, harder, and his hand popped free.

He almost blacked out from the pain. Taking deep breaths and forcing them all the way out slowly, the Phoenix Force warrior brought his mind back on track. His broken thumb throbbed as he gazed at it; the flesh around his wrist was torn, bruised and bleeding. The empty cuff dangled over his head, and drops of blood spattered onto his face as he slid a lockpick free of a secret pocket sewn into his pants.

Using his fingers, he worked on the lock holding his right hand. The cuff sprang open in a little over a minute.

James crossed the room, found a roll of strapping tape near a packing box and quickly bound his broken thumb to the rest of his hand for support. It limited his freedom of movement, but it also protected the thumb. He located a box knife in a side drawer just as someone came down the steps.

Moving silently, the Phoenix Force commando leaned into the sheltering shadows beside the door. When the man entered the room, James recognized him as one of his interrogators. The man stopped in his tracks, apparently thunderstruck that James could have escaped.

Before the man could raise an alarm James reached out for him with his wounded arm, flicked out the blade of the box knife and sliced the man's throat open from ear to ear. The ex-SEAL didn't drop his quarry until all struggles had died away.

As he knelt over the corpse, James could hear the echoes of gunfire warbling down the stairway. He took the dead man's .45, two extra clips, the Buck pocket-knife and his disposable lighter.

A shuffling noise alerted him that someone else was at the door. He lifted the .45 and found himself looking down the sights at Maria Alfaro. She had a pistol pointed at him.

For an instant they remained frozen in place, and James could see the cocaine in her system burning holes in her soul. He wasn't sure what kind of grip she had on reality.

Finally she lowered the pistol. "Thank God you're all right. I was afraid I might get here too late."

James got to his feet, not quite putting the pistol away. "What's going on upstairs?"

"I think your friends have arrived. And Churchill and his people are fighting among themselves." She took a shaky breath. "I want you to know I didn't have a choice about giving you up to them. They already suspected me. If I couldn't deliver Johnson, and

I was sure they'd know, I knew I had to give them something to buy myself some time.''

"So you gave them me.''

"Yes. You couldn't have gotten here on your own. Maybe your agency wouldn't have found this place if you hadn't been here. I was counting on Churchill to try to figure out who you were, and I was counting on your agency to find a way to track you down. If they didn't, I would have tried to break out on my own.''

"You took some pretty big chances with my life, lady.''

"I took some big chances with both our lives. But it had to be done. These people had to be stopped. Too many people are lost every day to drugs as it is now without Churchill and his group making things even worse.'' Her words were impassioned.

In spite of everything James couldn't find it in his heart to blame the woman. There were scars on her soul just as surely as there were scars on his. He was sure she'd lost loved ones to drugs just as he had, and the memory was bitter, something that would always drive them harder than other people.

He stepped forward and embraced her. "It's okay. We're going to beat this thing. Let's get out of here and see if we can help.''

Without warning she buckled in his grasp. He caught her before she fell, seeing her wounds for the first time.

CHAPTER NINETEEN

Houston, Texas

Carl Lyons tried to remain casual as he walked onto the docking pier at the Houston Port Authority. Inside every nerve was thrumming. He thumbed the transmit button on his headset. "Pol? Gadgets?"

"Here, Ironman," Schwarz called back.

"Ready," Blancanales replied.

"Haggerty?" Lyons called.

"We move when you give us the go-ahead," the MacTuff squad leader said.

From the go Haggerty had proved to be a good cop, a team player rather than a maverick. He kept his men in line, and he kept them professional. Instead of trying to go ahead with the assault on the *Jolly Jack* on his own—as many local law-enforcement heads might have wanted to do—Haggerty had been willing to work off Price's calls. It was another facet of the Stony Man mission controller that Lyons respected: she was able to turn up people her teams could work with when it was necessary.

The freighter was docked, waiting to be unloaded. Kurtzman had spiked into the port authority computer files and rescheduled the *Jolly Jack*'s unloading appointment to better coincide with the strike times of Mott, Phoenix and Bolan.

He carried a clipboard filled with bills of lading and tried to look bored as he closed in on the big ship. He wore a long windbreaker over his combat gear that hung low enough to cover the .357 wheelgun on his hip.

A mate hailed Lyons from the deck of the freighter. "You gonna get us unloaded in this lifetime?"

"We're working on it," Lyons bellowed back. "Keep your shorts on."

The mate waved at him in disgust and disappeared over the edge of the deck above Lyons.

"Okay, people," Lyons said, "let's get dangerous."

Ironman watched the hydraulic boom arm come around. He started up the rope ladder the mate had thrown over the side for him, glancing over his shoulder at the ball of cargo netting suspended from the boom arm as it swiveled toward the *Jolly Jack*. Men clung to the netting with their feet and hands. He didn't see a single weapon among them.

"Hey," the mate yelled as Lyons threw a leg over the top and went aboard, "we got our own crew to offload." He pointed at the cargo netting over their heads where a dozen men maintained their holds on the ropes. "We don't need those guys."

"The port's providing it," Lyons lied smoothly. "Our way of saying we're sorry for the computer error regarding your off-loading appointment."

Nearly twenty men sprang from the ship's holds. Not all of them looked like the adventurous seagoing type.

"Bullshit." The mate stepped forward, going nose to nose with Lyons. "I've been working this harbor a lot of years, and I never heard of anything like this. Who the hell are you?"

Lyons returned the man's stare, knew the guy was wily enough to pick up the cop scent that still lingered after all these years. "You know me."

"Cops!" the mate yelled. "It's a raid!" His hand darted to the small of his back and removed a chrome pistol.

Lyons slapped leather instinctively, the .357 Magnum filling his hand in the wink of an eye. It boomed as soon as it hit waist level. The recoil forced the weapon's muzzle up, and Lyons fired again. The second shot took the mate full in the face and pitched him onto the blood-slick deck.

Hitting the transmit button on his headset, Lyons ordered, "Sweep the decks." He lifted the .357 Python and drew target acquisition on his next opponent. He fired, punching a round into the man's chest and knocking him into the man behind him.

Sniper fire from nearby rooftops chopped into the crew. Men hit the deck, held their positions for a moment, then broke and ran.

The men clinging to the cargo netting—Lyons could see Schwarz and Blancanales among them—released their holds and dropped to the deck. Assault rifles and machine pistols up and tracking, they spread out in preformed groups.

"Hey, Ironman."

Lyons glanced over at Blancanales and caught the CAR-15 the man tossed to him. He stripped away the windbreaker to reveal the MacTuff uniform blouse underneath.

"Good hunting, Carl." Politician took off toward the wheelhouse to prevent any attempts at moving the freighter out of the harbor.

Schwarz and a member of the task force cut the cargo netting free. More of Haggerty's people provided covering fire while Schwarz and his assistant lugged the heavy bundle of rope over to the side of the ship. They secured it to the railing with giant S-hooks, then threw the end over. When it trailed down the side of the ship, it formed a broad rope ladder that would allow the rest of the force to clamber aboard.

Lyons ran to the nearest hold, burning two of the crewmen with short bursts on the way. He leaped over one of the falling bodies and pulled up at the entrance. The bowels of the freighter were unlighted.

His four-man team alighted around him, waiting for their orders. He took a pair of night-vision goggles from an equipment pack strapped to one man's back and donned them, then slung the CAR-15.

Heaving himself over the side, he hung by his hands, then dropped the fifteen feet to the floor below. He rolled, raked the assault rifle around and flipped off the safety.

The goggles turned the world green and black. Behind a line of wooden crates a pair of muzzle-flashes blossomed bright and deadly. Throwing himself to one side, Lyons rolled and came up with the CAR-15 tucked securely into the crook of his arm. He squeezed the trigger in a sustained burst that ripped the gunners away from their cover.

The MacTuff team dropped into the hold with him. Lyons waved two of them to the back to secure the bulkhead and sent the other pair to the port side of the freighter. He kept the starboard side for himself.

"The rear's covered," one of the men called a moment later.

"So's the port side," another man announced.

"Move out," Lyons commanded. "We don't want to miss any of these bastards." He moved at a slow jog, the rifle ready in his hands. "Haggerty?"

The sound of gunfire echoed inside the ship.

"We're in," the commander replied. "We're driving them to you now."

Lyons contacted the sniper leader and confirmed that the above-deck action had come to a halt for lack of targets.

Two crewmen raced toward Lyons, glancing over their shoulders. They didn't see the Able Team warrior until they were almost on top of him.

Lyons rose out of his crouch and buttstroked the nearer man into unconsciousness, then bounced a big booted foot off the other guy. The second crewman smashed into the bulkhead with a meaty thunk, then slid to his knees, gasping for breath.

Guiding the man into position with his empty hand, Lyons took a set of plastic cuffs from his equipment belt and secured the guy's hands behind his back, then did the same for the first man. A bullet spanged off the metal bulkhead and drove Lyons into hiding. More gunfire sounded on the other side of the freighter. He keyed the transmitter. "Haggerty?"

"Go."

"Be careful. They know we're here now."

"Roger."

Lyons returned fire, dropped another man, then watched the crew try to regroup. "Pol?"

"Yeah, Ironman."

"How's the wheelhouse?"

"We own it. This crate isn't going anywhere."

Lyons peered over the top of the boxes he used for cover at what was left of the crew. From his hurried count he figured there might be twenty survivors. He raked a smoke grenade from his webbing, pulled the pin and heaved the orb into the middle of the men, which generated muffled curses and fearful exclamations.

Lyons raised his voice. "That was just a smoker, gents. Think of what could have just happened. I'm giving you people exactly thirty seconds to pack it in, or I'm going to introduce you to the real thing."

Arguments broke out between the crewmen as they tried to select a spokesman.

"You're down to twenty seconds."

"How do we know you guys won't cut us down, anyway?" a man yelled back.

The ensuing heartbeat was pregnant with possibilities.

"You've got my word on it," Lyons said. "You want that in writing, you're going to have to drop the weapons, anyway. And you're down to ten seconds."

"All right, all right. We're coming out."

Rifles and pistols slid out into the open.

"Any tricks, if any one of you is holding out thinking you're going to break free, you all die. That's a promise, too."

More arguments broke out, then another handful of weapons dropped into the pile taking shape outside the crates.

"Okay," Lyons said, "everybody out and onto their faces. The sooner we get this part over with, the better the chances are that nobody else needs to get hurt."

The crewmen walked warily out into the open, then sank to their knees and onto their stomachs. At Lyon's suggestion they placed their hands behind their heads.

Five men from the MacTuff group closed in and quickly cuffed the sailors. Within minutes they had the men up and moving toward the upper deck. Lyons interviewed one of them long enough to find out where the psilocybin cocaine was hidden, then followed them up.

Solitaire Island, French Guiana

HOLDING ON TO the LCU's railing, Katz scanned the shore of Solitaire Island. They were still a quarter mile out to sea, but the security around the harbor had already started to tighten in response.

At first they'd been hailed by ship-to-shore radio from August's communications people. Katz had ignored the repeated commands to identify themselves. Once the LCU had powered up close enough to be seen, the communications had died away. There was no mistaking the military lines of the landing craft.

Two speedboats were cutting swaths through the sea tracking onto the LCU. Katz's field glasses had revealed mounted .50-caliber machine guns on board both vessels.

Katz hit his transmitter. "Phoenix Two and Phoenix Four, this is Phoenix One. Over."

"Roger, Phoenix One, you have Phoenix Two," McCarter replied. "Over."

"And you have Phoenix Four," Encizo said. "Over."

"Take your targets down," Katz instructed. "Phoenix One out." The headset clicked in his ear.

Less than a moment later the mined airfield and warehouse went up and the sound of explosions roiled out onto the harbor area. Debris blew straight up. The munitions had been planted with that effect in mind because it would let everyone on the island know that the sea didn't pose the only threat.

Machine-gun fire from the speedboats rattled across the thick metal sides of the LCU. Katz put the binoculars away and hunkered down slightly. "Helmsman."

"Aye, sir."

"Full throttle now."

"Aye, sir."

The landing craft shuddered as the powerful engines were kicked into full thrust. The LCU's nose dropped down into the water for an instant, then popped back up and lunged forward.

Forty SEALS and six jeeps were on the LCU with Katz, bringing the invasion force up to seventy men. The USS *Spearfish* was standing by with a secondary wave if necessary.

"Gunner," Katz called.

"Aye, sir." The SEAL rose to his position at the deck-mounted 40 mm machine cannon.

"You have your targets."

"Aye, sir." The gunner moved with the automated sighting and fired as the first of the speedboats raced toward them. The 40 mm warheads made a line of explosions that spumed water in twisting coils in front of the speedboat. As the craft turned to veer away, at least three of the rounds slammed into her amidships, setting off an explosion that ripped her to shreds.

The second boat turned tail and tried to run. More on target this time, the gunner picked off the craft as it crested a wave, blowing it to pieces with at least a half-dozen rounds.

Katz glanced at the harbor. Someone was out there trying to consolidate the security forces so that they could make a stand. Black smoke curled up from the wreckage of the airfield and the warehouse. The shore guns kicked sluggishly into action, drawing great gouts of water from the sea in a searching pattern that was closing in on the LCU.

He thumbed the transmit button. They were less than two hundred yards from the shore. "Come in, Phoenix Three. Over."

"You have Phoenix Three," Manning said. "Over."

"It's time to ring down the curtain. Over."

"Acknowledged. Phoenix Three out."

Katz rose from his crouch slightly. The success of Manning's theories was the linchpin that would tell how costly the invasion was going to be in lives for the Navy and Phoenix Force.

He waited. A round from one of the big shore guns rocked the landing craft when it hit only yards away. A wave of water erupted over the side and drenched the attack unit.

A series of rumbles came from the island, sparked by a chain reaction of underwater explosions. White foam billowed up around the island. The rumbling increased in decibel level until it sounded like sudden summer thunder.

The people on land acted as if they were experiencing an earthquake as the ground beneath them buckled and shivered. Without warning a chasm opened up, splitting through the main house and shaking down the outbuildings. Men, sand, trees and buildings dropped into the chasm as if filling a vacuum.

Katz hit the transmit button. "Ground units, report in. Over."

All five teams did, including Manning, amazement in their voices at the destruction that had been unleashed along the island's fault line.

"Helmsman," Katz called out.

"Aye, sir."

"Take us ashore."

"Aye, sir."

The LCU adjusted its approach and hurtled onto the beach with loud grinding noises as the rocky shore skated along the metal underside. The debarkation teams kicked down the boarding ramp and poured out onto the sand.

Katz took the shotgun seat in the lead jeep, clapping the driver on the shoulder to let him know the machine gunner had joined them. The driver popped the clutch and stepped down hard on the accelerator. The jeep hurtled out of the LCU, jumped over the ramp and bucked onto the loose sand of the harbor area.

The gunner with the deck-mounted 40 mm cannon kept firing into the buildings, and explosions ripped through the structures. Two men with assault rifles attempted to make a stand against the jeep. Katz kicked down the vehicle's window and knocked them both out of the way with a stream of .45 rounds from his Ingram MAC-10.

Small-arms fire never ceased chattering, and mortar teams among the SEALs already on the island heaved shells into pockets of resistance as Katz and other fire commanders called in coordinates. The SEAL driver heeled around the corner of a demolished building, pursuing a ground team that had used LAW rockets to take out two of the invading jeeps.

Katz got a brief impression of a yellow wall that was swelling up over him, then realized he was looking at a bulldozer. The driver tried to stop, but the jeep slid forward and collided with the bulldozer's scoop, flipping over.

Belted into the jeep, Katz rode out the crash, then cut himself free. As he got to his feet and secured his grip on the MAC-10, he heard the voices of the men closing in on him. He whirled around the jeep and laid down a blistering line of .45 rounds that chopped down three men in midstride.

The magazine empty on the machine pistol, Katz let it hang by its strap as he reached for his side arm. The SIG-Sauer P-226 settled onto the head of the driver of the approaching bulldozer.

Katz stood his ground and fired a full clip in rapid-fire. When he was finished, the hole in the cab's windshield could have been covered by an eight-inch pie plate. The driver crumpled to the cab's floor, and the bulldozer snorted and died.

"Yakov! Bloody hell, mate, are you all right?"

As he was reloading his weapons, Katz turned and saw McCarter running toward him. "I seem to be."

McCarter paused by the prone body of the SEAL gunner and pressed his fingers to the man's throat. He glanced up and shook his head.

But the driver was only stunned. Katz helped the man limp to the meager shelter of the flattened outbuilding and gave him the M-16 he'd been issued.

Encizo joined Katz, blood leaking from a corner of his mouth. "Webb August is getting away."

"Where?" Katz asked.

Following the direction the Cuban indicated, Katz saw a four-wheel-drive pickup charging into the jungle. No one was there to intercept it. The Israeli put his shoulder to the hood of the jeep. "David, Rafael, your assistance, please."

The three Phoenix commandos bent to the task, pushing and shoving the jeep until it rolled over onto all four tires. McCarter slid behind the wheel and keyed the ignition. It caught, but the engine idled raggedly.

Katz and Encizo climbed in and McCarter accelerated. The right front tire had a bad shimmy at any kind of speed. McCarter hung on grimly, aiming the jeep for the spot where the pickup had disappeared.

Action in the harbor was dying down as the SEALs secured their beachhead. Katz turned control of the invading forces over to the Navy SEAL team commander.

Branches whipped into their faces as they plunged into the jungle. McCarter had to struggle with the wheel as he steered around trees and boulders. Unexpectedly they plunged through a wall of bush and thumped onto a dirt trail.

"Obviously we missed something," Katz observed.

Encizo nodded. "I thought August looked like someone who had a definite destination in mind."

"Save the recriminations for the after-the-game analysis," McCarter said. "Those blokes haven't put anything past us yet."

Two hundred yards farther the trail ended abruptly. McCarter slammed on the brakes and Katz led the way out of the jeep into the clearing on top of a small, steep rise.

Six men were about to climb aboard a Bell helicopter, which was shielded by a canopy of camou netting. The helicopter's rotors were spinning, rotor wash flailing away at the leaves and branches. A man raised an assault rifle to his shoulder, shouted a warning and squeezed off a burst. Encizo cut the gunner down with a triburst.

Sunlight lanced into the clearing as the camou netting fell to one side. Webb August tried to crawl inside the helicopter while blindly firing his assault rifle one-handed.

Taking up a position behind a tree, Katz jerked a grenade from his webbing, pulled the pin with his hook, counted down, then lobbed the bomb under the helicopter. "Fire in the hole," he called as he ducked back.

A heartbeat later the grenade exploded, creating an empathic explosion within the helicopter that left it wrecked and twisted on the ground. The rotors came loose and went whirling madly through the trees, shearing off branches.

There were no survivors.

CHAPTER TWENTY

Near Dover, England

Mack Bolan hit the stone wall at a dead run, using the grappling hook and nylon rope to climb to the top. He paused for a moment on the wall, then was face-to-face with Cowboy Kissinger on the other side. Both men slipped on their gas masks.

The warrior hit the transmit button on his headset, lifting the gas mask so he could speak. "Snipers, report."

"One, able, sir."

"Two, able, sir."

"Three, able, sir."

The other three men reported in, as well.

"Be advised that you have friendlies in the field as of now."

The six men acknowledged him.

He rolled, dropped to the ground and raised the Mossberg pump as an Uzi-wielding hardman wheeled on him. He stroked the trigger, and the double-aught buckshot sent the man spinning away.

The 37 mm smoke canisters discharged by the Smith & Wesson riot control guns continued to blow red, black and yellow streamers into the air, mixed with the white CS gas. The Executioner ran through the carnage. Two Orientals fired at him from behind the relative safety of a captured food server. The woman kicked and screamed as she fought against them.

Unwilling to endanger the woman, Bolan pointed the shotgun at the canopy stand that sprouted from the center of a nearby table. He fired, and the tight pattern of shot sheared the aluminum pole in two. The wet canvas canopy collapsed onto the Orientals and their hostage, knocking all three to the ground.

Bolan shifted the Mossberg to his left hand and drew the Desert Eagle. Kissinger covered him as a small group of Churchill's security team took an interest in them. The weaponsmith jerked a grenade from his combat harness, pulled the pin, counted down and threw the bomb into the group. The explosive blew them off their feet. None got back up.

One of the Orientals clawed the canvas from his face and tried to bring up his weapon as he struggled to his feet. The Executioner put a 240-grain boattail through the man's forehead. When the second gunner surfaced, the warrior took him out of play, too.

Bolan turned at the sound of screeching brakes. A military jeep carrying more SAS troops came barreling into the yard. Four more would follow in seconds. They were the second wave of the attack, which would establish a spearhead that would claim the battleground.

He thumbed the transmit button on his headset. "Third team, you have your go." He glanced at the treetops a thousand yards away and saw Grimaldi's chopper rise into the dark sky like a giant black-eyed insect. Two more followed it, forming a flying wedge that was more for intimidation than anything else. Helicopter fire inside the primary killzone could end up injuring the friendly forces on the scene.

Bolan went to ground behind a concrete fish pond as a fresh wave of autofire searched for him. Bullets splatted into the water, gouging chunks from the concrete. The warrior crawled on his hands and knees, maintaining his grip on the Mossberg.

He came up without warning, bracketing the window where the gunners were taking cover. He pulled the shotgun's trigger, rode out the recoil and let it help him pump the next round from the magazine. Firing twice more, he cleared the glass from the window, then pushed himself to his feet and raced toward the manor house with Kissinger at his heels.

He slammed into place alongside the door, brought the shotgun up and replaced the shells he'd fired. Kissinger fed a fresh magazine into the CAR-15. Bolan looked at the weaponsmith and said, "Now." Whirling inside, the warrior took the left side while Kissinger covered the right.

Two of Churchill's men tried to break from the window. The Executioner cut the first man down before he could bring his weapon into play. The other gunner got off a pair of shots, but only one slammed into Bolan's Kevlar vest. The second discharge from the Mossberg caught the man in the chest and bounced him off a wall. Kissinger terminated another man.

Most of the interior of the building had been ripped to shreds by the fusillade of bullets. Stray rounds continued to slash through the house as Bolan and Kissinger made their way down a hallway. They dropped their gas masks onto the floor because they were no longer necessary.

The snipers had confirmed Churchill's reentry into the house. No one had seen the man come out.

At the end of the hallway Bolan found two men facing a closed door. One of them was working on the door with a fire ax.

"Drop your weapons," Bolan commanded.

The men turned, doing as they were told.

"Where's Churchill?" Bolan asked.

"In there," one of the men said. "There's a way out of here. A passageway leading to an escape tunnel and a Land Rover. The son of a bitch ran out on us."

"Down on the floor." Bolan waved the muzzle of the Mossberg meaningfully.

The men got down, holding their hands up when the Executioner instructed them to, and lay there while Bolan cuffed them.

"Take out the door," Bolan said to Kissinger.

The big man nodded, slung his assault rifle and delved into a pouch tied at his waist. He pinched off a section of a block of C-4 and stuck it to the door by the locking mechanism. Then he added a detonator switch and ducked back.

The explosion sounded loud in the room. Sparks and flames jumped at the opposite wall. When Kissinger waved the smoke away, the lock had been replaced by a big hole.

Bolan dumped his prisoners in the hallway, then lifted a foot, kicked the door in and entered. The room was empty.

"Damn, I hate these locked-room mysteries," Kissinger growled.

Slinging the Mossberg pumpgun over his shoulder, Bolan advanced on the library shelves. He built the house in his mind, tore it down and figured the most likely wall to house a concealed entrance. "Here," he said. He started scooping books from the shelves directly behind the desk. Unsheathing his Cold Steel Tanto knife, he tapped the butt against the wooden panels behind the shelves. Within seconds he found a hollow spot.

"I'm covering the door," Kissinger said.

Bolan nodded, already busy with a block of C-4. He ran lines at the top and bottom of the hidden entrance, then wired in a single detonator to both pieces of the plastic explosive. Activating the remote control, he jogged back out of the room and took up his position in the hallway.

"Striker."

Looking up, the warrior saw Calvin James stumble into the hallway from the other end. He looked worse for the wear, but he was walking on his own two feet and carrying a woman in his arms. A glance showed Bolan that the woman was Alfaro.

"She needs medical attention," James said. "It's pretty bad, and I've done all I can for her without medical supplies." He came to a halt in front of them.

"Let me take her off your hands," Kissinger volunteered. "You look plumb tuckered out."

Bolan tapped the transmitter button on the headset. "Major Adair, this is Striker."

"Go, Striker," Adair's calm voice replied.

"I need a Medevac unit double-quick," the Executioner said, watching James sag against the wall when Kissinger relieved him of the woman. "Two to transport, inside the house."

"Your people?"

"Yeah."

"They're on their way."

James nodded toward the library. The .45 hung at the end of his arm. Even banged up he still looked game enough to take on whatever came his way. "Churchill in there?"

"Was," Bolan replied. He thumbed the remote control.

The twin explosions roared inside the room. A blast of hot air cycled out into the corridor.

"I'm going to find out where he went," Bolan said.

"I'll go with—" James began.

Bolan cut him off. "You'll stay here and wait for that Medevac team. No offense, Calvin, but I can't afford to look out for you and me both down there."

James squared his shoulders and started to protest but realized the truth in the statement.

Taking up the shotgun, Bolan glanced at Kissinger.

"I've got them," the weaponsmith said. "You watch your ass down there."

Bolan turned and charged into the room, ran sure-footed over the debris and paused at the side of the gaping hole in the wall. Darkness swirled inside, riding the clouds of dust that had been stirred up by the explosion.

Taking a halogen flashlight and a roll of electrical tape from his pouch, he fixed the flash to the Mossberg's barrel and switched it on. He went in low, keeping his back to one of the hand-hewn stone walls.

"Striker." It was Adair's voice on the headset.

"Go," Bolan said softly.

"We're taking your people out now. Mind if I drop in on your little party?"

"Come ahead, Major."

Seconds later the bulky body of the SAS commander shadowed the library entrance.

Bolan went on. The tunnel sloped down, widening as the hewn walls gave way to a small cave. He listened intently, heard the crunch of loose stones under his boots, Adair behind him, and from somewhere ahead of him, the sound of running water. The smell of limestone and mildew was thick and cloying.

He continued to sweep the beam of the flash across the walls but saw nothing. Less than a minute later he hit bottom. No one was there.

Playing the flashlight's beam around the small cavern, Bolan discovered he was in a room almost fifty feet square. A stream flowed from the northwest, emerging from under a rocky wall and continuing down a tunnel running southeast. The water was dark, murky when the light touched it, but it looked deep enough to float a good-size longboat. Dull metal gleamed on the walls, and further inspection revealed them to be ringbolts set into the stone. A rusted anchor leaned in one corner among the shattered remains of a half-dozen wooden kegs and a rolled bunch of sailcloth.

"Smuggler's den," Adair commented. "Once an honored profession in this country. You find them in a lot of places." His own flashlight beam joined the Executioner's. "Your man Churchill really plays for all the angles, doesn't he?"

"Yeah." Bolan moved out to scout the terrain. A dark patch glistened on the stone floor. When he touched it, oil came away on his fingers. He jogged a short way along the narrow ledge following the stream and tried to look farther down the tunnel, but the flashlight beam was lost in the intense dark lying in wait there.

"No telling how far that bleeding tunnel goes," Adair said.

"It's got to come out somewhere." Bolan raced back to the library. "Send a foot patrol along after him."

"They must have some kind of vehicle. That was motor oil I saw on your hand back there, wasn't it?"

Bolan nodded as they came out into the lighted library. He took his map case from a slit pocket of the skinsuit. Flipping through the information concerning this part of Dover, he took out a geological survey map, wiped the debris from the desk with one sweep of his arm and laid out the document. "I want the team sent along to flush out Churchill if the guy tries to hole up instead of making a run for it. I'm hedging my bets."

"But you think he'll run."

"Yeah. From the coastline it's a twenty-one-mile jump across the Strait of Dover into France. If he gets that far, we could be looking at a whole new ball game." Bolan considered the map. "Parts of that cave and tunnel appear to have been hewn out by hand."

"That's not unusual," Adair said, studying the map. "As I said, privateering was a lucrative business in the sixteenth and seventeenth centuries."

Bolan sorted out another geological survey map, which zeroed in on the area surrounding Churchill's manor house. "True, but it leads me to believe that particular tunnel has access to the sea."

"You still have to find the other end of that rabbit warren in time, mate."

Bolan put the maps away. "Churchill's not going to escape. His chances of being able to rebuild this organization after the way we've shattered it are slim, but I want to leave him no chance at all." He changed the headset to the frequency monitored by the Stony Man troops and tapped the transmitter button. "Jack."

"Go, Sarge."

"Meet me out front."

"On my way."

Bolan ran through the house until he reached the front entrance. The battle in the yard had died away to sporadic gunfights. The SAS teams were obviously very much in control of the situation.

Calvin James and Kissinger were beside a gurney, working feverishly on Maria Alfaro. A SAS corpsman held up a plastic bottle of glucose while the fluid fed into the woman's arm.

"How is she?" Bolan asked when he reached James's side.

The Phoenix commando nodded. "She'll make it. She's a hell of a tough lady."

Bolan could tell the woman had made an impression on the ex-SEAL and wondered what the full story was. Price hadn't seemed well-informed concerning James's actions during the final stages of the mission.

Kissinger looked up and squinted at Grimaldi's approaching helicopter. "Going somewhere?"

"I'm going to tie up a loose end."

"Want company?"

"I've got Jack. You're needed here." He moved out at a jog, away from the medical teams so the rotor wash wouldn't create problems.

Grimaldi dropped the helicopter to within a few feet of the ground. Bolan leaped, caught the landing skid and hauled himself up, dropping into the copilot's seat.

"Where to?" Grimaldi asked. He pulled up on the stick and the main rotor grabbed airspace.

"Southeast." The Executioner quickly outlined the discovery of the smuggler's den below the manor house.

At full speed the helicopter winged toward the coastline. "That's a lot of area to cover," Grimaldi commented.

"Streams and rivers usually find the easiest route to the major bodies of water," Bolan said. "On the map some of them appear to twist and turn, but if you follow them for a couple of miles on foot they tend to head more or less straight. It's two miles from the house to the coastline. I'm betting whoever first established the smuggler's hideout chose this location because it was easiest to travel and had direct access to the sea."

"And the shortest distance between two points is a straight line."

"That's what I'm thinking."

"I'll buy it."

Moments later the coastline came into view. Grimaldi lost altitude, then skimmed low over the water while they searched the chalk cliffs for their quarry.

"There," Grimaldi called out. "I thought I saw something flash at ten o'clock."

Bolan turned his binoculars to the direction indicated, adjusted the magnification and saw an open-topped, military-styled Land Rover scaling the cliff face along a road that was almost nonexistent. A dark obelisk was a hundred yards behind them, an open mouth pouring out into the sea. He strengthened the magnification again, swept the four faces inside and found Churchill sitting in the passenger seat.

"It's Churchill," Bolan confirmed.

Before his words died away bullets starred the Plexiglass nose of the helicopter. Grimaldi pulled the craft up instantly, cursing at how close the bullets had come.

"They've got to come up," Bolan said as he put the binoculars to his eyes again. He scouted the twisting road the Land Rover was following and found where it peaked on the cliff face. He pointed. "Put me down there."

"Sarge..."

"There's no other way. This helicopter makes a big target. If Churchill gets by us, it'll take too long to organize a ground interception. By then he could be long gone."

The pilot heeled the helicopter over. It moved like a live thing in his hands, dropping with express elevator speed toward the top of the cliff where the wind and the sea had scoured the land clear of vegetation.

Bolan dumped the Mossberg, knowing that the pellets would prove ineffectual against the Land Rover's windshield. He swung himself out the door as

Grimaldi brought the craft to a shuddering halt a dozen feet above the ground.

The Executioner jumped, rolling and pushing himself to his feet on impact. Grimaldi cleared off, stirring up a cloud of dust and stinging sand that pelted Bolan's exposed flesh. With the helicopter leaving, he could hear the straining engine of the Land Rover as it crested the incline.

The warrior sprinted to meet the vehicle, driving his legs hard against the ground. He came to a halt where the road suddenly switched back and left a dangerous curve, where nothing but sheer cliff face and broken rocks waited a hundred feet below.

Bolan drew the Desert Eagle and squeezed the trigger as the Land Rover topped the last ridge less than fifty feet away. Dirt crumbled under his boots, and for an instant he thought he'd placed himself too close to the edge of the cliff. Then the ground held.

He put the first round through the windshield to let them know he was there. On the other side of the holed glass, Swaine Churchill gestured at him wildly. The two men in the rear seats stood and began to fire their assault rifles, but the bouncing vehicle made accurcy next to impossible.

The driver pressed down on the accelerator, closing the distance to forty feet, then thirty. Bolan guessed the driver intended to take him out with some kind of sideways skid. The Executioner stood his ground and brought the driver's head and shoulders into target acquisition as the Land Rover plunged toward him.

Rocks crunched under the big tires as the driver started to go into his skidding turn. Coolly the Executioner stroked the trigger of the big .44 and pumped a trio of shots into the driver. The windshield came apart and the driver slammed back into his seat, his head in fragments. Then the Land Rover went out of control, flipped over onto its side and skidded for the edge of the cliff.

Bolan suddenly realized he was trapped by the wall of steel hurtling at him. There was nowhere else to go but the sea, and a drop straight down to the rocks.

"Sarge!" Grimaldi's voice was harsh in his ear. The helicopter came up out of a diving swoop and hovered slightly below the cliff's edge.

Bolan dropped his pistol and jumped as the tumbling Land Rover closed in on him. Something thudded into his right boot, then passed by. There was a stomach-turning moment of free-fall, and his hands closed around the helicopter's skid. He glanced down to see the rear of the Land Rover plunging toward the sea and waiting rocks. The vehicle shredded on impact, and a gasoline explosion sent flames skyward.

"I'd say the blue-chip stock in the drug market just hit bottom unexpectedly," Grimaldi said dryly.

Straining with the effort and against the adrenaline letdown, Bolan hauled himself aboard the helicopter. "Churchill's gone," the warrior said, "but not the game. There's too much power and money to be made walking on the dark side. All we've done is buy the world a little time until the next predator comes along."

"Somehow it doesn't seem like enough."

"It has to be enough," Bolan said grimly, "because it's all you get." He settled back in the seat and watched the fire disappear behind the cliff as Grimaldi guided the helicopter back toward the manor house. People had been fighting that dark side within and outside of themselves since the dawn of mankind. It was that fight that made the war everlasting.

And as long as he felt he could make a difference fighting that dark side, the Executioner knew he'd keep himself on the front line. It was the only true home the warrior had ever known.